THE GOOD SAMARITAN

RC BOLDT

THE GOOD SAMARITAN

Please note: Liberties may have been taken with regard to legal and medical aspects, as well as the city dynamics of Cleveland, Ohio in order to accommodate the storyline.

Visit my website at www.rcboldtbooks.com.

Sign up for my mailing list: http://eepurl.com/cgftw5

THE GOOD SAMARITAN

RC
BOLDT

Dedication

Matty,
You're the love of my life, my best friend, and my rock. You are always my personal cheerleader and believe in me even when I'm fully entrenched in self-doubt. Thank you for single-handedly making me believe in happily-ever-afters by giving me my own.
P.S. I still love you more.

A,
We are so similar in that we love books, appreciate good storytelling, are foodies, are goofy as hell, and love to talk. It's almost like I grew you or something.
Oh, wait… ;)
I love you more than the whole world and universe. Always.
(Also, if you're reading this, please put the book down until you're legally an adult.)

Prologue

HIM

Evil thrives under the cloak of darkness. It's also where secrets are hidden in the depths.

I learned this long before I joined the ranks of the homeless.

Darkness, those shadows offering disguise, enable evil-doers. Those who prey on the weak and profit from their loss.

Darkness also masks our sins. It disguises everything we don't want visible in the light of day.

I'm a prime example of the latter.

I've become one with the dark obscurity, have melded into the shadows, to join the homeless.

I'm here, amidst the ragged, weary, unkempt population.

I'm here because this is the only way.

This is my mission. To not only look evil in its face and confront it, but to also protect those who cannot protect themselves. To leave only good deeds in my wake.

I must atone for my sins.

1

Faith

NOVEMBER

"Do you know what's more pathetic than a news reporter who has no life and spends most of her time at a bar, drinking with a priest and a bunch of cops and construction workers?"

"Ooh! I do!" Gordie, a man of the badge for more than fifteen years, raises his hand. "My mother-in-law!"

Boisterous laughter fills the bar along with numerous high fives, and I can't restrain my own snicker.

With my chin resting on my palm, I settle my gaze on Father James, the man who's been a father figure throughout my life. "That's not comforting," I manage drily.

"Cheer up, Faith." Father pats my shoulder. "It's not all bad, is it?"

"What can we help you with?"

"Do we need to go and scare the shit outta someone?"

"Maybe that new bosshole of yours?"

Random offers are tossed out by bar patrons enjoying an after-work drink, or those indulging in a quick meal with coffee before they return to their shift.

Father James and I exchange a look. He leans in close and lowers his voice. "What's really bothering you?"

I blow out a long breath. "My boss is skeezy in epic proportions. My new co-worker makes my skin crawl. My best friend has better hair and a much better social life than I do."

I squint as Dwayne, a young beat cop, draws near. "You know what you need?" he asks with a knowing smile.

I mash my lips thin and point my index finger at him with warning. "Don't even think about it."

Of course, he doesn't listen. They never do.

The bulk of the crowd roars with, "Group hug!" and I'm instantly swarmed by a handful of cops, some construction and road workers, the bartender, and a priest.

I know. It sounds like the beginning of a joke. But, alas, it's not.

It's my life.

Look, I haven't always been a "Debbie Downer." I honestly don't enjoy being morose and all melancholy. Sometimes, though, I need to have a full-fledged pity party and get it all out of my system.

My party just so happens to include an eclectic mix of individuals.

I said goodbye to normalcy when my mom left me to be raised by my crotchety grandmother at the age of nine. My father couldn't bear to stick around once he found out about me, and when you top that off with my own mother suddenly deciding nine years was her max capacity on motherhood, I was left with a gaping hole of vulnerability. Desperate for acceptance and hoping I wouldn't send yet another individual running from me, I did everything in my power to obey my grandmother and not be a burden.

Gran forced me to go to church with her every Sunday

morning, but things didn't change for me until the man sitting to my right took over.

Father James. He was met with a lot of resistance when he first came to St. Michael's. He wasn't "pure" or "ultra-conservative" like the others. His sermons include stories from his days serving in the Army or even after he got out and was unsure about his path in life. The older members of the church protested that he would bring down the entire parish with his "blasphemous talk," but I knew better. Even as a teenager, I knew I'd found a comrade. Someone who might understand me.

And I was right.

I volunteered to help Father when altar boys were suddenly scarce because their parents didn't agree with the humor in his sermons. And when he received the funding to build a shelter on the large plot of land beside the church, I championed his success. I helped plant flowers around the newly erected building and happily served meals on the weekends along with the other volunteers.

Gran was probably relieved I was out of her hair because she never gave any thought to me as long as I said I was helping Father. Countless times, he'd bring me to the Tavern and sit beside me on the barstools, and we'd share a meal of fish and chips or whatever the cook's special might be.

I'll never forget the argument I overheard one day when I came home from school my senior year. I stood frozen with my feet rooted to the spot outside the screen door of Gran's small house. It was never a home, and it was never *my* house. She'd made sure to remind me of that over the years.

"She will not waste her life on this rubbish! Her mother threw her life away, and I won't allow her to do the same!"

I jerked back as if she'd slapped me, the pure anger

and hatred of her words flowing out from the house and cinching tightly around me.

"She has a gift." Though Father didn't raise his voice, there was a steely edge behind it. "You want to see her ignore that?"

"They're just drawings," Gran practically spat out. "Nothing special."

The silence washed over me. *Nothing special.* The words played on a loop in my head, and I fought the urge to claw at my ears to erase what I'd heard.

Nothing special.

Those words haunt me to this day.

I'm jostled back to the present when Dwayne's beefy arms tighten around me once everyone else has returned to their seats. "You gonna be okay?"

His tone is sober, at odds with his usual jovial personality, and I nod. He releases me with a pat on the back. "Chin up, girl." He walks back to his table, rejoining his buddies to likely discuss the tall skyscraper where they're installing windows.

Father grins at me, his neatly trimmed gray beard showcasing his smile. He shrugs, eyes alight with amusement and affection. "Family. Gotta love 'em, right?"

I make a derisive sound but end up smiling, because I wouldn't trade them for anything.

"I have to get going." Planting a quick peck on his cheek, I slip off the barstool and slide on my jacket. "Work calls." Without a word, Harry, the bartender and owner, presents me with the hot coffee in a to-go cup and wrapped-up cheeseburger I'd requested earlier. I accept them with a grateful smile, and he winks before retreating to refill other patrons' drinks.

"Be safe, Faith," Father says.

"Always."

With a wave and a round of goodbyes from the others, I exit the bar. I scan the surrounding area for the man I saw when I arrived a few minutes earlier. Finally, I spot him seated against the cold, unforgiving brick surface of the nearby building.

His jeans are well-worn, but something about him stands out among the other homeless people I've crossed paths with. I can't quite pinpoint it. It may be that his stature alone practically radiates strength. His clothes can't mask the muscular physique beneath the fabric.

I hesitantly approach where he sits on a piece of cardboard on the cold ground. His hooded sweatshirt is pulled up over the low-sitting ball cap, which masks much of his face. The only view I'm afforded is his sharp jawline covered by a short dark beard and a pair of full lips.

I stop a foot away from him. He doesn't look up at me, but I know the moment he realizes my intent to approach because his shoulders stiffen slightly.

With care, I set the coffee down before placing the wrapped burger on top of it. Even though the shelter has been around for a while now, something compels me to reach into my pocket and withdraw one of their cards with the information printed on it. I slip that between the burger and coffee lid. Maybe he'll stop by and get some assistance.

"Hope this helps a little."

I turn to head to my car that's parallel parked a few feet away when he speaks.

"Thank you."

His voice sends a jolt of something potent through my entire body, nearly causing me to physically jerk in surprise. It's so gravelly and rough, yet with clear sincerity.

"You're welcome."

Once I'm inside my car, I start the engine and sit for a

moment, staring out the windshield. "Back to the grind," I mutter beneath my breath.

I'd be lying to myself if I said my motivation for going back to work after my lunch break was because I love my job. But it pays the bills and provides health insurance.

The latter is what I need more now than ever before.

ANONYMOUS MAN SAVES SCHOOLCHILDREN
AT BUS STOP FROM CAR

"He came out of nowhere and pulled the kids out of the way. I can't imagine what might have happened if he hadn't jumped into action..."

2

Him
DECEMBER

He drags his left foot. It's slight enough one might not detect it, but it's a weakness just the same.

He doesn't belong here. I knew it the moment he walked through the doors and sauntered up to the registration desk of St. Michael's shelter. His eyes and the way he purposely broadened his shoulders to bump into others are telling. He strives to intimidate.

The difference between us is, I don't have to work at intimidation. I don't need to throw my weight around as a signal to others.

I'd hoped to get some rest tonight, but I'm not certain that's going to happen. Not with him here.

"Darrel," Father James starts off, "you know the rules here." The older man gives Darrel a hard look as if silently warning the guy. "This is your last chance. If I hear or see anything that's not kosher on your end, you won't be allowed back. Understood?"

Darrel gives a lackadaisical nod, clearly dismissing the priest's words much as an unruly teen would to their parents.

The thug's body language tells me everything I need to know. This might be his last night spent at the shelter, but he plans to make it worth his while. I assess Darrel, attempting to determine where he's likely stashed a weapon beneath his clothing. Possibly in one of the deep, bulky pockets of his winter coat or beneath the pant leg of his right ankle. As my eyes track up his form again, analytically, my gaze clashes with the priest's, and I quickly avert my eyes.

Keep your head down, stay quiet, and keep to yourself. That's been my mantra. I never draw unnecessary attention to myself. If I can blend in with the shadows, it works to my benefit.

Sure, there'll always be shit starters. That's to be expected. But overall, I'm left alone.

But now, trouble has landed itself at my feet. In the form of Darrel.

He's got quite the rap sheet on the streets. First and foremost a thief, he deals drugs, is known to rough up women, and uses his fists on those smaller or easily intimidated to prove his powerful influence.

Word has gotten around that he's killed a few dealers to get them out of the way so he could move up the ranks faster.

And now he's fucking up my night to sleep, which pisses me the hell off.

I hand over my ticket for the cellophane-wrapped turkey and cheese sandwich and bottle of water. I stuff both in the inside pockets of my coat. I learned real quick to sew extra pockets by a man I'd run into early on. Old Man Hank.

The former Marine Corps sergeant was the kindest soul and would give a woman or child his last stitch of clothing off his back. That man carried a sewing kit and extra fabric scraps on him along with super glue.

Let me tell you, those items weren't strictly for sewing up fabric. Hank had saved me many a time early on when I'd crossed paths with knife-happy punks who thought ten to one was a fair fight. I got my hands on a sewing kit and super glue soon after.

Ironically, it had been the same night I discovered Hank had fallen victim to a gang member—Timmy Shanks, if the rumors are accurate. Shanks had been hell-bent on earning his fucking teardrop tattoo, so he'd sliced open Old Man Hank's throat.

I can tell you what Timmy's name will change to if we ever cross paths: Fucking dead.

"For our new guests, the shower line's over here."

One thing I appreciate at this shelter is how they treat people here with dignity. No one is looked upon as though they're worthless just because they've fallen on hard times. Or don't have a roof of their own. Or stand in line in the bitter winter of Cleveland, Ohio, for a chance at a warm place to lay their head for the night rather than risk freezing to death outside in some damp, dark alley. Father James runs this, and word is he manages to work miracles, garnering private donations to keep this joint running on all cylinders.

"Mass starts at six thirty."

I internally cringe at the voiced reminder. They don't make it mandatory to attend their church service, but it's encouraged.

Doubtful they'd like me to venture inside their chapel. The place would probably burst into flames the moment the toe of my worn-out boots touched the holy surface.

The use of tickets at St. Michael's shelter allows it to remain organized and orderly. I gratefully accept a new, clean dark blue thermal shirt and what appears to be a brand-new pair of dark gray boxer briefs. Socks are in demand, so there's a shortage right now, but they offer an extra knit beanie, which I'm thankful for since I'd given mine to a young teen boy I'd seen huddled beside his mother the other night. The wind barrels through the downtown area, and every little bit of extra warmth helps to combat the biting chill.

I hand over my shower ticket and accept the small but neatly folded towel that fills my nostrils with the scent of fabric softener along with the small paper-wrapped soap and shampoo like one would see in hotel rooms. Quickly, I gather my winter coat and other outerwear along with the pack I carry on my shoulder. This sucker holds everything I own, and I stow it all in one of their lockers before securing the simple keyed lock and palm the key.

"If you have valuables, do *not* let them out of your sight," the shelter employee reminds us as they stand by, ensuring everyone showers accordingly. They take personal hygiene seriously here, but it's because they actually care and don't want the entire joint—or us—to become infested with bed bugs.

I strip down and place my key for the locker in one boot and bring it in the shower stall with me.

I lay my towel over the top of my boot and place it in the corner where I can keep an eye on it. I unwrap the soap from its wrapper and place it on the soap dish. As soon as I turn on the shower, I take a quick moment to relish in the sensation of the warm water washing over my body. I quickly lather up my entire body, attempting to rid myself of the effects of my time spent on the streets. Where keeping warm meant stuffing newspapers inside my coat and between my socks and boots.

I work the shampoo in my hair and beard, mentally

reminding myself I'll soon need to trim my beard. The longer it gets, the itchier it becomes. After I rinse clean, I turn off the water and dry off as quickly as I can to let the next guy have his turn.

Once I'm dressed and have brushed my teeth, I stop by the locker to grab my sandwich and drink. I slide my key inside the Velcroed inner pocket of my pants to ensure it won't be lost and make my way to the cafeteria tables set up for everyone to eat.

They're serving hot soup, but I've grown weary of it. It might warm me briefly, but I'd rather have the basic turkey and cheese sandwich and water. The "poor man's miso soup" they're currently serving in the kitchen doesn't have enough spinach in it to provide more than the barest amount of protein.

I down the sandwich and bottled water and survey my surroundings, sure to keep an eye on Darrel, who's busy stuffing his face. A few fluorescent lights above the small galley opening leading to the kitchen prep area are burned out and could use replacements. I rise and saunter casually over to the guy with the clipboard. William—according to his name tag—is tall and so skinny he looks frail but always has a ready smile on his face, lifts his eyes at my approach.

"What can I do for you?"

I lift my chin, gesturing in the direction of the rectangular light fixtures above us. "You have replacement bulbs for those? I can help if you have a step ladder."

His eyebrows rise. "You're volunteering?"

I offer a curt nod. "I am."

His expression is grateful. "Beneath the cabinet there"—he points the tip of his pen in the direction off to the left—"and the step ladder's collapsible and stashed over there off to the side." He points a few feet away beside a volunteer who's handing out waters from the cases piled up nearly five feet high beside him.

"Got it." I tug on the hood of my sweatshirt in an attempt to shadow my face more. It's not completely unreasonable for this since it's quite drafty in this place, but I do it for more than that purpose.

It's a challenge not to draw attention to myself, but I can't overlook something that needs to be done. Especially not in a joint like this with people who actually care about the work they're doing.

Within five minutes, I've changed out the light bulbs and disposed of the old ones in the oversized trash cans nearby.

"Thanks..." William trails off, and the expectant lilt in his tone is obvious. He's waiting for me to supply my name.

"No problem." I nod and turn away slightly. "Anything else you need?"

"I...don't think so, but I'll be sure to let you know if I do." He offers a kind smile, and his mouth parts to say more, but he's interrupted by another worker.

I take that as my way out and amble down the main hallway. I don't even realize it until I pause at the double doors leading outside the shelter.

The sign on the doors reads "This way to the cathedral."

This is where I've always stopped.

Suddenly, I realize why something has me contemplating pushing through those doors and striding along the covered sidewalk a few yards over to the cathedral.

Inhaling deeply, I slide up my sleeve to check my watch, and I realize the time. The date.

A short laugh that's more anguished than humorous rushes out with my murmured words. "Happy Birthday."

I shove my hands in my pockets, and something inside

butts against my fingers. Frozen, I'm jarred by the coincidence as I withdraw a card from my pants pocket, the pad of my thumb grazing the worn plastic lamination of the card Old Man Hank had given me the last time I'd seen him.

Without another thought, I shove through the door before I can second-guess my intentions and rush through the bitter cold until I tug open the old, heavy wooden doors of St. Michael's Cathedral.

As soon as I step inside, the heavy weight of the door closes with a soft thud behind me, and I'm overwhelmed at the sight of stained-glass windows and ornately carved wooden beams crisscrossing the twenty-foot ceiling. I've never been a churchgoing guy, but this place instantly rouses a sense of awe and reverence from within me. The enormous marble pillars are striking, let alone the carvings of certain Biblical events, as well as the ornate stained-glass depictions of Jesus. They hold my attention so fully that I barely register the fact I've entered the sanctuary until I slide into the last pew and quietly settle myself on the wooden bench seat.

I link my fingers together in my lap and stare sightlessly toward the altar, where Father James appears to be wrapping up his sermon.

Without realizing it, I whisper, "I miss you. I'm so damn sorry."

I wince, closing my eyes as if to ward off the overwhelming pain that still radiates through me to the marrow of my bones.

I ignore the sounds of footsteps retreating from the other pews in the front of the cathedral while I attempt to regain control of my emotions.

Once I finally open my eyes, I notice the cathedral is vacant except for Father, who readies the altar for the next use. I study the man who's so dedicated not only to this church but also to the shelter. He looks mid-sixties, gray hair cut short and neatly parted on one side, with a neatly trimmed beard. He's tall and still looks like he takes good care of himself.

After he's finished, he steps down and strides down the main aisle, drawing near. He surprises the hell out of me when he stops at the corner of my pew.

"May I join you?"

It's on the tip of my tongue to refuse—it really is—but I'm ultimately on his turf. I might be homeless and viewed as worthless to most, but one thing I'm not is blatantly disrespectful.

I dip my chin in a barely imperceptible nod and move over to afford plenty of room for him to slide in beside me.

He lowers himself and lets out a long sigh but doesn't immediately speak. Our silence isn't entirely comfortable, but it isn't completely awkward, either.

"This is your first time here in the church, isn't it?" Father James poses the question in a conversational way rather than a manner that puts me on the defensive.

"Yes, sir."

He nods. "I've seen you at the shelter before." He reaches a hand out to me. "We've never officially met. I'm Father Joseph James."

I grasp his hand, and he's got a firm grip I can respect.

"Nice to meet you." That's all I offer. Not because I'm trying to be a dick, but I don't have a name to offer. Not anymore.

I lost that right.

Luckily, the priest takes it in stride. "Anything special bring you here tonight?"

I shake my head but stop and withdraw my hand from my pocket, still grasping the object Old Man Hank had given me. I peer down at it and wish I knew why the hell he'd thrust it at me the last time I'd seen him alive.

I wonder if he knew something was about to happen to him.

"I used to be anti-church, anti-religion for the longest time." The priest's words surprise me, and I turn his way, squinting in disbelief. If this is some ploy to get me to become a believer…

He waves me off with a soft chuckle. "I can see it on your face, son. Trust me, there's no gimmick here. Just truth." He lets out a long sigh and gazes up at the beautiful wooden beams along the ceiling. "I was in the Army, a medic, and I'd seen far too much by the time I'd turned twenty-two. Too much death. Helplessness. Lack of faith."

He pauses so long, I'm not sure he plans to continue. But he does.

"I'd lost my way." The edges of his mouth tilt upward in a faint smile. "Until I came across a young nineteen-year-old who'd lost his legs." He shakes his head, seemingly caught up in the memory. "I'd braced myself for his reaction once I broke the news to him after he woke up."

Father James turns, and his eyes land on me. "He nodded and asked for a few minutes alone to digest things. And when I came back in, he was already planning how to rig a contraption to do pull-ups and strengthen his upper body so he'd be able to maneuver himself better and learn to adjust to his new reality."

He peers up at the enormous wooden carving of the crucified Jesus hanging from the ceiling with a thoughtful expression on his face. "He said to me, 'Doc, I just gotta have faith. 'Cause if I don't have that, I don't have anything.'

"When I'd asked him what religion he was, he waved me off with a small laugh, looked me dead in the eye, and said, 'It doesn't matter what you have faith in—Baptist, Catholic, Methodist, Lutheran, whatever—you just gotta have it.'" The priest purses his lips thoughtfully. "It planted a seed of sorts. I realized I needed to be rooted in something but wasn't sure what. So when I got out of the Army, I did a little soul searching and decided to go to the seminary and dedicate myself to the Lord."

I mull over his words and gaze ahead at the pillars of marble, the silent reverie of the church surrounding me.

"Saint Jude."

I turn to him in question, confused by his words.

He nods toward my hand—"Saint Jude"—and gestures to the small card I've been holding.

I glance down at it, so worn from being handled that the print on it is now illegible.

I shrug. "A friend gave it to me, but it's so worn I didn't know what it said or what it even meant."

"Ah." Father James flashes a kind smile. "Saint Jude is the patron saint of desperate and lost causes."

An unsettling jolt shudders through me as I stare down at the card in dismay and a little shock. Why had Hank given me this? Did he somehow know?

"Sometimes, people lose their way, but the important thing to remember is that it's always possible to find the road back." He tips his head to the side. "The path may be a bit difficult to navigate and hard to discover, but it's still there."

His words settle over me, and we sit in silence for a moment before he lightly slaps his palms on his knees. "Look at me yammering on. Shall we head back?"

"Yes, sir." I follow him out, and he locks up the church behind me. We cross the walkway to the shelter, and when we approach, I hold the door for him, and he thanks me.

Once we're inside, I slide my hand inside my pocket to ensure I still have my locker key.

"Have a good night, Father." I begin down the hall toward the bunks in the large auditorium-sized room. I'm nearly to the corner and about to enter when his response reaches my ears.

"Sleep well, Jude."

3

Jude

The dreams—or nightmares—are always the same. She stands there all alone, out of reach, crying out for me. And I'm helpless, unable to move to save her.

To save them.

The snoring from the guy beside me amplifies, rivaling the decibel level of a damn freight train. It rips me from the throes of the dream, but then I'm unable to fall back asleep. His snoring grows even worse, louder, and it's a wonder the damn roof hasn't blown off yet with the way he's going at it.

This is the price I have to pay, but the expression on the older man's face when I'd offered my bunk bed to him in exchange for his sleeping mat—the ones offered when bunk spaces run out—was worth it. He looked like he might not make it through the winter, his back hunched slightly, fingers gnarled and callused to hell and back. The way his eyes widened before filling with heartfelt gratitude indicated I did the right thing.

It takes me longer than I'd prefer to shake off the fog

of weariness from being sleep-deprived, but as soon as it begins to subside, I sense it.

If anyone ever claims it's impossible to sense or see evil, they're full of shit. They've never witnessed true evil at work, never stared into its cold, dead eyes.

I know without any confirmation who lurks in the shadows while others sleep.

Darrel.

My movements are lithe, stealthy, and soundless. My eyes adjust quickly to the darkness, and I know exactly what he's going for. An older, overweight man sleeping on a lower bunk in the other section of the room has left his bag and boots beside his bed. He should have used the bag as a pillow or at least kept it closer. He's practically asking for his belongings to be stolen.

Definitely a newbie move, but it doesn't make it acceptable for Darrel to take them.

I intercept him just as he reaches down to grab the bag. With swift movements, I place my hand over his mouth and manacle his arms with my own wrapped around him. I duck my head to whisper menacingly in his ear.

"Pick on someone your own age and size, Darrel."

Rage pours from him, and he attempts to break free from my restricting hold. Though I'm homeless, it doesn't mean I've let my body get soft. I continue my pull-ups and push-ups and ensure I stay active in order to maintain my strength. Not only to be able to hold my own but also to make certain I can protect others who might need me.

"I'll let go as long as you promise to be a good boy and go back to your own bunk and sleep." There's no mistaking the derisiveness in my tone.

His breathing is erratic and labored with anger, and when he doesn't immediately acquiesce, I clench my grip over his mouth tighter, causing my fingertips to dig into his flesh. Finally, he gives a subtle grunt of agreement, and I cautiously loosen my hold.

He whirls around on me, but I stand firm, confident. He's a damn pissant compared to what I've faced in the past.

Darrel steps forward, purposely invading my personal space, and gets in my face. He hisses at me with breath that can rival the stench of the filthiest of vagrants I've crossed paths with. "You have no idea who you're messing with, boy."

With no emotion crossing my features, I stare back at him. "The same could be said for you."

He snorts a laugh full of disgust and foolish bravado. "You better watch your back. This ain't over." Darrel shoves past me, purposely knocking into my shoulder.

I immediately grip his throat and squeeze painfully tight, pressing him back against the post of one of the bunks. With my nose to his, I make sure he gets my message loud and clear.

"If you have any fucking sense, you'll know it's not wise to threaten me." He makes a choked sound when I add more pressure to his larynx. "It's you who'd better watch his back."

I hold his eyes for another beat before I release him abruptly and step away. He falters but regains his balance in the nick of time. His eyes flash with hatred before he stalks away.

It's not over. Not by a long shot. I know I've stirred up a damn hornet's nest, but no way could I let him get away with this shit.

Not on my watch.

MORNING COMES TOO SOON.

Everyone's required to vacate the shelter's grounds by nine, but I'm always up before that. I've already brushed my teeth and have my pack strapped to my back, ready to head out. It's snowed about a foot and a half since last night. Thankfully, the plows have been out and cleared the roads some, but the snow's still falling.

As much as I hate any reminder of my past, I'm grateful for these boots since they've seen me through a few winters already. Steel-toed, waterproof, and insulated, they're one of my prized possessions. And they come in handy at times like these.

I trudge along, eager to make it to my destination as early as possible so I don't offset my normal times at my other stops.

Intent on heading past the front and around the back of the house for the bag of ice melt stored there, I'm not the least bit surprised when the front door cracks open barely an inch. I should have known better than to think she'd let me sneak by without insisting on a visit.

The steam from her breath as she speaks through the crack of the door is a visible contrast to the bitter-cold temperature.

"You still showed up, did ya?" Pauline cackles and shuts the door. The sound of the chain sliding loose from the inside seems to resonate in the mostly quiet stillness out here, and she opens the door again. "Come in here before I freeze my damn arse off." She waves me in, her large unrestrained breasts jiggling beneath her housecoat.

As much as I'd like to refuse, I already know she won't accept it. She's a stubborn old coot, but her heart's in the right place. Which is why I allot enough time for her in the mornings.

I lower my head and carefully make my way up the two

snow-covered steps, stomp my boots on the thick doormat, and enter the warmth of her house. I move aside for her to shut the door and lock it. "I can go ahead and get started on your walkway." I tip my head toward the outside, insinuation clear.

Let me do what I came to do. Nothing more.

She waves me off. "It's a Tuesday, honey, and a cold one. I need some hot cocoa first. And I need some company." Pauline heads in the direction of her large kitchen.

I peer down at my boots, warring with myself. I don't like taking them off because I hate the risk it poses for a quick escape. But her carpeting is pristine, more along the museum lines…

"Get in here already. Keep your boots on if it makes you feel better."

I can't help but shake my head at her mind-reading skills as I follow her into the kitchen.

"Have a seat. I'll make us some hot cocoa." She pours some milk into a small pot on her stove. "And none of that garbage from a powdery mix." She shakes her head with disgust as if instant hot cocoa is an abomination.

"Yes, ma'am." I settle myself onto an old chair covered in some sort of plastic to maintain its original condition.

"Always so mannerly," she muses with her back to me as she busies herself getting mugs for us. "I like that about you."

"Can I help with anything?"

Pauline spins around, and those crinkles at the corners of her eyes become more prominent when she smiles at me. "Thanks for asking, but no." She sets a cloth napkin on the table in front of me and one at her spot before turning back to the kitchen counter. "Such a sweet man," she murmurs under her breath before her features take on a sour expression. "Not like my grandson."

Our rapport is much like that movie *Groundhog Day*—the same thing time and time again. It's not that she's senile, because Pauline is wicked smart. Sharp as a tack. She's also the most persistent person I've met.

The fifth time I brought her newspaper to her door from where the young kid had flung the plastic bag to land at the end of her driveway, she'd had what she called a "stakeout." She'd been sitting by her front bay window, waiting to discover the identity of her "newspaper helper," who saved her a trip down the drive with her walker.

Let me tell you, Pauline could give the most intimidating drill sergeants a run for their money, which became evident when I initially attempted to evade her. She persisted, preying on the fact that I couldn't leave her damn newspaper to get soaked in the slight dip at the end of her driveway, let alone leave her to make the trip and risk getting hurt. She insisted I come in and sit for a moment. Then it was for some iced tea. She's intuitive and understood immediately that my pride was still intact. That I never wanted handouts.

I'd refused her money, and somehow, in her insistence on giving "a lonely woman who won the damn lottery when it comes to having a good-for-nothing grandson," she would discreetly shove money in the loose pocket of my pants. Let me tell you, the woman could've been a famed pickpocket in her former life because most times I didn't detect her slipping me the cash.

Once she bid me goodbye, she would call out, "Be sure to check your pockets, honey," before abruptly shutting and locking the door.

Sneaky little bugger, that one.

It's another twenty minutes until I've drunk my "authentic" hot cocoa and chatted with Pauline—which really means she talks while I sit and listen—before I get outside and unlock her garage to start spreading the ice melt along the walkway and her driveway.

"Oh, honey?"

I'm standing in front of the detached garage a few feet away from her house. This may contain her rarely used car, but she keeps the place immaculate. Her garage is so damn clean, you could practically eat off the cement. But I can't seem to drag my eyes away from the object hanging on the hook beside the large bag of ice melt.

"I got my lazy grandson to drop me off at Bass Pro Shops while he went and did God knows what." She waves a hand dismissively. "I found that nice jacket and thought it would bring out your eyes."

My eyes flick to hers, and she tosses her head back with a loud cackle. Because we both know she's full of shit.

"My eyes, huh?" I mutter dubiously. I return my gaze to the deceptively thin-looking jacket that I know is Gore-Tex, the high-quality brand of all-weather wear that's warm as hell. This thing had to set her back easily about four hundred bucks. Dammit, she must have noticed the numerous patches I've tried to affix to my coat.

Without turning back, I call out, "You realize my eyes aren't gray, right? And you know I can't accept this."

She snorts. "Well, too damn bad. You're gonna take it with you, or I won't invite you back for any more visits. And we both know you'll get lonely and end up practically meowing at my damn door. Just take the damn thing already and get to work so I can watch you from the window and brag to the ladies I play cards with about my yard servant's strapping muscles."

Her cackling abruptly ends the moment she shuts the door.

HOLY HELL. That damn jacket is comfy and warm as hell, the fabric resistant to the bitter chill from the harsh wind.

Once I finish coating the areas with ice melt, I ensure there's enough in the bag for next time before I lock up behind me.

"Come here, honey, and get this before you go." Pauline stands at the door, bundled in a large afghan, and waves a wad of cash in her fingers.

I step up to the door and level her a stern look. "You gave me a jacket, ma'am."

"Nonsense." Her expression is stern and practically dares me to make her chase me down the driveway, walker and all. "You'll take this and give me no arguments." She shoves the money at me.

With a resigned sigh, and because I know exactly what will happen if I try to refuse a stubborn woman like Pauline, I accept the money and thank her.

"I appreciate it." I pause and reach to place the money in the inside pocket of my thick coat to secure it. "Anything else I can help you with?"

She grins at me. "Yes. Go find yourself a good woman who needs more than the ice on her driveway melted." She wiggles her eyebrows and lets out a cackle.

"Yes, ma'am." I nod, and a corner of my mouth tips up barely as I stride along the now-cleared walkway.

"Be safe."

I lift a hand in a wave.

Safe is objective. And it holds a certain irony when a person's homeless.

I NEED to change my routine. Desperately.

Predictability is dangerous, but I'm torn. I can't let

these people fend for themselves. They don't have anyone else to truly depend on, and if something happened to them… *Shit.* I have enough on my conscience as it is.

But they've begun to tuck money away for me when I drop by to help them. It's not that I don't appreciate their kindness and generosity—I do. But it's not why I do this.

It's never been for the money.

I make a silent vow to put the bulk of the eighty dollars to use. It's nearly time for the big fundraiser for St. Michael's shelter. God knows that place can use all the help they can get. Especially since the people there are a rarity and treat us like humans. They care.

With the money securely stowed in my pocket, I internally war with myself and contemplate splurging and spending a few dollars on a cup of homemade soup from one of the small shops a few blocks away.

It doesn't take but a moment to realize that's a ridiculous notion. A single glance at me would likely have them escorting me off the premises.

I need to take care of the necessities first, so I head off toward one of the better laundromats and put a small portion of the money toward my laundry. Now that I'm showered and clean, it's time to match everything else so I can make it last a while.

THE SCENT of freshly laundered clothes is indescribable. The sensation of clean fabric covering your body is even better. I've spent over four years on these streets, and nothing could possibly surpass the feeling of cleanliness.

I carefully make my way behind the small cafés and stores, striding along the alleyways. I'm out of sight to many, not important enough to warrant a second glance—

sometimes not even garnering the first look—because this is where I can go uninterrupted. Unwatched.

No one cares about me. I'm not being surly or petulant. It's simply a fact. We never want to look something in the face when it's a frightening possibility. Anyone could become homeless. The majority of the population is one paycheck away from it. No one wants to admit just how scary that is.

I hear the hushed voices before I see them, and the anguish and shame in the woman's tone has me slowing my pace.

"Mommy, can I please have the Power Rangers light-up shoes?"

"Baby, they're expensive, and Mommy doesn't have that much money to spare."

The child, not much older than seven or eight, lowers his eyes dejectedly. "I know." He tugs at the collar of his well-worn coat. His hair is more on the shaggy side, and the hem of his pant legs stop at the very top of his socks. "I just wish the kids at school would stop making fun of my shoes."

The mother has dark circles beneath her eyes. She's dressed in a uniform for the local diner a few blocks away, but that's not where I recognize her from.

I've seen them at the shelter.

She crouches down to speak to him, affectionately smoothing back his hair from his face. My eyes are drawn to the soles of her own shoes, which are worn so thin, the color of her dark socks are faintly visible in certain spots.

"I'm trying, sweetie. That's why I'm working extra shifts. But certain things cost a little too much right now." She forces a smile, and it doesn't reach her eyes, which are still deeply shadowed with worry. "We have to make sure we have enough for food."

The young child doesn't meet her eyes, but he nods slowly in understanding.

I hover in the shadows, watching them, and when they embark for the discount shoe store nearby, I carefully withdraw the wad of cash I've accumulated from Pauline. Counting off the designated number of bills, I tuck the rest away safely. First, I head toward the grocery store diagonal to the shoe store before quietly entering the small store and weaving through the aisles and displays of shoes.

Twenty minutes later, I stand back and watch as the mother walks out, her son happily skipping beside her, and they are each holding a bag purchased with the gift cards left for them, as well as having one from the grocery store stowed in the woman's pocket.

When she smiles down at her son and quickly swipes at the tears trickling free, I peer up at the overcast sky and nod.

At moments like these, I feel as though they're looking down at me and helping me carry out this mission. Ensuring I do my penance.

Other times, I can't help but wonder if they're looking down and cursing my existence.

4

Faith

JANUARY

"You want me to report on the scandal with the former mayor and the underage girl he allegedly had an affair with?"

This is one of those times when you reiterate someone's words because you're either not entirely sure you heard them correctly, or you're desperately hoping you misunderstood.

For me, it's the latter. I'm hoping—practically praying—my boss doesn't mean what I think he means.

"Is there a problem, Connors?" He narrows his spectacled eyes on me. "Plain English: Dig up the dirt on this story."

Let's get one thing straight. Before Anthony took over, our paper had been a respected, reputable news source.

Now, it appears he's single-handedly turning it into a tabloid rag. The worst part is, I can't do anything about it. I need this job, and it's the best paying position I've had at a paper. If the *Akron Journal* were hiring, I'd consider applying there even though it would mean leaving everything behind here in Cleveland.

Basically, I have to suck it up and hope that someone replaces Anthony soon. It's not likely, but I need to keep my head down and my nose to the grindstone.

"Yes, sir." I push the words out between a clenched-teeth kind of smile. Sometimes, that's all I've got to offer.

Especially for him.

He waves a hand, shooing me out of his office. "Get to it."

I rise from where I've been perched on the edge of the chair across from his desk and quickly exit his office. The faster I get away from him, the less likely I feel that the nasty grime from his black soul can attach itself to me.

A little melodramatic, but I always feel dirty and a shade tainted when I'm around him.

Settling into my desk chair in the safe confines of my cubicle, I heave out a sigh of relief.

"Hey, gorgeous."

Speaking of nasty grime…

Without turning to face him, I focus my attention on centering a legal pad and pen on my desk. "What do you want, Evan." I don't pose this as a question because I feel like between him and Anthony, I'm being drained of all civility in a slow, agonizing process.

And don't be mistaken. Evan *always* wants something.

"Happened to hear about your latest assignment. How about I trade you the superintendent story for the mayor one?"

I prop my elbows on my desk and massage my temples, trying to stave off the beginning of a headache. "Why?"

His heavy hands drop to my shoulders, and I jerk in alarm, shrugging them off. Spinning around in my chair, I pin him with a glare. "Don't touch me." With a hushed voice, mindful of others within earshot, I add, "Ever."

He holds up his palms in surrender, but his smarmy

smile is still in place. Ever since he transferred in from Atlanta, he's been sniffing around, trying to be friendly. There's something untrustworthy about him. It's nothing I can pinpoint, but it lingers around him.

But I'm grateful he'd caused me to turn around to face him because another episode occurs, and I'm forced to read his lips.

"Just thought I'd save you from having to deal with a misogynist like the mayor." He shrugs as if it's no big deal. As though he goes around doing good deeds all the time.

He's stating facts I'm aware of. The mayor is a well-known misogynistic asshole, and if I was granted an interview with the man—and that's a huge if—I'd more than likely have to knee him in the balls for grabbing my ass.

The superintendent, however, has been accused of siphoning school monies into his personal accounts for lavish gifts and trips instead of using it for necessities like desperately needed renovations and the upkeep for the buses. That's a story I could really sink my teeth into.

I stare into Evan's face. His fake tan contrasts with his glaringly bright bleached toothy grin.

"If you okay it with Anthony, I'm all for it."

"Done!" He shakes his fist with excitement. "I'll get the okay right now." Without a second to spare, he darts off, and I scoot my chair around the edge of my cubicle to watch him. Sure enough, he enters our boss's office and disappears for a matter of a minute at most before exiting with a triumphant grin on his bronze face. He flashes me a thumbs-up, and I merely nod and return to my desk.

Maybe I dodged a huge bullet this time with his help, but I still don't trust him.

GOOD SAMARITAN CHANGES TIRES FOR TWO TEEN GIRLS

"He told us to keep our doors locked the whole time. And he didn't want any money or anything. It was like he was really worried about us and wanted to make sure we were safe."

5

Jude

FEBRUARY

I've made my way to the outskirts of the downtown area near Lake Erie and the park overlooking the water. There are quite a few others who hunker down in the park's wooded areas rather than try their hand at overcrowded shelters. I'm planning to put my old thermal sleeping bag to use tonight. I've always felt more at ease outdoors. Something about the fresh air makes me feel more alert.

It's late—far later than I intended—because I stopped to drop off a few necessities for Curtis in case the weather took a nasty turn.

He and I first crossed paths when I'd found him after he slipped on a patch of ice. His thick-soled orthotic shoes were no match for the frigid temperatures. He'd dropped his eggs, busted open his bag of flour, and bruised his bananas. I didn't question why he'd been out walking a few blocks to the small grocery store alone. I'd witnessed it plenty; the older population either have no one who can help, or they're too stubborn and prideful to ask for help. I was grateful I happened to be nearby when he tripped because I'd immediately gone to check on him.

He'd been embarrassed and disgusted with himself, and after ensuring he wasn't hurt, I'd helped him to his door and told him I'd be back with his eggs, flour, and bananas that had spilled alongside the sidewalk.

It meant I had to go without a meal for a few nights, and with bed bugs running rampant throughout the city's multiple shelters, it meant no supplied meals. But it had been worth it when I'd caught the look on Curtis's face.

He'd taken my dirty hand in his own without any thought and squeezed it tight. "You're a good man," he'd told me.

I didn't have the heart to tell him he was wrong.

Now, striding down the wide sidewalk past the Fifth Third Bank, Fox News 6, and the office for *The Vindicate*, the area's largest newspaper, I cut through an alley to get to the park. It's in the sketchier part of town, and at night, things just get worse. I'm on high alert and continue at a clipped, quick stride when I hear it before I see it.

A car stalls, sputtering just as the driver steers it barely off the road, the headlights a beacon in the dark.

It's not a pricey model, but in this part of town, it's bound to gain attention. I cautiously approach and peer in the passenger side window.

A dark-haired woman sits, her palms smacking the steering wheel in apparent frustration. I gently tap against the window to get her attention.

She jerks and stares at me, eyes wide, startled. I hold up my palms and speak through the window.

"I'm sorry to startle you, but I wanted to check and see if you're okay."

"I…" She winces, expression brimming with embarrassment. "I ran out of gas."

"I'll get it for you." I tip my head down the street in the direction where the gas station is located. "It shouldn't take me long." I glance around before turning back to her. "Make sure your doors are locked. And get your cell phone out in case you need to call for help. If anyone bothers you, promise me you'll dial 911." My tone is stern and demanding because this is the worst part of town to have car trouble in.

She nods quickly, her eyes not leaving my face. "I promise."

Satisfied with her response, I rush off in the direction of the gas station. Luckily, it's a pretty slow night, and I get in and out with a small plastic container filled with gas for the woman's car. When I approach the car, I move slower so as not to scare her. She hits the switch inside the car to open the fuel door for me, and I fill the tank with gas.

Once the container is emptied, I tighten the cap and secure the small door. I bend down and peer through the passenger window. "Go ahead and start it up."

She cranks the engine, and it starts flawlessly. With a relieved smile, she cracks the window barely an inch. "Thank you. Oh!" She reaches for something and rummages before grimacing up at me. "I only have two dollars cash."

I wave it off. "Don't worry about it. Just get home safe." As an afterthought, I add, "And don't let it get so close to E next time."

"Thank you." The softness in her voice catches me off guard because it holds a genuine appreciation. "I don't even know your name so I can thank you properly."

An inner war instantly begins within me. On these streets, I'm nameless, but something compels it to spill past my lips.

"Jude."

Her tentative smile is like a breath of fresh air. "Thank you, Jude."

"Drive safely." I nod and step back from her vehicle.

I wait and watch as her taillights fade from sight before I get my ass in gear to return the gas can and head to the park.

The memory of her smile lingers, flashing on repeat in my dreams throughout the night.

BEING aware of my surroundings through keen observation is vital. In some cases, it can mean the difference between life or death.

The only neighbor in my vicinity is a woman I'd estimate to be in her late fifties. Although she seemed well-attuned to this lifestyle, I didn't recognize her from around this area.

Apparently, someone else picked up on this knowledge.

"Give me your fucking stash!"

The not-so-hushed demand wakes me. They can't be much more than a few yards away.

My sleeping bag is well-concealed since I chose a spot the average person would shy away from. Between two thick tree trunks, I'm on a pile of dead leaves that provides a natural cushion between me and the ground. Most people want a cleaner spot or one that doesn't require being close to trees or anything pertaining to Mother Nature.

Everything is still damp from the earlier snowfall, masking the sound of my approaching footsteps.

"I'm not gonna ask again. I'll cut your goddamn throat." The recognition of that voice has me hastening my steps.

Like hell he will. My "neighbor" doesn't deserve to get her throat cut. That much I know.

Darrel's running his mouth so much he doesn't even detect my approach. Which is exactly how I prefer it.

Within the blink of an eye, I disarm him, throw him on the cold, damp ground, and press my knee against his spine.

"What did I tell you before, Darrel?" I cluck my tongue. "Didn't your mama teach you to make good choices?"

"Don't you talk about my mama!"

I press more weight on his spine. "How 'bout you stop being a fucking bully and thief, then? Otherwise, someone might have to pay a visit to your mama after all."

He doesn't appreciate my threat in the least and mutters a string of obscenities about what he'll do if I go after his mother.

"I'll kill you, motherfucker!" His cheek is pressed hard against the firm ground, partially muffling his words. But the sentiment is clear.

It doesn't faze me. Instead, it further incites the rage inside me. The one I try to suppress.

But it's no use. I refuse to stand by and allow Darrel to do this to her.

I refuse to have another death on my hands that I could've prevented.

My tone is lethal, steely when I bend and lower my face to his. "You can't kill someone who's already dead."

Then I grab the six-inch knife and drive it through his hand and into the hard ground underneath it.

His howls don't register; they're simply white noise. Once I ensure the woman's unharmed, I suggest she move on. She immediately nods and rushes to gather her belongings. I walk away and quickly pack up my stuff, ignoring Darrel's cries intermixed with curses and threats.

They roll right off me because I spoke the truth.

I might have blood pumping through my veins, but everything inside me is dead. I'm not ready to fully leave this earth just yet, though.

I haven't fulfilled my penance.

6

Faith

FEBRUARY

"Call me if you need me, okay?" I hover at the door, hating that I have to leave him. Granted, he has the horrid man-cold right now, but I still worry about my best friend and roommate.

He's even gone so far as to only put a little gel in his hair. This is huge for a man who uses more products in one sitting than I do in a full year.

It could also be that I haven't dated in what seems like an epoch, but whatever.

"Go on, or you'll be late." Max waves his hand. "Get to work. Love you."

"Love you, too." I start pulling the door shut, and it's nearly closed when he calls out, "And don't forget to fill up your car!"

I lock the first-floor apartment door and stride to my parking spot.

The same car that ran out of gas just last night.

I quickly slip inside and toss my soft briefcase on the passenger seat before I crank the engine and turn on the defrosters. Thank heavens we didn't get more snow dumped on us last night. I grab my large ice scraper from the passenger side floorboard and tug the collar of my winter coat up farther to ward off the bite of cold air. I scrape at the annoying glaze of ice on all my car windows until I feel I can safely navigate my car.

Once I'm inside and buckled in, I head to work. But my mind replays the events from last night the entire time.

The man who'd come to my rescue had been a bit… intimidating, to say the least. Not because he was a vagrant, but because of the way he carried himself. His broad shoulders and the overwhelming intensity of his stare, evident even in the dim light from the nearby street-lights, led me to believe his physique was just as powerful beneath his thick, dark winter coat. His jawline was strong beneath his dark beard, and I found myself wondering about his hair concealed beneath that black knit beanie. I couldn't shake the feeling that I'd seen him before.

His voice was deep and gravelly as though it was rusty from disuse because he didn't speak much. But his lips are what drew me in, what had me so transfixed. The way he spoke each word so carefully, mesmerizing me with the sharp contrast of his white teeth.

I'd been too distracted, stressed, and had forgotten to fill up my car. It had been an idiotic move since I drive past some not-so-savory neighborhoods to get to and from work.

But he'd come to my rescue. He hadn't wanted to take my measly two dollars as payment, which surprised me because it was obvious he needed it.

Jude.

I just wish I knew how to find him to repay him.

Once I've parked in the lot designated for the paper's employees, I slip out and catch myself looking for the banana, muffin, and bottled water I used to bring each morning for Hank, the homeless gentleman I'd come to look forward to greeting in the mornings.

When I heard through the grapevine that he'd been murdered, I'd been devastated. He had been one of the kindest souls around. I'd tried to offer him money many times, but he'd always refused. Instead, he requested, with what I'd come to think of as his sparkle in his eyes, that all he wanted was to see me smile.

My lips tilt up at the corners as I recall Hank, and I wonder if he was watching out for me last night.

I wonder if he had anything to do with Jude coming to my rescue.

"CONNORS! IN MY OFFICE!"

My boss's bark is the jolt to my system caffeine could never rival. The man has the uncanny ability to startle me when I'm deep in thought or concentrating on an assignment.

He also doesn't believe in using the intercom system on our phones.

Blowing out a long breath, I rise from my chair and exit my cubicle to walk the few feet to his large office.

I hover in the doorway. "Sir?"

"Come in. Sit." He waves his hand without glancing up, keeping his attention transfixed on his computer screen.

I lower myself onto one of the two chairs across from his desk and fold my hands in my lap.

"You got my email that you're assigned that boring-ass story on St. Michael's shelter, right?" He screws up his face in what appears to be disgust. "Upper management is making us do that," he mutters.

I furrow my brow, unsure where this conversation is going. "Yes, sir, I got your email."

"How's the story coming along?"

"I have an appointment to head there later today. Rob's also going to take some photos of the place before they open the doors to show the contrast better from empty to capacity. Then I'll get some interviews."

"After you wrap that up, I have something else I want you to look into."

He slips off the thick black-framed glasses that he believes make him look trendy or hot—major fail, there—and levels a look at me. I force myself not to shift nervously beneath his heavy gaze. He grasps the screen of his desktop computer and swivels it my way.

"Look at this. See these headlines?" He clicks his mouse on each internet window to open them, and the headlines of each newspaper website are similar.

Rumor of a Good Samaritan and ***The Good Samaritan saves shut-ins from the harsh, extended winter weather*** are in bold font.

I lock eyes with him. "I've heard some rumors about a person helping some shut-ins but nothing really noteworthy."

He nods slowly. "That's what I thought." He leans back in his chair. His plain white button-down shirt stretches across his potbelly. The buttons threaten to bust, and there's already a small coffee stain on his light gray tie.

It finally dawns on me that he's using past tense. "Thought?" I pose carefully.

He purses his lips. "Until I stumbled upon a police report." He slides his glasses back on and picks up a paper, reading from it. "They discovered a man in the woods of Erie Park who had multiple stab wounds." His eyes meet mine. "Turns out he not only had a rap sheet, but he wasn't exactly popular among the homeless population."

I mull over this news. "And you think the same person—the Good Samaritan—is responsible? Turning vigilante?"

He shrugs. "Who knows? What I *do* know is that it's a hot story and one we need." He links his fingers behind his head and leans back in his chair. "If we broke the news on his identity, that would mean a huge boost in readership and ratings." His gaze settles on me.

I know there's more here, so I wait him out.

I don't have to wait long.

"And if you get the story, that means a considerable bonus for you."

Whoa. Now that's not what I was expecting. At all.

I lean forward in my seat. "And by considerable, you mean…?" Because, make no mistake, I could certainly use the extra money a raise could provide. It would make a huge dent in the amount I need to save.

"I mean a three percent raise."

Three percent… I'm already mentally calculating how much more that means I'd bring home after taxes.

God, that would ease the burden considerably.

I nod. "I'm on it."

His mouth curves into a satisfied smile. "Knew I could count on you."

Slightly dazed, I exit his office and head back to my cubicle.

Unfortunately, Evan appears out of nowhere, like a shark when there's blood in the water.

Barely able to withhold an exasperated sigh, I do my best to ignore him as he trails me.

"What's up? Boss called you in his office, huh?" he prompts expectantly. "What did he want?"

I drop into my desk chair and finally raise my eyes to his. "He just wanted to talk about the shelter piece."

He narrows his gaze as though he can sense I'm not being entirely truthful. "Right." His tone is ripe with doubt.

I turn my attention back to my work and my computer. "I need to get back to this." I'm clearly dismissing him, and we both know it.

He's always sniffing around, ready to pounce and steal other people's assignments. But mostly, he sticks close to me. I don't understand why he's singled me out among the others, but for whatever reason, he views me as his biggest competitor.

Evan leans in, his mouth inches away from my ear. His stale coffee breath assaults my senses as he taunts, "I know there's a story, and I'm not afraid to go after it, Connors."

Then he's gone.

To haunt someone else.

Some days, I really hate this job.

"THIS PLACE IS HUGE. No wonder they need help funding it." Rob surveys the vast building serving as the shelter. "Must be expensive as hell to heat and cool." He shakes his head. "Let alone the cost of food for everyone."

He photographs the outside of St. Michael's shelter first—and quickly, due to the harsh wind pelting us—before we walk up to the main entry. They keep the entrance locked during certain hours for the safety of the staff while they prepare for each evening.

William, a tall, wiry man in his early forties, greets us when we ring the doorbell and welcomes us inside.

"Faith." He flashes me a wide smile and envelops me in

a hug. "So good to see you." I feel terrible I haven't been around in a while. This job has sucked the life out of me.

William gives us the official tour of the facilities, explaining their everyday schedule and the services they offer. Most of the information I already know, but I asked him to treat us like any other visitors in an official capacity.

Once William's finished, I ask Rob to take more photos of the shelter before they open their doors for the evening. By the time four thirty rolls around, a line has already formed outside the entrance. The earlier people check in and register for the shelter's services, the higher their chances are at getting a better sleeping assignment—the bunks rather than the mats on the floor—for the night.

I offer to assist with serving the dinner, and William gratefully accepts, leading me over to an older woman with a familiar face.

Terri, the shelter's cook, flashes me a bright smile. "Faith!" She draws me in for a hug and pats my back gently. "I've missed seeing you around." Her whispered words send immediate surges of guilt through me.

I ease back with an apologetic look. "I know. It's been…a little rough lately."

She nods, her features etched with sympathy. Quickly shifting gears, she clasps her hands together. "Well, I appreciate you volunteering to help tonight." Her expression sobers, and she lays a hand on my arm before lowering her voice. "It's nice not having to go through my usual spiel and reminder that these people aren't to be looked down upon just because they're homeless."

"Oh, of course. I would never…" I trail off at a loss for words.

Her smile is near blinding. "Oh, I know, sweetie." She turns and grabs large plastic gloves. "Put these on, and I'll get you started serving the chicken and dumplings."

I don the gloves and follow her over to the large heated serving platter, waiting for the people to begin cycling through the dinner line. As I survey the mass of individuals entering the large room, I swear I catch sight of a man in a thick winter coat who looks familiar. As quickly as the glimpse is, he's gone, and I'm left wondering if I imagined him.

"YOU DID A WONDERFUL JOB." Terri releases a long but satisfied sigh. We served nearly eight hundred individuals tonight, ensuring they received a hot meal on a cold evening.

"It was my pleasure." And I mean it. Tonight was a wonderful experience, to be able to serve others who are experiencing tough times. I need to make this a priority especially since I attend St. Michael's church next door. I learned from Terri that many of the long-term food donation agreements have fallen through. Hopefully, this story will bring more attention to this shelter and allow them to garner new businesses to partner with for donations.

Rob sidles up with his camera already secured in the bag. "I got a ton of great shots."

"Great." I blow out a long breath and glance at the clock on the wall. "I think I'll see if I can catch Father James before I leave."

Rob hesitates. "You want me to wait and walk out with you?"

I wave him off. "No. You head out. I'll be fine."

He gives me a little salute. "See you in the morning."

"Drive safe."

I turn to Terri. "When does Father James normally finish up with mass for them?"

Terri checks the time. "Right about now, actually."

"Oh, great. I wanted to chat with him before I left."

"Thanks again, Faith. Hope to see you soon."

I relish the hug she wraps me up in. "I do, too."

I'VE ALWAYS FOUND STEPPING inside St. Michael's Cathedral to be inherently soothing. Some might say it's the ornate decorations, the stained glass, the carved wood, and the marble, but I know better.

I can practically feel the goodness, an ethereal quality, when I step inside as though I sense a holy presence. I can't quite explain it, but a calmness—a serenity—instantly washes over me.

Lord knows I can use some of that with the stress I've had lately over the uncertainty of my future. I never could have predicted I'd have to make a decision of this caliber or that I'd be dealing with such a powerful blow with the capability to change my life forever.

Father James is at the front of the church, preparing the altar for tomorrow morning's service. I quietly slip into a pew at the rear of the church and use my foot to ease the kneeler down. Lowering myself onto the padded leather, I link my fingers together, bow my head, and pray.

Lord, please watch over those in the shelter and those who decide to brave the streets this winter. I pray for my friends' safety and health. And, selfishly, I'd like to pray for myself, too, Lord. I pray that my—

My thoughts draw to an immediate halt as goose bumps rise on my skin. It's not from the cold, however; this is far different. It's the sense that someone's attention is riveted on me.

Slowly, ever so cautiously, I turn my head to the left.

Shock reverberates through me, and an audible gasp escapes my lips.

It's him. The man who helped me the other night. Except now I'm afforded a better look at him without the shadows of night masking so much.

Before I realize what I'm doing, I've risen from my seat to approach him at the far end of the pew. Once I reach within a foot of him, I stop and falter, nervousness ricocheting through me. His eyes don't veer from mine. The edge of his mouth tips up the tiniest fraction, and he waves a hand, gesturing to the empty wooden seat beside him.

"Feel free."

Without the barrier of my car's window, his voice is clearer now, though it still has that rough, gravelly quality to it.

I lower myself to sit beside him and find that I'm caught off guard by his clean, masculine scent. Immediately, I reprimand myself for being judgmental toward a person who's homeless. "I want to thank you again for the other night." I break off with a nervous laugh. "I swear, I'm not normally so…forgetful."

His eyes are a deep, stormy blue, like a tumultuous sea during a storm. Framed by dark lashes, they survey me in a way that makes me feel like he can see right into the heart of me. As though he detects everything I attempt to keep beneath the surface—all my worries and fears. I allow my gaze to skim over his straight nose and along his dark beard. His hair, almost black in color, appears a bit damp as if he's freshly showered. Parted lazily on one side, it's nearly chin length.

His lips part to speak, and I can't help but marvel at how lush his bottom lip appears in contrast to the top. "You're welcome."

"I'm Faith, by the way." I offer my ungloved hand to

him, and for a split second, he hesitates as though he's going to refuse to shake it. As though he has an aversion to touching me.

Finally, he reaches out his right hand, and the instant he grasps mine, I'm overwhelmed by the sensation of his rough calluses in contrast to the firm warmth of his touch.

How a stranger's touch can elicit comfort is puzzling to me.

Once he relinquishes his hold on my hand, I find myself bereft and strangely yearning his touch.

A man I don't even know.

Good grief. All this stress must be frying my brain cells, too.

I curl my fingers tightly against my palm as if to somehow preserve his touch.

"Jude."

I jerk my attention from him to discover Father James standing at the end of the pew near the man's side.

Father smiles at me. "Faith. So nice to see you." His eyes flick back and forth between me and Jude. "Do you two know one another?"

I part my lips to answer, but Jude beats me to it. "No, sir." He rises abruptly and mumbles a hushed yet polite, "Excuse me." Father steps aside, and we both watch the man slip through the large wooden doors with a stealthy quietness.

"He's intriguing, isn't he?"

I return my attention to the older man settling onto the pew beside me.

"You know him?"

Father stretches an arm along the back of the wooden pew and shakes his head slowly, thoughtfully. "I can't say that I know him, actually. Not well at all." His gaze focuses on the altar in front, and his brows pinch together. "He's different than the others. I can't quite put my finger on it, but there's just something about him…"

"Different as in…dangerous?"

Please say no.

Father turns and rests his gaze on me. "No, I don't think he's dangerous to you." He studies me for a beat. "Have you two met before?"

I glance around the empty church before answering. "He helped me when I ran out of gas on my way home from work."

He frowns with concern. "You ran out of gas?" He blows out a long breath and smooths a hand down his neatly trimmed beard. "Oh, Faith. You need to be more careful."

I scoff. "Tell me something I don't already know. But with work and…everything else, I've been a little spacey lately." I slouch against the hard wood of the pew. "I tried giving Jude money—granted, I only had two dollars on me—but he refused. I mean, money might be tight for me, but it surely isn't as bad as…" I trail off and peer up at Father James.

His mouth curves upward into a faint smile. "I think he's prideful. It's common. Especially among a lot of the men."

We fall silent, our attention resting on the ornately carved depictions of *The Last Supper*. We remain this way for so long that when he finally speaks, it startles me even though he murmurs his words softly.

"You know I'm always here if you want to talk." There's a pause before he adds, "Or if you'd like me to pray with you."

I nod. "I know. And I appreciate it." I twist my lips ruefully. "No offense, Father." I turn to him and muster a pathetic excuse for a smile. "But I'm not so sure prayers are going to fix things in my case."

"I'm here if you change your mind." He reaches for one of my hands resting in my lap and gives it a comforting squeeze, then he tips his chin upward. "And He's always around, too, you know."

I nod. "I know. Thank you."

He releases my hand and rises. "I'll walk you back through the shelter so you don't have to walk the long way around to where you parked in front."

As I accompany Father James to the shelter, I can't help but wonder if I'll see Jude again. And if I'll ever get a chance to repay him.

7

Jude

MARCH

Mother Nature has decided to change her ways and stifle her wintery vengeance—at least by Cleveland's standards. The temperatures have reached the low forties, and it's been a nice reprieve from the harsh, extended winter.

I've discovered a perfect perch for the evenings; one I'm surprised others haven't stumbled upon. Not sure how long that'll last, so I'm taking advantage of the safety and peacefulness. This brick building has an odd layout. The bottom serves as a covered parking area which butts against the solid brick of another building surrounded by overgrown evergreen shrubs. The overhang from the parking area for the nearby hospital provides more shelter and shadows for me. It might be a tighter squeeze to fit in here, but it's worth it.

Every time I settle in for the night, she crosses my mind. Faith. My rough skin against her silky softness was a jolt to my entire system. Even more jarring was the realization she didn't appear to view me as some homeless bum or a loser. She looked at me with gratefulness etched across her face as though I was a good man.

My mind replays the way she regarded me that night in the church. It felt as though she could actually see me, the person, the human beneath the well-worn clothing and the unruly beard. She didn't view me as a lesser being or as faulty. Her eyes, a deep golden-brown hue with traces of green, tracked my movements and absorbed each word I spoke with an intensity I've never before experienced. No one has ever listened so attentively when I've spoken.

I felt like an asshole for skipping out on her abruptly that night when Father James approached, but she made me uneasy. I've not had that kind of reaction to a woman in years. And I have no name. I have nothing to offer. And right off the bat, I can tell she's the kind of woman who deserves everything in the world…and more.

She's the kind of woman who doesn't need to get wrapped up with the likes of me.

As much as my heartache has subsided along with a portion of grief, I can't deny the ever-present guilt that shows no signs of ebbing.

I give in to the urge to doze off since I've been fighting a damn cold. I'm hoping a little extra rest will help. It's barely dusk and far earlier than I've ever settled in for the night, but judging by my sluggishness and aches, it's necessary. As soon as I close my eyes, sleep pulls me under almost instantly.

My eyes flash open suddenly, and I estimate I've been asleep for a few hours judging by the pitch-black sky and the glowing streetlights. However, that's not what roused me. It's an uncanny awareness, a foreboding that floods my senses.

The sickening crash of metal fills the air, lingering like a waking nightmare that won't release you from its clutches. What soon follows are the piercing sounds of sirens wailing in agony and the flash of red and blue lights reflecting off the nearby buildings. A part of my body begs to go back to sleep, knowing I need it.

But I can't.

Someone might need help.

I rise quickly, securing my belongings within my pack even as I walk at a fast clip. Shifting my bag's straps over each shoulder, I navigate the side streets, the sound of cries and authoritative voices serving as my beacon.

Once I approach the scene, I shove aside my own nagging discomfort and ignore the deep ache in my body. Instead, I focus my attention on the crushed and mangled cars from the multiple-vehicle accident. Paramedics are outnumbered, and a handful of others are milling around, trying to help. The semitruck driver appears dazed as if in the full throes of shock while sitting on the curb as one police officer questions him.

A sports car is sandwiched between an SUV and an older pickup truck with steam wafting from beneath its hood. The truck, whose hood is mashed into the side of the semitruck, had apparently been carrying metal pipes in the truck bed, most of which are now scattered in disarray along the wide city street. After noting one of the metal pipes piercing the windshield of the sports car and driven into the driver's body, I cautiously approach the passenger side door, where a woman is slumped against the seat. I know I can't get to her unless I bust out the back window.

I give a solid rap of my knuckles against her passenger side window. "Can you hear me? I need to get you out of the car."

She stirs, and her lips part before her eyes flutter open.

"Can you tell me your name?"

"V-Veronica."

"Okay, Veronica. I'm going to break the back window

to get to you, okay? Don't turn around. Keep facing the front for me."

She appears dazed and not entirely coherent, but she nods, assuring me she understands in some capacity.

The trunk looks like an accordion, and I desperately attempt to pry it open farther in hopes that it contains what I need. I work my arm between the gap and feel around in search of the object, and my fingers wrap around the cool, hard metal of the tire iron.

Bingo.

Carefully withdrawing the tool from the trunk, I rush back to the sports car and shrug off my pack, placing it on the roof with the thick, cushioned straps hanging down along the rear window. With one strong swing of the metal, it collides against the fabric of one strap, creating a fissure in the glass. With two more carefully executed hits and a well-placed shove of my pack against the spider-webbed glass, it collapses inward in partial sheets.

I ease my way into the car, my large frame cramped by the small interior, and unfasten her seat belt. Her slumped companion's eyes are wide open, staring sightlessly, his upper body pierced with the metal pipe and neck twisted at an odd angle. His airbag appears to be deflated, another casualty from the pipe's impact.

I ensure my voice is smooth and calm in an attempt to distract her from noticing. "Can you move your legs?"

"Y-yes."

"I'm going to gently run my hands over you to check for any injuries, okay?"

"Okay." Her voice still sounds a bit dazed but more coherent than a few moments ago.

I carefully press along her side and around her ribs. She doesn't make any sound aside from her harsh breathing.

"It hurts…when I breathe." She winces and brings a hand up to the center of her chest over where the seat belt crosses her body. "And I can't breathe through my nose."

"You may have torn some cartilage in your chest when the seat belt held you back on impact. And your nose is broken from the airbag deploying." I pause briefly before continuing. "Can you move both your arms?"

"Yes."

"Okay, Veronica. I want to get you out of this car, but the doors aren't working in our favor right now. Do you think you could move your seat back for me? If it hurts too much, don't do it."

"I think so…" Her right arm reaches for the lever beneath her seat. I hear the release and watch as she slowly edges the seat back.

Once she's as far back as the seat will allow, I glance around, hoping there will be an available medic to help me remove her from the vehicle.

I lightly lay a hand on her left shoulder. "Veronica, I'm going to try to find another person who can help me get you out of here since it's a tight squeeze, and I don't want to chance—"

Her hand settles on mine, fingers clamping down as though I'm her only lifeline. "No, please." She swivels her head to lock eyes with me, panic in the depths. "Please don't leave me."

"I won't—"

"Hey!" an authoritative voice rings out.

I duck and maneuver my upper body out of the car and gesture for the person to hurry over. "I need help getting her out of the car. She has some apparent minor injuries, but I'm not certain she doesn't have anything internal. I didn't detect internal bleeding."

The male paramedic eyes me with a mixture of wariness and skepticism as he draws near. I know what it looks like, what *I* look like, but he needs to lay off his judgments and help me get this woman out.

With painstaking care, we manage to remove her from the vehicle and load her onto a stretcher by the time his partner approaches.

That's my cue to leave, and just when I take a step away, Veronica calls out.

"Wait! Is Michael all right?" Her eyes appear a bit wild now that her shock is beginning to wear off, and a panicked expression takes its place.

"Ma'am, we need to get you to the hospital. The other paramedics will tend to him."

He's either a newbie, or he sucks at disguising the truth in his voice.

She knows it. I watch as the realization washes over her, transforming her features instantly.

The agony and heartache are etched upon her face.

The man lifts the one end of the stretcher with his partner, but she reaches out for me. Her fingers catch the fabric at the end of my sleeve and curl around it, drawing me to a sudden halt. When our eyes lock, she utters two words which aren't necessary.

"Thank you." A myriad of emotions flicker in her gaze. Gratefulness, fear, and grief.

The two latter emotions, I'm all too familiar with.

I nod and wait for her to release her hold. Once she draws her hand back, I confirm paramedics have things under control before I venture on my way.

WOMAN STILL ON LOOKOUT FOR THE MAN WHO CAME TO HER RESCUE

"There's no telling what might have happened if he hadn't come along. Everything was shut down, and I was trying to make it to my parents' new house with my infant and got turned around because of the near whiteout conditions. I'd lost my cell phone charger, and my car died on me—basically everything that could've gone wrong had."

Regina Morris of Pottsville, Pennsylvania, said she hopes to find her rescuer and thank him personally. Her car broke down during the frigid snowstorm months ago, and a man had appeared out of nowhere, ready to help.

"His poor beard was iced over, but he told me he was going to get help and rushed off in the direction of the fire station two blocks away. Firemen came with blankets for my baby and me, and we stayed at the station and rode out the storm.

"Wherever he is, I want him to know that he's an angel, and my daughter and I owe him so much."

If anyone has any information regarding this story, please email us at newsdesk@thevindicate.com.

8

Faith

MARCH

Be aware of your surroundings at all times, especially at night, they say.

Well, that's easier said than done when you feel like the weight of the world is on your shoulders. When you have a million different thoughts flitting through your brain, wondering how you're going to solve problems that have no readily apparent solution in sight.

Like when you're desperately trying to hide how your body's failing you and attempt to perfect lip reading. How your hearing comes and goes in waves.

In my case, it's mostly going. Disappearing like the water in a slowly draining sink as it ekes away, getting lesser and lesser. Until no water remains.

It's genetic. Those were the doctor's words as if that would soften the blow. Because even though I'd had very little hearing loss throughout my childhood, it wasn't enough to warrant alarm. Gran had brushed it off, and I hadn't had any obvious effects, so I certainly never had concerns.

Until about two years ago.

I'd been in a meeting at work, and people were going around the large boardroom table, each contributing to the discussion. Suddenly, it was as though someone magically turned the dial down on the volume for my surroundings.

Until they were muted entirely.

It might not seem like a major issue initially. I mean, how many times had I fantasized about being able to mute Evan and his annoying, snarky self? *Countless.*

But when it began to happen more frequently, with longer periods of the "unexpected silences," I knew something was terribly wrong.

After being referred to the specialist, the look in her eyes, the one everyone knew was the *I hate giving bad news to patients* look, confirmed it.

The moment you're faced with losing your hearing altogether when you're only twenty-four years old is terrifying. My thoughts were all over the place.

I won't be able to listen to my favorite music.

I won't be able to interview people "normally."

I will never get to hear my baby's voice, to hear their first words.

I'll never be able to hear my husband tell me he loves me.

Granted, I don't have the latter two, but I'd always imagined my future including a husband and a child.

Instead, I was tested, and it was determined that cochlear implants might be able to help me. There are never any guarantees, of course, but it was hopeful news.

Until I realized it came with a ridiculous price tag.

My insurance isn't the greatest, so my out-of-pocket expenses are atrocious. Which is why I've been trying to save up and scrimp when I can. To tuck extra money away.

The Good Samaritan story can change things for me. Not only does it promise me a raise, but my name attached to the breaking news of the individual's identity can mean more opportunities.

I'm mulling this over as I head along the mostly deserted sidewalk to my car. Since I was running late this morning, the station's lot was already full, so parking a few blocks away was the only option. I decide to take the shortcut—to dart through one of the shorter, wider alleys to get to where my car is parked.

I should know better. Especially being a Cleveland native.

But I fall victim to my own self-absorbed thoughts. The woe-is-me mood is affixed to me like cling wrap.

Of course, that's when it happens.

The strong grip on the back collar of my coat yanks hard, catching me off guard and immediately sending panic coursing through my veins.

This is what they warn you about. What to do when you're attacked from behind when you're not expecting it.

And every damn thing we're supposed to do to resist and escape vanishes from my mind.

I'm frozen in shock, petrified.

The shove against the harsh brick building is enough to have me seeing stars and wincing from the impact my body and head have just sustained. Throbbing pain radiates through my skull.

Steely fingers wrap tightly around my throat, and his face is so close that it's out of focus. A knife digs into my skin, and the faint trickle of blood along the column of my neck serves as a cool wetness amidst the brisk night air.

All I can manage to concentrate on are his lips. The movement of them as he speaks his threats.

He slams me against the unforgiving brick surface, once, twice, and a third time. "Don't you fuckin' think about screamin'," he hisses, his spittle flecking my skin. With each blow my body sustains, I battle against my vision fading to black. "You think you're so much better than me, don't you, bitch?"

If this were any other scenario, I'd have laughed and given him one of those *you're ridiculous* looks. Because I don't think I'm better than anyone else. Especially now. If anything, I *know* I'm not better.

I'm faulty. Defective.

But the tightening of his fingers around my larynx isn't allowing me a chance to speak. To defend myself.

He doesn't care.

His other hand offers me a short reprieve from the knife at the side of my throat. He shoves aside my unbuttoned jacket and grips the front of my blouse, jerking in a downward motion. The buttons immediately give way as the fabric rips under the pressure.

It may be weak and the polar opposite of brave, but my initial wish is to die right now. Because the option of being aware of what's to come? I honestly don't think I am strong enough to survive that. He's angry and wants to take his anger out on someone.

And I'm the chosen victim.

My skirt is tugged and pulled to the point where I vaguely register the chafing from his rabid insistence on removing it from my body. He uses the knife to slice through the fabric, and I brace myself for it.

For the violation. For him to mutilate me. I've covered stories like this. Horrific accounts that have left me with nightmares.

You never think it'll happen to you.

Until it does.

He places the knife against my throat, digging into the already open wound created by the sharp blade. If I fight against him, it means that knife at my throat can cut into my jugular. It's a choice I never thought I'd have to make.

Choosing the risk of a brutal death versus enduring the worst violation anyone could ever experience.

I close my eyes and mentally utter a prayer. I pray that Max doesn't have to identify my body. That Father James knows how much I love him like the father I never had.

I pray that they find this monster before he does this to someone else. That maybe he'll leave evidence behind.

Allowing only a single tear to escape, I open my eyes, prepared to use all my force to jerk the side of my neck into the sharp point of his knife.

Except I don't get that far. As though anticipating my intent, he slams me against the rough brick wall so violently that my vision fades to black.

I register the sound of my own whimper echoing in my ears, and I succumb to the darkness that overtakes me.

9

Jude

I'm coming down from the adrenaline rush from helping that woman—Veronica—and heading back to my spot. I need to try to get some rest because I feel like shit.

The soles of my boots are nearly soundless as my feet eat up the sidewalk, and I stride quickly through the alleyways in a shortcut.

That's when I feel it.

The hairs on the back of my neck stand on end, and I slow my breathing even further, attempting to calm the surge of adrenaline at the instantaneous awareness that something is awry.

The sound of a woman's clicking heels on the asphalt reaches my ears, the downtown buildings creating an acoustic oasis. But that's not what lights a fire under my ass. It's the faint sound of someone trailing her. The slight scuffing of sneakers following close behind.

My feet carry me in quiet but rapid strides in the woman's direction. My ears perk, keeping track of every single nuance of sound I can possibly detect.

I draw still when her footsteps suddenly fall silent. With

my head cocked to the side, I try to catch a hint of sound to send me in the right direction.

That's the moment I detect a faint whimper followed immediately by the low rumble of a man's voice.

Then I'm off, running, grateful for my speed but also cursing this damn cold and how it has affected my head and made me slower than normal. Approaching the alley I believe they're in, I slow and cautiously turn the corner. It's ironic that this is only a few blocks from the hospital, and the sight I'm faced with immediately tells me I'll be making a stop there.

After I take care of business.

His hand is wrapped around her throat, the woman's body mostly limp, and he slams her against the ground.

She looks like she's taken quite a beating already and appears barely conscious, her jacket ripped open and blouse torn apart, likely from the knife-wielding asshole. A dark, expensive-looking briefcase is carelessly tossed aside. He's shoved her skirt up around her hips to grant him enough access. He's got his dick out and looks ready to roll.

Too fucking bad for him because I'm not about to let that shit happen.

I drop my bag from my shoulders. The sound grabs his attention, and he whips his head around to stare at me.

"The fuck you want?" The faint light from the nearby streetlights illuminates his face, and he squints at me dangerously. I notice the tiny teardrop tattoo at the corner of one eye.

Forcing a casual tone, I wave a hand toward the woman lying on the filthy ground. "Just thought maybe you'd wanna share?" I allow my eyes to gloss over her form. "She's a fine piece of ass."

"Yeah." He lifts his chin with pride. "But I got to her first." He turns back to her and releases an evil laugh.

"She's mine." He drags the blade of his knife down the center of her chest, the sharp tip cutting into her flesh and leaving a faint bloom of red in its trail. "You're Shanks's girl now, ain't ya?"

At his smug murmur to his victim, the rest of my surroundings fades away. *Timmy Shanks*. My eyes are suddenly drawn to the knife in his hand, now noticing the faint light reflecting off the blade where it's engraved.

A K-bar. But not just any fucking K-bar. This one was issued by the Marine Corps and later engraved on the shaft. I know this because one night when we'd both slept in the wooded park, Old Man Hank had shown me. Told me how his buddy had it engraved with the Marine Corps logo for him after he'd gotten out.

I stride over just as he's about to thrust his dick into the woman. My body moves of its own accord, and I wrap an arm around his neck, drawing tight. His gasps do nothing, make me feel nothing, unlike the woman's earlier sounds. He's fucking scum.

I squeeze as hard as I can, and his body goes limp. After a few more beats, I release him, prepared to let his body drop to the ground so I can see to the woman. He's nearly down to the concrete when I realize my mistake.

He's played me.

The knife makes a direct hit before I can move out of the way. It pisses me off—my stupidity, succumbing to this damn cold that's making me lose my edge, and this fucking asshole who stole Hank's life and prized possession.

I rear back and slug him as hard as I can. When my fist connects with his face, there's so much anger and pain behind it that it has far more force than even I expect. Timmy reels back, and his head knocks against the brick building behind him. He slumps instantly, his body crumpling to the filthy ground. I wait a beat, unwilling to be played the fool again. Only when my swift kick to his calf elicits no reaction, aside from his body slumping farther, does a fraction of the tension in my body ease.

I grip the handle of the knife and pull it out of my side. The flow of blood tells me this is going to be a bitch to patch up, but I'm breathing easily, so I don't think he nicked a lung. I grab some nearby newspapers someone's tossed beside one of the dumpsters a few feet away and stuff them beneath my shirts and clothing, pressing it against my skin. It'll have to do for now.

Grabbing my pack, I kneel beside the woman to check her pulse but jerk my hand to a stop.

Faith.

I hadn't realized it was her until now. With an unsteady hand, I place my fingers on the side of her throat and can't restrain the whoosh of air that spills past my lips in relief. Her pulse is still steady, but there's a chance she might have a serious head injury. I withdraw the jacket Pauline gave me from my bag and gently pull it over Faith's body to ensure she's somehow covered.

I gather my pack and can't restrain the wince at the pain that accompanies my movements as I slide the straps over my shoulders and jar my injury. I snag her thin briefcase; it dangles from my fingertips as I carefully heft Faith in my arms and begin rushing in the direction of the hospital.

Her eyes flutter open a fraction, and her lips, even amidst the bloody split along the bottom one, part as a whisper breaks free.

Pupils dilated, sudden panic etches her features, and one hand fists at my jacket. "Jude."

"I've got you."

That's all I can say. I can't promise to stay after I hand her over to the doctors. I can't jeopardize things even though I want nothing more than to continue holding her and relish the fact she's still alive. Reveling in the fact that she's in my arms and not shrinking away from me in horror or disgust.

Her eyes fall closed, and her fist relaxes its grip as she slumps against me.

Fear for her reverberates through me, warring with the searing pain from my knife wound. I don't understand why this woman elicits such a reaction from me. But the fact she does and the worry it causes me that she's fallen unconscious again tell me what I need to do.

I force myself to concentrate on things I can control. Walking. Getting her to the hospital. I can see the signs, illuminated in the night, the red and white glow serving as a beacon.

Ducking my head, I shift her weight in my arms to draw my hood over my ball cap and help disguise my features from any cameras on the nearby streets and intersections.

Once I enter the automatic doors of the hospital, I duck my head away from their surveillance. Although there's not much need tonight due to the still-present pandemonium resulting from the massive pileup.

"Just found her outside, lying there."

Nurses and an orderly rush over, and the woman is gathered onto a gurney along with her briefcase. I casually ease away from the bustling activity, allowing myself to get lost amidst the ruckus.

As soon as the doors slide closed after me, I pick up my pace as much as I can endure. My breathing becomes ragged far quicker than normal, but I push through the pain because I need to ensure no one's following me.

I have nowhere to go. I don't know anyone who knows how to patch me up.

No one who might actually do so without turning me away and leaving me to face the authorities.

Finally, once I'm nearly certain the coast is clear, I slow my pace and grab some discarded newspapers littering the sidewalk nearby. As I approach the small area I'd vacated what seems like only moments earlier tonight, I stumble, and it's at this moment I realize the side of my black hoodie is drenched with my own blood.

"Just need to sit down for a moment," I mutter to myself and gracelessly settle in a heap. Hands fumbling, clumsy from blood loss, I pull the duct tape from my pack and attempt to pack a wad of newspapers against my wound and tape it against my skin.

"GET UP."

The soft voice sounds far away as though it's echoing in a tunnel.

"Get up, sweetie."

The voice—a familiar one I haven't heard in years—sounds marginally clearer, but nothing like it normally does in my nightmares. It causes a deep ache in my chest, and I want so badly to open my eyes, to part my lips to respond, but I'm too weak. Nor am I brave enough to risk looking and dealing with the disappointment of not seeing her here.

Something wet touches my cheek. I swat at it and miss. My head is so foggy; my body utterly weak. The wet nudge happens again. It takes a concentrated effort to drag open my eyes.

When I finally manage to focus my gaze, I'm caught by surprise. A dog whines and nudges me with its wet nose again as if to say, *Get up, you lazy bum!*

"What do you want?" My voice sounds rusty to my own ears, my mouth parched, tongue like sandpaper. Shockingly enough, I realize I managed to sleep till the morning.

He whines again and nudges my jaw with his nose. He wants me to move. I know enough to realize animals have a keen sense, and I shouldn't ignore it.

I try to clear my head of the lingering cobwebs, the foggy sensation, and rise to my feet. Pitching forward, I nearly lose my balance, and the dog saves me by pressing his body against my legs to steady me.

Out of my periphery, I notice a few beat cops strolling down the sidewalk across the street with coffees in hand. Then I hear the telltale rumble of thunder. Glancing up at the rapidly darkening sky, I know we're in for one hell of a storm.

"Ah, thanks for saving me, buddy." The last thing I need is to get tangled up with them and have them asking me questions. Especially since I'm certain they'd notice the damp bloodstain along my left side and the drenched newspapers.

I peer down and take in his soulful eyes but also scan his body.

He's lean as though he manages to get just enough to eat—likely scavenging—but that's not what draws my surprise.

One leg—his left hind leg—is crooked. But it doesn't appear to slow him down one bit, aside from his slight limp when he moves.

"I don't know where you came from, but I'm sure grateful."

With my new companion nudging me, I brace myself against the brick wall of the nearby building. It takes everything to bite back the painful groan at each movement I make.

"Where do you think I need to go, buddy?" I murmur softly.

But then it hits me. The realization that one person might be able to help me and keep me safe.

I take a step, wincing with the movement. "This is a shot in the dark, you know."

I say that more to myself than to my canine companion.

A few drops fall, wetting his fur, and it seems like only seconds later, the sky opens up and a deluge of rain hits.

Rushing as fast as my feet can carry me across the few city blocks, we arrive at the door.

A place I never expected to visit.

A place I hope won't make me face my past. Won't force me to return there.

The parsonage.

The home of Father James.

10

Jude

I rap my knuckles against the door, leaning against the weathered siding covering the parsonage. I'm risking it all by coming here, but I don't have any other choice. I know enough that the wound on my side needs medical attention—more than I can attend to.

The sky is pitch black from the storm, which is unusual for this time of midmorning. I unscrew the bulb on the light enough to make it go out. The last thing I need is to draw more attention to myself.

With a groan, I press a hand against my side, my palm instantly wet from the fresh blood continuing to seep through the layers of clothing and attempted buffer of newspapers.

It seems like a decade passes before the sound of clicking locks reaches me, and the door opens a crack.

"Jude?"

I press my lips thin at the rush of pain that brings with it an onslaught of dizziness. "I'm sorry. I don't have anywhere else to go."

There's a beat of silence, and when Father James finally speaks, his voice is hard, firm, unlike normal.

"You're not involved in drugs or anything illegal, are you?" His brows slant together sternly.

Exhaling slowly through the pain, I swallow hard before I answer. "No, sir. I ended up on the wrong end of a knife…trying to save—" I'm unable to finish as I gnash my teeth together to fight against the combination of nausea and pain washing over me.

He mutters, "Hell," before opening the door and rushing to help me inside. Father locks up behind us and leads me inside his home.

"Let's get you in here and lying down…"

The last thing I recall is laying my head on the softest surface and being surrounded by the scent of fabric softener.

IT'S HAPPENING AGAIN.

It's one of those nightmares where a part of me recognizes it as such, yet it feels so real I can't turn it off.

It's the same scenario each time. A massive gap in the earth, a trench separating us. She's on one side, and I'm on the other. She cries out my name, begging me to save her. I try to move, but my entire body is frozen in place. My feet feel as though they're cemented to the ground, and I'm unable to move even an inch to reach her.

I'm helpless to do anything except watch as the gap between us widens farther, and she finally disappears from sight. I yell out her name, frantically searching, desperate for even a glimpse, only to find nothing.

She's gone forever, and I'm still rooted to the spot. The

toes of my shoes are at the edge, and the earth begins crumbling beneath me.

"Easy, easy. You're safe, Jude."

The male voice echoing in my ears has a familiarity but not enough to set me at ease. I don't understand why I'm being called Jude. That's not my name.

"Easy, son. Easy." The man's gentle tone holds a comforting quality that seeps through me. The soft furry object thrust against one of my hands is warm and soothing.

I allow myself to be drawn away from the nightmare and into the darkness as his voice fades, sounding farther and farther away.

I SHIFT, and a sudden awareness washes over me. The scents surrounding me are different, contrasting with the distinct odors I've become accustomed to. The way unclean skin smells. The scent of rotten food. The stench of filth and excrement of others.

None of that is here.

My eyes flutter open, and I wince at the harsh presence of the light.

"Look who's finally decided to join us."

My initial response is to jerk upright in alarm, but my side immediately screams out at that choice. I groan and discover I'm lying in bed, shirtless, in only boxers. A large bandage is secured to the area below my ribs, and I gingerly run my fingers along it. The tightness tells me I'm likely the owner of a set of stitches. Finally, I focus my gaze on the man sitting in the chair beside the twin bed.

Of course, he's not the only one in the room. The dog

who's decided to become my new companion is perched right alongside me, blue eyes beseeching.

"Hey, you." I reach out my upturned palm, and he nuzzles me. His instant touch is comforting, setting me at ease. Yet I can't ignore the heavy scrutinizing weight of Father James's stare.

I scan my surroundings, noting the light streaming through the curtains on the small window. "How long have I been out?"

"Two days."

I clench my jaw. *Fuck.* "I'm sorry." I shake my head with regret. "I didn't think I would be that much of an inconvenience."

He quirks a brow, and there's a mixture of amusement and challenge in his tone. "Did I say you were?" He settles an affectionate look on the dog. "Your little companion's had a bath and been checked out by the vet, too. Turns out he's a Blue Great Dane. Vet said this breed has an uncanny ability to sense danger."

Interesting. That certainly explains his help the other night.

With care, I lift my body upright and slide my legs over the side of the bed. "I should get out of your hair. I'm sorry you had to go to so much trouble."

He throws up a hand to stop me, his forehead creased. "Stop. You can't leave just yet. If you're that intent on going, I insist you let me feed you before you head on your way."

I part my lips to protest, but the words catch in my throat at his stern expression. I press my lips together firmly and nod. "Yes, sir."

He rises from his seat, and it jogs my brain. "Wait." Alarmed, I try to figure out how to ask him without giving away too much. "Have you…heard anything about the woman?" I try to keep my tone free of any traces of emotion. "Have you heard about Faith?"

I should've known better.

He eyes me with interest...and something else I'm unable to decipher. "I got a call about one of our parishioners being in the hospital. A victim of an attack."

I remain silent but maintain eye contact.

"You know anything about that?" He arches an eyebrow in question.

Choosing my words carefully, I offer, "I didn't attack her."

He stares at me, and it's uncanny how his eyes feel as if they have the ability to peer right into my soul.

If I still had one, that is.

"Will she be okay?"

There's a beat of silence before he answers with a slow nod. "The trauma caused a pneumothorax—a partial collapse of her lung. They had to insert a chest tube, but everything seems to be resolved now. She's expected to recover fully."

I can't restrain the tiny whoosh of breath I expel in relief. Something catches my eye just then, and I notice the telltale bandage on the top of my hand. I flick my gaze to him in surprise.

"There were signs of infection, so I started you on an IV." He lifts a shoulder, eyeing me pointedly. "You're not the only one with secrets, Jude."

I press my lips together firmly, knowing I won't—can't—rise to the bait. My lack of response doesn't appear to faze him, though.

"I washed everything you had as a preventative measure since we don't need you getting any dirt or germs anywhere near that incision."

Pausing in the doorway, he doesn't turn around. "I

plan to visit Faith in the hospital if you feel up to tagging along. After we eat lunch, though." He steps out of sight, but I catch his good-natured muttering. "Need to fatten you up." There's a pause, then his voice sounds further away. "Too many damn muscles for your own good."

"I WAS there to pray over her before she regained consciousness."

Father folds his laundry while I sit on the couch at his insistence that we talk. "She's like a daughter to me, that one." His mouth curves upward, and his eyes take on a certain brightness I've not witnessed before. "She's had a rough go of things but hasn't given up."

As he sets a folded pair of socks on top of the pile of clean laundry, his expression sobers, and he takes a seat in the chair across from me. He leans forward, the light from the nearby lamps making his nearly bald head shine. Elbows resting on his knees, he links his fingers, and when he raises his pale blue eyes to lock with mine, I already know I'm not going to like what he's about to say.

"I hope you understand that I had to leave you under someone's supervision so I could be with Faith."

Fuck.

Tension expands through me much like a rapidly moving cloud from nuclear fallout, nearly paralyzing me.

Am I at risk?

I already know they didn't take anything from my pack. I'd inspected it earlier before I'd finally dragged myself out of bed to use the bathroom. There were no signs of anyone detecting the secret compartments.

I don't offer a response because if there's one thing I've

already confirmed about Father James, it's that he's an intelligent man. Astute as hell.

"You're safe here, Jude."

"Am I?" I challenge softly.

His response is part sigh, part chuckle. "Of course. But I feel it necessary to mention the person who watched over you was a friend of mine. Pat Hollcom."

Father inhales deeply before releasing it slowly while sitting back in his chair. "He's a former cop, retired now." His lips twist, expression tinged with sadness. "He lost a partner and couldn't recover from that. Got out early."

A damn cop watched over me. Just fucking great.

"I wanted you to know it won't be an issue."

I mull over his words for a beat, rolling them around in my mind before I finally ask, "You believe that?"

"I do."

His immediate response should put me at ease, but it doesn't. Trust is earned. Sure, the man patched me up when he could've just as easily let me bleed out on his doorstep, but normally someone wants something out of the deal. Tit for tat.

"He won't take me in?"

Father shakes his head slowly. "No reason to do that. Especially since I told him you saved our girl."

I raise my eyebrows at his curious phrasing. "Our girl?"

A slow, sheepish smile spreads across his face. "That's how we all think of her. Faith has been around us since she was a teen." He turns and focuses on what I hadn't noticed adorning the wall. A photograph of a bunch of people, some in police uniforms, others in plain clothes, Father James with his arm draped across the shoulders of a young teenage Faith with the backdrop of what appears to be a bar. She smiles wide, the happiness on her face illuminated by the glow from the candles on the enormous birthday cake in front of her. *Happy sixteenth birthday, Faith!* is written in neat icing script.

"We all love Faith like she's our own. Would do anything for her." His voice is softer, gentler. When I turn to look at him, he's still gazing at the photograph as though lost in the memories it holds.

He rises from his seat and grabs his basket of clean laundry. "After lunch, we'll go and visit her at the hospital so you can see her for yourself." He pauses at the doorway of his bedroom and glances over his shoulder. "I know she'll want to thank you."

I CAN'T RECALL the last time I brought flowers to a woman. Hell, I can't remember the last time I bought flowers, period.

My intentions aren't entirely noble, though. I'm afraid that someone at the hospital will recognize me from the other night. With this bulky arrangement, I can hide my face. Never thought the day would come when I'd have a priest's assistance in masking my identity as we strode through a hospital.

"Hello, Father."

Numerous people nod their hellos to Father James as we navigate through the hallways on our way to Faith's room.

My palms are sweaty—fucking sweaty like I'm a damn teen on his first date—and my heart ratchets up a few notches. What the hell is it about this woman who has me feeling so off-kilter?

The door to her room is partially open, and it's quiet inside. Father raps his knuckles on the door twice before a hushed male voice calls out, "Come in."

A man is here with her. Probably her boyfriend. Or fiancé. All I can think is that he'd better be treating her right. Like a fucking queen. With the utmost care.

I follow Father inside and notice the curtain separating her space from the other patient's area is open, and that hospital bed is empty.

"Faith," Father speaks in a soothing tone, approaching the side of her bed, and grasps her hand gently. "How are you feeling?"

She grimaces, not immediately noticing me as I hang back and drink in the sight of her. She's lying in her bed, slightly reclined, hair the color of brown sugar fanning the pillowcase. Her eyes have life in them—a vast contrast to the last time I saw her. She's still a little pale, and the bandage along one side of her throat causes a swell of rage to rush through me at the memory of what almost happened to her.

"I've definitely been better. They said the swelling in my brain has subsided, thank goodness. Hopefully, I'll be out of here soon."

"She's not the most patient person in the world." This comes from the man who's around the corner of the wall on her other side. When I step forward, he comes into view. He fusses with the covers on her bed, tucking her in, and my entire body stiffens.

He's not at all who I pictured for her. With an athletic build, he's tall but not as tall as I am. His hair is perfectly styled, his fit body dressed in a button-down shirt that's pressed and pristine, his jeans molded to his body. Hell, even his black shoes are polished. *What the hell?*

She rolls her eyes at him, their comfort with one another evident. "You'd be the same way if you were me."

I shouldn't have brought these damn flowers. *Fuck.* Maybe I can back out without anyone noti—

Father James chooses this moment to turn and wave his hand, gesturing me to come forward. "Jude. Come here and join us."

I ignore the heavy weight of the other man's eyes on me as I approach where Father stands at Faith's side.

Her sharp intake of breath causes my chest to tighten painfully. *Shit.* She probably doesn't want a stranger here. Probably doesn't remember me anyway. With more concentration than it requires, I set the vase of flowers on the nearby table.

"I just wanted to bring these by. Hope you heal up soon." I'm already halfway turned with my eyes trained on the exit when she speaks.

"Wait!" The urgency in her tone draws me to a sudden stop. "Please…don't leave yet." Her voice fades, drifting from a fierce urgency to timid.

I turn slowly, and when our eyes lock, an awareness shimmers between us. It's the strangest sensation I've ever experienced.

She watches me, her eyes beseeching. When I take one step toward her, she darts a look at the other men. "Could you both give us a moment?"

"Of course."

"I don't thin—"

The protesting response comes from her companion, who eyes me suspiciously.

"Max," she says in a placating tone.

He stares at her incredulously. "Do you even know this guy?" He waves a hand in my direction. "He looks like he came in off the streets."

Spine stiffened, I lift my chin defiantly. "Probably 'cause I did." I refuse to back down—refuse to be made to feel like a worthless piece of shit.

It might be true, but he doesn't need to know that.

"He saved my life, Max."

His eyes widen in disbelief, flitting back and forth between me and Faith. He appears to war internally with what he wants to say next.

Finally, his shoulders slump, and he shakes his head, features pinched tight. Without responding to her, he advances on me and stops, jabbing a finger in my direction.

"You'd better not try anything shady."

With that, he storms out of the room. Father James raises his brows as if to say, *Well, that was interesting*. He pats my shoulder once as he passes me before following in Max's wake.

She regards me with a hint of apprehension. The fingers of one hand tightly grasp the blanket covering her body, and as I allow my eyes to travel up along the blanketed outline of her body, my gaze stutters over the bruises along the column of her throat.

I clench and unclench my jaw as pure, unadulterated rage flows through me at the sight of those marks on her skin.

"I just…" She falters, her voice fading before she clears her throat to continue. "I want to thank you." Her eyes lift to mine, and the shimmering tears in the depths are like a gut-punch. "They told me the rape kit came back negative, but I keep thinking—" She breaks off as her voice cracks. "If you hadn't come along when you did…" Her bottom lip quivers slightly before she clamps her mouth tightly as if afraid to show her raw emotion.

I draw closer to her side. "Don't think about that. Any of it. Just concentrate on healing."

She reaches a delicate hand to me, palm upturned. I watch, dazed, like an out-of-body experience, as I draw my hand from the pocket of my pants and place my palm against hers.

Her fingers tighten slightly, and an eerie sensation washes over me. Her eyes are troubled, and she glances in the direction of the doorway before turning back to me, and whispering, "I see him every time I close my eyes."

Fuck.

Her words cause my chest to crack open wide, pain radiating through me.

"Don't." My tone is sharper than I anticipate, and I inhale deeply before softening my voice. I maintain our locked gazes while I speak. "Don't give him that power. He doesn't deserve it." A single tear escapes and trickles down her cheek. At the sight of it, my knees grow shaky, and I carefully lower myself to the chair beside her bed and swallow hard past the lump in my throat.

She nods slowly, and her voice is thick with emotion. "I'll think of when you held me in your arms. Kept me safe."

I can't tell if it's her or me who increases the strong clasp of our hands. All I know is, this is the first touch I've experienced in years that makes me ache, yearning for more.

It's at this moment the shift happens.

With my other hand, I use my thumb to gently swipe away the tears cascading down her cheeks.

I'm still on a mission, but my objectives have changed.

I have a penance to endure, yet now I have another task.

I vow to do everything in my power to keep this woman safe.

Even if it's from myself.

Bob Tallmedge, visiting from Florence, Kentucky, insists he saw a homeless man jump into action when a man with a probing cane carried by many who are blind appeared to have trouble managing the crosswalk of the busy downtown intersection.

Due to road construction, traffic has been considerably more congested and drivers less patient in this particular area. After the man, later confirmed to be legally blind, was nearly hit by an oncoming car, he was approached by the Good Samaritan who helped him cross the street.

Tallmedge claims the two walked for a while, passing numerous shops along Caswell Street before turning the corner. "My wife went into one of the nearby stores. While I waited outside for her, I noticed the Good Samaritan who'd helped the blind gentleman coming back toward me." Tallmedge says he stopped the man and thanked him for being so kind and tried to offer him cash as he'd appeared to have "fallen on rough times." The man politely declined and went on his way.

11

Faith

A part of me is mortified that I've broken down in front of him. Jude is practically a stranger, yet I feel more at ease with him than I've felt with anyone in years. My shoulders shake as I sob silently, failing in my attempt to pinch my eyes closed and staunch the flow of tears.

It's the touch, the slightest sensation of the callused pad of his thumb against my cheek that causes me to freeze.

I open my eyes, and our gazes lock. He's leaned closer, and I detect the slight mint in his breath and that same freshly showered scent I noticed when I'd seen him in the cathedral. His eyes, the shade of a tumultuous sea during a storm, flicker with a multitude of emotions as they stare deeply into my own. But one emotion in particular stands out.

Anguish. For *me*.

Our hands are still joined, and I'm gripping him so tightly that I fear it might stop his circulation.

His gentle touch wipes away my tears, and the soothing sound of his gravelly voice washes over me as I fix my attention on his mouth as he speaks.

"Shh," he whispers, his full bottom lip mesmerizing me. "Don't waste those tears on him."

"Jude, I—" I stop the instant he stiffens.

His eyes are pinched closed.

"Are you…okay?" I ask hesitantly.

The moment his eyes flare open, I'm robbed of breath, the embers of heat in the depths stirring something deep within me.

His gaze drifts to watch his thumb as it traces another tear to the edge of my top lip. The slightly roughened pad skims across it in a caress that has my mouth parting.

"Don't cry. You're safe now, Faith. I promise."

It's surreal how his words manage to burrow deep within me, somehow easing the heavy weight of fear that's been plaguing me.

People make promises all the time, and so many are broken. Yet Jude's promise makes me believe he's speaking the truth, and that he won't go back on his word.

"What the hell did you do?"

I jerk at the sudden sound of Max's angry demand. His steely glare is focused on Jude, who moves away from me. When he tugs his hand free of mine, I instantly register the loss.

Max strides over, bristling with anger. "You made her cry."

"Max, he didn't—"

"Easy, now." Father James steps up, his tone calm. "I'm certain Jude didn't do anything wrong."

It's clear my friend is warring with emotions, his loyalty and protectiveness at the forefront.

"I should get going." Jude takes another step back. He casts me an apologetic look before he turns to leave.

"Wait. Jude?" I don't speak until his eyes meet mine.

I'm not certain what makes me say it, but I feel an urgency I can't deny. "I'll see you…soon?"

He doesn't say a word, his face devoid of any flicker of emotion. After a beat, he nods and walks to the door.

"I'll be right there in a moment." Father directs this to Jude before he offers me a kind smile and gives my hand a gentle squeeze. "You need anything, call me."

"Thank you," I say softly.

As soon as he's gone, the silence between Max and me is nearly stifling.

He drops into the nearby chair, slumps his shoulders, and leans his forearms on his legs. Fixing his gaze on the floor, he releases a long sigh. "I don't like him, Faith."

I toss him a sharp look. "I don't understand why." Anger lines my tone. "The man rescued me."

His eyes lock with mine, gaze holding steady. "Because anyone can see there's more than meets the eye with him. He's…" He trails off with a shrug.

"Do you really think Father James would bring someone dangerous along with him?" I challenge. Narrowing my eyes, I continue. "Just because he's a little rough around the edges and in a tough place doesn't mean he's dangerous."

Max blows out a long breath, lowering his chin, and links his fingers together. "I'm not an idiot, Faith. I saw the way you looked at him. And how he looked at you, too." He shakes his head, and one side of his mouth tips up partially. "He's got that rugged look, but anyone with eyes can see he's a decent-looking guy." His expression drops, features tightening with worry. "I just don't want you getting hurt." He closes his eyes as if in pain. "Especially with what you're dealing with."

His words are like sharp knives, delving painfully deep. He's the only person who knows what I've been going through pertaining to my hearing loss and what I'm striving to do.

"There's nothing to worry about, Max." And it's true. We sit in silence, the only sound the faint bustling from the hallway outside.

I can't hold back. I have to know.

My tentatively whispered words seem to echo in the quiet room. "How did he look at me?"

Max slowly raises his head to meet my eyes but doesn't answer right away. His gaze searches my features for a beat before he finally murmurs softly, "Like you were everything he'd ever wan—"

"Knock, knock!"

Our eyes whip in the direction of the doorway. Mine are horrified, whereas Max's expression is one of curiosity.

I stare back, wishing I could shrink and this hospital bed would swallow me whole. Just to avoid Evan Phillips.

He strides in, looking like he owns the joint, and tosses a lone carnation onto the hospital tray table. "How's the patient doing?" He attempts an expression of concern, but I know better.

"Evan, this is Max. Max, this is my co-worker Evan." My monotone introduction speaks volumes even if I hadn't already vented to Max about the smarmy jerk.

Recognition dawns on my friend's face as he eyes Evan analytically. "Nice of you to bring Faith flowers."

The obvious jab doesn't register, and Evan leans against the foot of my bed as if he's right at home. "So, those two men who just left? They friends of yours?"

I don't like this one bit. With his attention fixed on me, I can't shoot Max a warning look without being obvious, so I try to play it off, praying Evan didn't overhear our conversation before he arrived.

"Yes." I pause for a millisecond. "Listen, Evan. I appreciate you stopping by, but I'm worn out and would really like to rest a bit before they finally get around to releasing me."

His eyes narrow as if he can literally sniff out a lie, and for a moment, I wonder if he's going to challenge me. Only he would have the audacity to do so.

Luckily, he doesn't. Instead, he straightens and grins with a little salute. "You two take care. Let me know if you need help with work stuff, Faith." He winks, and then he's gone.

Max stares after him, and neither of us speaks for a long beat.

"He's trouble."

His softly spoken words are such truth yet also feel like a dangerous omen. I merely exhale a long breath and close my eyes to cleanse my mind of Evan or my attacker. Instead, I conjure up the memory of Jude, of his hand in mine, of his tender touch on my face while he soothingly wiped away my tears.

It's this memory that settles me to sleep.

12

Jude

"You shouldn't leave just yet."

He's been pulling this ever since we got home from visiting Faith in the hospital. It's been a week now. Granted, I wanted to make sure my stitches were healing well and there were no signs of infection, but I also don't want to overstay my welcome.

This isn't part of the plan. I need to have space. Be outside in the open. A night at the shelter is one thing, but I don't deserve to have something long term like this.

"I need your help with something anyway."

I toss a questioning glance at Father James's retreating back as he heads to the closed door where I now know he keeps the medical supplies.

A shit ton of them.

I don't ask—haven't asked—because it's none of my business. Sure, it's a bit odd for a priest to be hoarding what appears to be anything from hospital-grade equipment and scalpels to bulk hypodermic needles and vials of various medications to bags of saline, but I'm not in the position to question or judge.

"What kind of help?" Soft footfalls reach my ears, and I peer down to find the dog we've since named Scout standing at my side. I stroke his back, and he nuzzles my pant-clad thigh.

"I have someone coming in to see me, but I'm going to need an assistant for this job."

I walk over and brace a hand against the doorway while watching him choose certain supplies and set them out.

"I'm not well-versed in this sort of thing."

He turns his head, his gaze scrutinizing. "I think you know enough." Returning to his task of carefully arranging the supplies and bandages on a tray covered with a paper towel, he smirks. "Besides, I figure we'll be even after this."

I cock an eyebrow. "Think so?"

He nods, finished with his prep work, and turns to fully face me. "I do. Each of our secrets will be locked up tight."

"ALL SET, Jim. Come back and see me in about a week unless anything changes."

"Thank you so much, Father." The older man, probably somewhere in his fifties, hands him a wad of cash.

Father glances at the money with a frown. "That's too much."

"Take it. Please." Jim holds it out, insistent. "I know it's going toward a good cause."

With reluctance, Father accepts the payment and nods. "Thank you."

"No, thank you." The man slides off the small chair and rises. "You saved me once again." He nods at me, and with a wave, he strides out of the room, and we hear the door of the parsonage close quietly behind him.

Father busies himself, cleaning up and disposing of the used supplies with care. I place what wasn't needed or used back inside the labeled drawers and cabinets. We work in silence before he lets out a long exhale.

"Go ahead."

I shake my head without so much as a glance in his direction. "Not my business."

He cleans and wipes the area down with strong-smelling disinfectant before turning his attention to me.

"Jim is self-employed—runs a small roofing business—and when his insurance premiums skyrocketed, he had no choice but to cancel." He leans back against a wall and crosses his arms. "I put the bulk of that money toward the shelter's food costs. What I don't have to spend to restock this stuff." He lifts his chin to gesture toward the stored supplies. "But I can't stand by while good, hardworking people struggle with medical issues I can easily help them with when they've either lost their health insurance or can't afford an office visit, let alone treatment for something as simple as stitches or wound care.

"The stigma left on the Catholic church from the abuse scandals meant tithing decreased in addition to the reduced donations for the shelter…" Father blows out a long breath. "I've had to resort to other means to help make up the difference."

The defensiveness to his tone is evident. In response, I lift a shoulder in a half shrug and raise an eyebrow. "Isn't this along the lines of 'only the sinless are allowed to cast the first stone'?"

He chuckles softly. "How right you are. But I appreciate your help with him just the same." He tips his head to the side slightly. "And you know I'm always here if you need to get anything off your chest."

And just like that, the room feels like it shrinks exponentially in size, closing in on me.

"Noted." I glance at my watch before heading toward the door, where I pause. "It's time for me to take Scout for his walk. Need anything?"

"No, but thank you." He hesitates for a beat. "You'll be back, right? At least tonight?"

Now I'm the one who grimaces with hesitation.

He's quick to volunteer, "I have another person coming by tomorrow after the evening mass at six."

A thought strikes me suddenly, and I look at him thoughtfully. "What's the shelter's kitchen running low on? Anything in particular?"

Father James purses his lips in thought for a moment. "Honestly, we can use just about anything." With a furrowed brow, he asks, "Why do you ask?"

I shake my head. "Just wondering." I have an idea I've been mulling over, something I've noticed lately.

"Enjoy your walk."

I don't respond, but as I tug open the front door of the parsonage, I'm reminded again just how astute the old man is when his voice calls out to me.

"If you end up speaking to her this time, be sure to tell Faith I said hello."

I pull the door closed behind me, shaking my head at the barest hint of amusement lacing his tone.

I'VE BEEN HOMELESS for fifty-one months and six days. I decided on this penance and planned to live on the streets to experience what it must have been like to be ignored and dismissed, to feel nonexistent.

Just as they had.

I return to the area near where I was raised and feel as though I've come full circle. Experiencing the hunger that's so fierce you imagine your ribs will clang together like pots and pans. Enduring the bitter-cold winter months in the typical northeast combined with lake-effect snow. Surviving the scum of the earth who rejoice in the thrill of preying on others.

Each day, I strive to help those in need. I try to be the man I should've been and save others from hardship or death, all in hopes that someday I might wash off the blood from my hands.

Some might think I'd feel whole again by now, that I'd have gained some semblance of closure, but it hasn't happened. Though the grief has lessened, the guilt remains. I haven't paid enough for my wrongdoings.

The bright sunshine warms us as I hold Scout's leash and he ambles leisurely along the downtown sidewalk. He sniffs a small square patch of flowering bushes. His ears perk up, and he lifts his nose in the direction of the outdoor patio at one of the more frequented coffee shops, Uncommon Grounds, cocking his head to the side.

I know what he's trying to say. We've been coming out this way each evening around this time because she's been busying herself by stopping here. I've been keeping an eye on her during the day as well, but staying out of sight so I don't spook her. Just on the periphery. Enough so I can see for myself she's safe.

Now, as we pause a few yards away from the patio area, I take advantage of this moment to observe Faith. Sitting at a small table with an umbrella to provide shade from the sun, she has a pencil in hand and a sketchbook splayed open on the table. Peering closer, I wonder if my eyes are playing tricks on me because her hands seem to tremble. As soon as I notice it, she clenches her fingers, gripping the pencil tighter. *Huh.* Maybe I imagined it.

At a nearby table, a young woman holds a small toddler on her lap, and an older woman I assume to be the grandmother laughs as the mother tickles the little girl, eliciting giggles. Faith's head turns, observing the trio, and something flickers across her face—an almost sad wistfulness, possibly—before her lips curve into a soft smile. A smile that likely holds more power than she realizes, because her smile reaches deep within me to the darkened depths, attempting to force light there.

As if sensing my attention, she glances up, and I stiffen in response. Because I'm me. Homeless. A guy with nothing to offer. A guy who doesn't even deserve to breathe the same air as her, let alone do something as simple as bask in her damn smile.

Yet I want to. This is the first time since I've been on the streets that I've wanted more.

It's selfish as hell. No doubt about it.

She lifts a hand in a tentative wave, and I find myself wishing her eyes weren't covered by sunglasses.

Scout and I approach and step up a few feet away from the small wrought iron table where she's seated. "Hey."

She offers a polite smile, one tinged with nervousness.

"Hi, Jude." She glances down at Scout. "And who's this cutie?" With an outstretched hand, she says, "Hello there."

"This is Scout." My dog nuzzles her hand, and for the first time ever, I find myself jealous of him.

I'm jealous of a damn dog. All because he gets to feel her touch. Easily. Freely.

"Why don't you two join me?" She closes her sketchbook and places her pencil atop it.

I hesitate, wavering, because it's not wise to form any sort of bond with her. Yet having her close provides a sense of soothing comfort, especially when the other chair at her small table is right beside her. It'd be rude to slide it farther away. I'm many things, but rude isn't normally one of my traits. Plus, she's been through hell already. The last thing I want to do is upset her.

I can sit for a moment, then I can report back to Father James that she's all right.

Yeah. It's a bullshit excuse, but I'm giving in this once.

I lower myself onto the other chair beside her and rest my forearms on the hard surface of the wrought iron table. Scout settles down between us, placing his chin on his front paws.

"I was wondering if you'd ever decide to join me."

It takes a moment for her words to sink in. I jerk my eyes up to find her watching me, head tipped to the side thoughtfully.

Shit.

I avert my gaze, instead choosing to scan the area. "Noticed that, did you?" So much for being incognito. Then again, when it comes to this woman, I keep experiencing a lot of firsts, veering off onto an unfamiliar path.

The soft warmth of her palm sends a jolt of awareness rushing through me, and I drag my eyes back to her.

Her voice drops to a gentle murmur. "You're kind of a hard guy to miss." There's a brief pause, and she withdraws her hand from mine. "So, you've appointed yourself as my bodyguard, huh?"

I shrug in response, playing it casual. Safe. "We just happen to cross paths, I guess."

She lets out a little laugh, and the sound wraps around me like a comforting embrace. "If that's how you want to play it." Sobering, she leans forward. "Although, I have to be honest. I feel a lot safer just being near you and knowing you're watching out for me."

After a brief pause, she tips her head to the side, her gaze watchful, tone hushed. "I'm really glad you were there that night." She ducks her head. "I should have been more aware. Especially since it's the shadier part of town."

I never imagined being homeless would give me such an infallible cover, but in this case, it has. Because it's expected that I'll be roaming the streets.

She holds out her arm, palm facing down. "Even though I'm supposed to be recovering during this time off from work, I haven't been able to get rid of the trembling, the moments when panic tries to get the best of me." She breaks off, retracting her arm and placing both hands atop her sketchbook. "Except for when you're around."

It fucking guts me that she's dealing with the repercussions from that night. Rage barrels through me as my hands clench into tight fists, wishing I could go back and kick that asshole's ass again.

"Hey." Faith grasps one of my fists in her hands, her fingers gently working to unclench my own.

I jerk away from her touch, not wanting to taint her with my anger. She presses her lips thin and leans back, holding her hands up in surrender.

"Sorry. I didn't mean to make you uncomfortable..." She trails off with a nervous laugh. "When you live with a guy who's a touchy-feely Greek, it kind of rubs off. My gran was a hug-once-on-holidays kinda lady and—"

"You live with a guy?" My tone comes out sharper than I intended, but for whatever reason, her living with a man—the one I met at the hospital, who's either a boyfriend or a fiancé who's too cheap to put a ring on her finger—causes a burning sensation to spread in my chest and irrational jealousy to course through my veins.

Faith slides her sunglasses up to rest on her head now that the clouds have moved in front of the sun. She peers at me, her features etched with surprise. Her eyes are wide, regarding me curiously.

"Max is my roommate."

"Not your, uh"—I clear my throat and glance away —"boyfriend?" I refuse to admit how my entire body tenses as I wait for her answer.

"Not even," she says with a tiny laugh.

I turn my gaze back to her. "How long have you two known each other?"

Fuck. What am I doing? Why am I asking her this? I can't do this. That's not how this should work. I can't form attachments of any kind.

"Since college." Her smile is thoughtful, and her eyes take on a faraway look as though lost in memories. "He was the model for the art class I was taking, and we had to sketch him. We ended up talking afterward and have been friends ever since."

"So, you're an artist?"

She wrinkles her nose and shakes her head. "No. I'm not that talented, and Gran told me it would never pay the bills. So, I majored in journalism. The rest, as they say, is history. Now I work at the local newspaper *The Vindicate*."

I flick my gaze to her sketchbook before returning it to her. "I'd love to see your sketches."

A flush creeps across her cheeks, and she ducks her head. "They're not that great. I mean, it's really just a hobby." She shrugs as though it's nothing more. But it's the way she shrugs and the look on her face that tell me that's a lie.

"Please?" I glance at her sketchbook. "I'd be honored if you'd share them with me."

Something in my tone must sway her, and she purses her lips before flipping to a specific page and turning it my way.

Holy shit.

The fine details in her pencil sketch are breathtaking. The tiny dimple in the toddler's cheek sitting at the table nearby, the shading of the mother's faint lines of tiredness around her eyes. The expression on the mother's face that illuminates her love for her little one.

"This is amazing." I lift my eyes and discover her watching me intently as if trying to gauge the truthfulness of my words.

"Think so?"

"Absolutely." I pause, allowing my eyes to absorb each well-placed pencil line and shading. "I don't know much about art, but I bet this could be more than a hobby."

She offers a wistful smile. "I once thought about trying to be brave and sharing it, maybe having it displayed in a gallery someday…" With a tiny laugh with a slightly embarrassed tinge to it, she glances away.

"You should show these to someone."

She gives a noncommittal shrug. "Maybe someday."

I hold her gaze, and something deep within compels me to say, "You should do it before it's too late. There are no guarantees in life."

I learned that lesson all too well.

She appears surprised by my admission. To try to brush off the awkwardness, I turn my attention back to her sketches and flip to the previous page.

"Wait! No, I—"

All breath is robbed from my chest at the sketch on this page. My lips part in amazement, the slightest niggling of discomfort accompanying it, but I can't bring myself to look away.

The sketch is of a man, his jawline sharp, nose straight, and lips full. His hair is slightly tousled around his face as if it's recently been at the wind's mercy. The thick beard outlines his mouth, drawing more attention to his lips. But that's not what gives me pause. It's his eyes. By the way she's drawn them, it's clear the man is tortured or troubled by something. Yet Faith has somehow managed to make this person look…beautiful.

"I'm so embarrassed."

I finally drag my eyes from the sketch to peer over at her, and she's hiding her face in her hands.

"Why?"

Dropping her hands, she winces. "Because I know how this looks. Pathetic. Creepy. Like I have some sort of… crush or something." She looks away as if nervous.

Do you? an inner voice wants to ask.

But that's far too dangerous.

"I should get going." I rise abruptly and hold the sketchbook out to her. I've got to get out of here before I give in to whatever bizarre pull there is between us. "And, Faith?" I gesture to the sketchbook. "It's a compliment. Because I know I don't look like that."

She accepts the book with an indecipherable expression. I push in my chair and turn away with Scout's leash in hand.

If I wasn't paying attention and not already so damn in tune with this woman, I would've missed her softly murmured words.

"To me, you do."

13

Faith

APRIL

I've been off work for a week—paid leave, thankfully—and I've forced myself to get out of the house each day. I've alternated between dropping by the Tavern and traveling downtown to my favorite coffee shop. I'm certain everyone would rather me restrict my visits to the bar, judging by their continuously worried expressions, but I felt as though their concern was smothering me. Not to mention, the weather has allowed me to sit outdoors on the small patio area of the café and indulge in my favorite hobby.

Drawing has always been something I've loved. I can lose myself and decompress while I sketch. It's been soothing to have the ability to sit for a few hours and either observe my surroundings and recreate them on paper or draw something from memory.

Max has been worried about me, but I insisted I'd be fine and even more vigilant while out. Which is probably why I noticed Jude's presence.

I'd sensed someone watching me and, initially, panicked, having flashbacks to that night. When I'd stopped in front of a large store window, pretending to peer inside, I'd scanned the reflection. It took me a moment to notice him, but that was when my breath caught in surprise.

Jude.

I'd pretended to go on my way with no outward indication of his presence. But I kept an eye out for him.

With the comforting knowledge that he was watching over me, I desperately wanted to know more about him. He was mysterious, yet his eyes told a story all on their own. Those blue eyes were haunted with an utter sadness illuminated in their depths. Never before have I ached this much, wishing I could ease someone's pain.

He doesn't see himself the way I do. I may not know much about him, but I do know he's a good man. A man who saved my life. A man who could have just as easily kept walking, much as the average person would, too uncomfortable to take a risk by getting involved. Especially in a dark alley.

But not Jude. He'd taken action and carried me to the hospital.

What I wasn't aware of, what he likely hadn't planned to disclose to me, was that he'd been injured in the process.

"He's fine now—he healed up well—but I keep making excuses for him to hang around."

Father James and I sit alone in the last pew now that everyone from the final mass has gone home. He's tightlipped about the extent or type of the injury Jude sustained, which strikes me as odd. But I shrug it off, considering how much the man risked to help me.

"He's been watching over me," I admit quietly.

No surprise edges into his expression, and he merely nods.

I tip my head to the side. "You knew?"

A faint smile plays at his lips. "It was pretty easy to

figure out." He leans back and drapes an arm along the back of the wooden pew on the vacant side of him and focuses his attention on the altar. "Jude is complex. Closed off. Guarded. There's much more than meets the eye with him, and he'll do everything in his power to distract you from noticing that."

He draws in a deep breath before exhaling slowly, his brow furrowing. "In all my years in the military and priesthood combined, he's the most tortured soul I've ever encountered. He's bound and determined to carry his burden and not allow anyone else to help with the load, regardless of what it costs him…" Father trails off and turns back to me. "But when it comes to you, it seems to spark something within him."

I worry my bottom lip before I offer, "I think he feels obligated for some reason. Because of what happened and…maybe what almost happened."

He doesn't immediately reply but studies me thoughtfully before changing the subject. "Do you feel ready, well enough, to return to work?"

I nod slowly. "I do. I mean"—I let out a small sigh—"I have a story I need to work on. A lot is riding on it."

"Oh?" Father James has always enjoyed when I tell him about the interesting stories I've been tasked with reporting on. "What's this one about?"

"Well"—I chuckle lightly—"people seem to be chattering about this Good Samaritan person lately. Anthony wants me to find out who he is."

"And you said a lot's riding on it?"

I glance down at my folded hands on my lap. "Yes," I murmur softly.

We sit in silence for a bit, both of us seemingly lost in our thoughts. With a gentle sigh, he settles his slightly wrinkled hand over my still linked ones.

"Just remember, Faith. Everyone has secrets. It's the ones we hold close and keep hidden that are the most dangerous. Because those"—I drag my eyes up to meet his somber ones—"can be the most damaging. Whether to their heart or our own."

I swallow hard past the sudden lump in my throat because although I've never confessed my secret to him—Max is the only one who knows—I feel like Father already knows. Or suspects.

He knows I have a devastating secret. And maybe that's what draws me to Jude. Out of everyone else, he's the only one who might understand because he carries the burden of a painful secret similar to mine. One that's changed the course of our lives. One that's derailed us.

One that's ensured our future is no longer bright and full of life as we once imagined.

IRRATIONAL. That's what this is—what I'm doing. The hospital psychologist who spoke with me suggested I attend counseling after what happened. She warned me I might be tempted to do something reckless. Something irrational, perhaps.

She wasn't mistaken. This can easily be classified as reckless. But I'm still doing it.

I'm following Jude. It's late, and I snuck out after I ensured Max was asleep for the night. It's about one thirty in the morning, and if I had to be at work in the morning, I'm not sure I'd have given in to the temptation to try to find out what makes Jude tick. To observe him.

Actually, that's a blatant lie. When it comes to this man, I'm unable to resist any temptation.

I follow him as he strides with purpose within the

shadows of the alleyways and nearly silent downtown streets. I'm armed with my pepper spray. That sucker is in my hand, and my finger's already resting over the button, ready to ward off anyone who might be a threat.

He just turned a corner, heading behind the local grocery store. I know there's no other exit, so I wait for him to emerge. There's some noise, almost like a clanking sound, some hushed voices, and then…nothing. I wait a bit longer before I decide to follow him.

As soon as I turn the corner, a large hand clamps down over my mouth.

I bring up my arm to spray my assailant, but he's far too quick, pressing his body against me, between my legs, and forcing me against the building. My entire body goes rigid, and I frantically attempt to break free from his hold.

"What the hell, Faith?" the man hisses.

My eyes adjust to the darkness of this particular spot, and I stare back at Jude. His features are tight with anger, jaw clenched, eyes boring into mine. He slowly removes his hand from my mouth and drops it to my shoulder. "You should know better."

God, I feel stupid. What was I thinking, trying to be stealthy when he's a man who's lived on the streets for God knows how long?

My breath surges past my lips in harsh pants from the adrenaline rush. "I just wanted to know more about you." I lower my eyes, unable to look at him straight on.

"*Fuck.*" The muttered expletive has me returning my gaze to him. His eyes drift to my mouth, to my parted lips, where I'm trying to tamp down my ragged breathing. This time, his voice is gentler when he speaks. "You can't go around like this. It's not safe. And if anything happened to you…"

I raise my eyes to his in challenge. "What if something happens to you? It's dangerous for you, too."

An edge of his lips quirks up faintly. He reaches out and tucks a few strands of my hair back behind my ear, and a shiver of awareness skitters down my spine. "No one's ever worried about me before."

His tone carries what sounds like a hint of wonder or amazement. And it's at this moment I feel it happen.

The walls I've built up, the way I've continued to guard myself and my heart to prevent hurt and disappointment on both sides, begin to give way ever so slightly.

Because I'm staring back at the first person who might understand what it's like to face the prospect of a bleak future.

Our gazes remain locked, and I wish I knew what he was thinking. Finally, after a long beat, I glance around the deserted area, and a thought hits me. "Hey, you wouldn't happen to come across anyone who's going out of their way to do nice things for people, would you?"

He backs away from me and drags a hand along his bearded jawline as if agitated, and tucks his hair behind his ear. His heavy gaze settles on me, and I work hard to resist the urge to fidget. "Someone's doing that?"

I can't quite decipher exactly what it is in his tone, but it's…odd. I brush it off because, after all, this man is a prickly one.

"Apparently so. I'm assigned the story. To find out who the Good Samaritan is. There's gossip that he's going around doing these good deeds, but it's always anonymously."

Something flickers across his face. "Maybe they're doing it anonymously because they'd like it to stay that way."

I narrow my eyes. "Do you know this person?"

He presses his lips thin and shakes his head before answering tightly. "Afraid I can't help you there."

My shoulders slump slightly with disappointment. I figured being on the streets, he would be more likely to notice someone going around and helping in various ways.

Staring off toward the end of the alley, Jude's lips move, but I can't hear what he's saying.

Dammit. It's happening again.

I step closer. "I'm sorry. I didn't quite catch that."

He levels a look on me. "I said give me a moment. I have to leave a message with someone." With hands on my shoulders, I battle against the shiver from his touch alone. He steers me back toward the sidewalk and the large streetlight nearby. "Go stand there, under the light, and have that pepper spray ready, just in case."

In the next instant, he's gone.

"WHERE DID YOU DISAPPEAR TO?" I arch an eyebrow. "Not planning to tell me?"

Jude lets out a little huff. "You're stubborn. Anyone ever tell you that?"

I smile wistfully. "My mom used to say that when I was little."

We walk along the sidewalk toward the all-night diner nearby where I parked.

Melancholy washes over me, and I find myself admitting, "She used to tell me I was headstrong. Stubborn. But that it would suit me well when I was older." I shake my head with a little laugh. "She said to choose wisely when to be stubborn because it could hurt me if I didn't."

He tosses me a curious glance. "And have you?"

"Chosen wisely?"

He nods.

I give a half shrug. "Sometimes."

We draw to a stop near my car, but I don't want to say goodbye. Something about this man comforts me on a deeper level.

"I, uh…" I lower my gaze to my shoes before giving myself an internal pep talk. I raise my eyes to lock with his, the intensity startling and catching me off guard. "I was wondering if you'd like to head inside"—I tip my head in the direction of the diner—"and grab something to eat with me."

His lips part, and I instantly know he's going to turn me down.

This is what I get for stepping out of my comfort zone since things ended with my ex-fiancé, Todd.

I hold up my hand to stop him. "You know what? I shouldn't have put you on the spot." I force a laugh. "I mean, I look horrible and everything, and—"

He stares at me like I've lost my mind. "You think you look horrible?"

I look down and gesture my hand over my outfit, which consists of yoga pants and a large, roomy hooded sweatshirt over a T-shirt, paired with sneakers. "Not exactly appealing, I know."

Suddenly, I'm being crowded as he steps toward me and lifts my chin with his finger. Dark blue eyes clash with mine, and his ferocious expression catches me off guard. His lips part, and slowly, he utters words that are spoken so fervently, so emphatic, they wrap themselves around my heart.

"You're a beautiful woman. Never doubt that." He shakes his head slowly. "Doesn't matter what you're wearing." His eyes skim my features; his thumb grazes my jawline.

A group of college kids exit, laughing and breaking the moment. Jude looks alarmed, as if surprised by his forwardness with me, and takes a step back.

I shove my hands into the pockets of my hoodie and force a casual tone. "Well, I figured I could buy you a cup of coffee at the very least." I tip my head to the side with an impish grin. "Maybe even a full-fledged breakfast if you can put up with my company."

He studies me for a beat, and I internally beg him to say yes. Just so I can have a little more time with him. In hopes that maybe, just maybe, he'll grant me a glimpse of what he keeps hidden beneath the layer of mysterious aloofness.

What no one else gets to see. *That's* what I want.

He glances around before releasing a sigh. Then he tilts his head in the direction of the diner.

"Shall we?"

I have to bite the inside of my cheek to restrain the satisfied and utterly happy grin aching to spread across my face. Instead, I simply nod and step forward, but before I can reach for the door, he catches my wrist in his hand.

I whip my head around to stare at him in surprise.

He releases his hold, and his tone has a sternness to it but without any bite. "A lady should never have to open her own door in the presence of a man."

He tugs open the door to the diner, but I can't force myself to move just yet. Instead, I take a step toward him, ignoring the wariness that inches into his eyes. I cup the side of his face, his beard rasping against the inside of my palm. I raise to my tiptoes and press a light kiss to his other cheek and whisper against his warm skin, "Thank you."

The sentiment is brimming with more than its average run-of-the-mill simplistic nature. We both know it holds so much more.

When I back away, his eyes remain closed, as if he's trying to relish in my touch, in my words, in my kiss. I'm slow to remove my hand from his face and am warring with myself to do so when he places his palm over mine. His eyes finally open slowly, and the depths hold an overwhelming fire of emotion. With his hand on mine, he slides it down his cheek, still in a light grasp as our joined hands hang between us. The touch feels so natural. So casual. So *real.*

He dips his head and whispers, "Anytime."

COMMUNITY HIGHLIGHTS

Don Bullard—owner of Fiore Pizzeria located on Centre Street downtown, which offers jumbo slices of pizza with one topping for a dollar—now claims people are paying it forward to those in need.

"Anyone can come in and pay ahead for a slice, write a message on a Post-it, and hang it on the wall. Then someone in need of a hot lunch is welcome to come and take one of the notes from the wall to redeem it for a slice," Bullard says.

He claims they've already fed what has to be over a hundred individuals, many of whom confessed to be homeless and desperately trying to get back on their feet.

14

Jude

This place is teeming with cops. I can sense it. And it makes me nervous as hell. Not to mention, I notice the looks we're garnering. My damn overgrown beard and hair, my attire contrasting with Faith's. Even in a sweatshirt and yoga pants, it's clear as day we run in different circles.

"Don't look too excited to be here. I might get a complex."

Faith's muttered words cause me to jerk my eyes away from the coffee I've been staring into.

Only she's not looking at me now, either. Her index finger is picking at the small edge of the adhesive paper banded around the napkin-wrapped utensils.

"I'm just..." I run a hand over my hair. "Not used to this."

Hazel eyes fly to mine in shock. "To sharing a meal with someone?"

I lift a shoulder in a half shrug. "Basically." Or having a bona fide conversation.

She holds up both hands. "I'm not judging, trust me." Her tone is threaded with a hint of embarrassment. "I mean, I have a guy roommate who looks more put together than me on even my *best* days, I have pretty much no life, and my father figure is a priest, so..."

I frown. "Why don't you have much of a life?"

Her eyes go wide, eyebrows shooting up in surprise, and she laughs. "Out of all of it, including the part about a priest basically being my father, you choose to question that?"

For the first time in a long while, I have to work hard to fight the start of a smile.

A sigh spills from her lips, and she shrugs. "My job is pretty demanding and, well…" She hesitates for a beat. "I've been dealing with some personal things."

She makes no attempt to elaborate, and hell, I know it's not my place to pry. Taking a small sip of her coffee, she studies me with unnerving intensity. "You look well." Her eyes flick over me, and I wonder how she sees me. If she sees a homeless man who hasn't sat down and had a cup of coffee with someone in years, let alone a woman.

I wonder if she can somehow see beneath the surface. If she can see—or merely sense—the pain I carry.

"Well…" A curt laugh breaks free, and I hate how awkward and nervous it sounds. "I *did* shower."

She grins, a sudden sparkle in her gaze. "Well, that must be it." She lowers her eyes to peer down at the contents of her coffee mug. "Maybe you should do it more often." There's a brief pause. "Maybe land a date or something."

My laugh is a touch brittle. "Do I really seem like the kind of guy who's out looking for a date?"

Her eyes lock on me, regarding me in an unnerving way. With a tip of her head to the side, she says, "How about you tell me what kind of guy you are?" She laces her fingers around the mug. "Tell me about yourself."

I shake my head and stare down at the well-worn table. "Nothing to tell."

She makes a dismissive sound. "I beg to differ." She leans in closer. "You're the incredible man who stepped into action when I needed help." Our eyes meet, and she stares back at me with a myriad of emotions flickering in the depths. "You helped me when no one else would...or could."

I open my mouth to protest, but she lays a hand over mine. "You're a good man."

I clamp my mouth shut. Out of the corner of my eye, I notice two men rise from their booth on the far side of the diner. When they shift and slip on their blazers, the florescent lights reflect off the shiny badge at their hips. The one with a slightly receding hairline catches sight of Faith and nudges his buddy before they fix interested stares on me.

I drain the contents of my mug before abruptly setting it down on the table. "Thanks for the coffee, but I need to go."

Startled, she appears as though she's about to protest, but I slip out of the booth before she can.

"GOOD THING I'm still in decent shape." Father James flicks me an amused look. "And I have friends who I can call at a god-awful hour to help me."

I wince. "I apologized for that." And I did. I felt like shit having to leave him like that, but I couldn't risk Faith catching on to things.

Especially after she'd mentioned doing a story on "the Good Samaritan." I know I'm probably putting too much thought into it, letting paranoia take hold, but if word is getting out about what I've done…

"I'm just giving you a hard time." Father slaps a hand on my shoulder, his expression sobering. "I know you said Faith wanted to talk to you. That's more important."

"I feel bad you had to deal with all that."

We'd "rescued" eight roasting chickens and four enormous bags of still-good produce that were tossed in the dumpsters behind the local grocery store downtown. The chickens were still frozen. I'm amazed all that was discarded.

"My buddy and I stowed it at the shelter. It was more of a conundrum trying to fit everything in the car." He chuckles. "Travis couldn't actually help me, so he watched me move it to the trunk of the car and then followed me back to the shelter to help unload it."

I furrow my brow, confused. "He couldn't help you?"

"He's a cop, and it's technically trespassing." He slides onto the chair at the kitchen table and opens his Bible to the bookmarked page. "I certainly didn't want him to get into trouble for that."

A cop. Fucking stellar.

I lean back against the wall and tilt my head toward the ceiling and close my eyes.

"Worried I told him about you?"

My eyes flare open, but I continue peering sightlessly at the old popcorn ceiling. "Did you?"

"Jude." He releases a long sigh. "There's always bound to be talk among the gossipy women in my parish when they notice someone entering or leaving my home."

Alarm and another emotion I despise—fear—rushes through my veins. I push off from the wall, my entire body rigid with unease. "I should go. I don't want to—"

"Stop."

It's not so much the word as it is his tone that has me

freezing in my tracks. I've never heard him use such a commanding voice, especially with me.

I eye him warily as he rises from his chair and approaches. He stops within a foot from me, and I realize he's granting me that space, a reprieve, or an escape if I choose it.

"I've been here for twenty years." He lowers his chin, appearing thoughtful. "I'm not your typical priest. I didn't come to the seminary fresh out of school. And I sure didn't arrive a virgin." A hint of a smirk plays at his lips. "I've dealt with more than my share of people who thought I wouldn't be a good fit, but I like to think I've proven them wrong because I bring a different perspective. Something unique. I show people how sometimes the paths we choose aren't always the ones we're meant to stay on, and it's okay to take the backroads. Follow your heart and soul, if you dare.

"I want everyone to feel welcome. To know we don't all have to look the same or have the same background. I don't care if I have alcoholics or former drug addicts in my church. What matters to me is they're here for a reason, and it's up to me to ensure they don't walk out those doors feeling doomed. It's up to me to make sure I communicate a message they can take with them and feel uplifted." He shrugs. "If they never come back, perhaps it wasn't a good fit, but at least I know I've done my best."

He blows out a long, measured breath. "I've experienced pushback, and it doesn't scare me. Do you know why?"

I don't answer, merely offering a curt shake of my head.

"Because what's in here"—he presses the tip of his index finger to his chest—"tells me I'm doing right. And it has yet to lead me wrong."

His words hang in the silence between us.

Finally, he turns away, walking back to the table.

"You haven't given me a reason to think I was wrong. That's why I don't give a crap about the gossips." He reclaims his seat. "But, Jude?"

"Yes?"

He turns his head to look at me, his features intensely fierce. "Don't prove me wrong."

15

Faith

APRIL

"I only wanted to—"

The door closes softly in my face.

That's the third time it's happened today. The *third.* And it's not because I lack professionalism.

At least I got a cup of coffee before they showed me to the door.

Swiftly, I spin around and descend the two shallow steps leading to the driveway. "If you think that's enough to deter me," I mutter under my breath, "then you're sorely mistaken."

Dead ends. Every one of them. After the local police had shared information in hopes that our collective efforts might produce faster results, I thought these would be legitimate leads. A few neighbors had reported seeing a man around their neighborhood while others had claimed a few shop owners downtown had been helped by the Good Samaritan. Two other reports included details of a woman who insisted on anonymously paying for other people's meals at three different restaurant locations.

One thing I learned long ago? Don't completely discredit reports. Especially when they all have a common denominator. The person doing these "good deeds" is mainly active in the downtown area by the shops and cafés and the nearby neighborhoods.

I'm onto something. I can sense it.

It doesn't mean, however, that my frustration hasn't gotten the best of me for today.

The sudden gloominess and dark clouds rushing in don't bode well either, and I decide to make a stop at Uncommon Grounds for a coffee and grab a table along the back wall so I can mull over my notes and determine my new plan of attack.

I sip my latte and relish in its warmth as I read through my notes. I can't shake the feeling I'm missing something that's staring me right in the face.

A sudden prickle of awareness washes over me, and I sense someone's attention on me. *Could it be Jude?* The rush of anticipation and excitement at seeing him again instantly deflates when I look up and lock eyes with an older woman using a walker slowly making her way toward me. She's dressed to the nines, and her gaze never leaves mine. The unabashed interest in her light blue eyes is a bit unnerving, but I assume that she recognizes me from my recent front-page story, so I paste on a smile.

"Hello, young lady." She greets me with a wide smile, and it makes me think she has a secret I've yet to be clued in on.

"Hello."

"You wouldn't mind too terribly if I rest my feet for a moment at your table, would you?"

"Not at…all." Before I've even finished answering, she's dropped herself down into the chair, and a man I now notice behind her accepts the walker from her and moves out of sight as if to give us privacy.

"I loved your article about the former superintendent

of schools." She lets out a low whistle. "You addressed every pertinent question the people wanted answered." With a head nod as affirmation, she adds, "Well done."

Her eyes flick to my notepad, and I realize she can see where I've written *Who is the Good Samaritan?* and jotted some quick notes beneath it.

I shift my arm to cover it, and her gaze lifts to meet mine. "We all have secrets, don't we?"

I furrow my brow because I'm caught between wondering if she's asking a rhetorical question or if she actually expects me to answer.

Luckily, she continues, granting me a reprieve. She settles her hands on the table, linking her fingers whose knuckles appear swollen as if riddled with arthritis. Her gaze is inquisitive with an odd touch of steeliness behind it.

"Sometimes you have to make a choice whether those secrets do more good being exposed or whether they'd cause more hurt. Because once revealed, no matter how innocent that secret might be, it's now vulnerable and defenseless to others who may wish to taint it."

I'm honestly at a loss for words because this is such an odd exchange. Especially with a woman I don't even know. The muffled sound of a cell phone ringing interrupts, and she reaches into the right pocket of her pants. "Excuse me for just a moment, please."

She shifts in her seat, and I scan the shop while I wait on her to finish, musing about this impromptu "visitor." It's a bit awkward—this woman seeking me out and chatting with me—yet something about her is almost comforting. I wonder if she has grandchildren she dotes on. It seems likely, and I imagine she's a spitfire of a grandmother.

As I survey my surroundings, I keep coming back to the front windows, hoping for even a glimpse of Jude.

God, I'm pathetic. Antsy over the mere sight of a man

I don't really know. Yet there's no denying I'm drawn to him in a way that's thrilling yet simultaneously terrify—

"Looking for your beau?"

I jerk my gaze from the windows to settle back on the woman. "I'm sorry?"

Amusement sparkles in her eyes. "Are you looking for your beau?"

I laugh tightly, a bit embarrassed. "Oh, no. I don't have one."

She cocks her head to the side and studies me in a way that makes me feel as though she can see beneath everything. As if she knows my secrets.

Which is ridiculous. She's an absolute stranger.

She lightly raps her knuckles on the table with a knowing smile. "I wouldn't be so sure of that." Her expression sobers, and it's so sudden it makes me stiffen in alarm. "Just remember." Her eyes hold mine with an urgency that crackles in the air between us. "Everyone has secrets. But they're meant to be shared, not revealed." She rises from her seat, and immediately, out of nowhere, the man from earlier arrives by her side. He supplies her walker, but she doesn't immediately turn to accept it. Instead, she stands, peering down at me. She points at my notepad, and her voice has a steely calmness to it.

"Think of your own secret, Faith. Would you want what you keep hidden revealed without your permission?"

She grasps the silicone handgrips of her walker and turns toward the exit, but stops and shifts back to me. Reaching over, she places her hand on top of mine. "Do the right thing. Make the choice you can live with." Her mouth tips up slightly at the corners. "The rest will work itself out. Trust me."

Minutes later, I'm still sitting at the table, dazed and

replaying the entire conversation in my mind. So many questions race through my mind.

Think of your own secret, Faith.

She didn't say secrets. She only spoke of one.

As if she knows exactly what mine is.

16

Jude

APRIL

"*Jude.*"

I jerk my head around at Terri, the shelter's cook. She stares back at me, eyes brimming with tears.

Shit. What did I do?

Unease trickles down my spine, and I'm about to apologize—even though I'm not sure why—when the older woman rushes forward and wraps her arms around me.

"Thank you."

Awkwardly, I pat her back. "I can't imagine what the response would be if those pounds of potatoes had been roses."

Terri rears back to peer up at me, her features laced with surprise. "Did you just use humor?" Her lips form a wide smile, a hint of teasing in her tone, and she swipes at the tears on her cheeks before giving my chest a quick pat. "I knew you had it in you." She turns on her heel and heads over to start prepping the food I'd rescued from the dumpsters in the middle of the night. I turn away to finish putting the rest of the packaged meats in their large walk-in freezer.

"All you need is faith."

Terri's mumbled words are faint but unsettling nonetheless.

Because silently, a deep, well-hidden part of me agrees. Not in the spiritual sense but Faith, the person.

Once I finish, I slip out the rear door of the kitchen and head to make my rounds for the day. I have to stop at Pauline's and check on her. I've hated slacking on my duties, especially for her.

On my way through the back alleyways, I notice a young man pacing out back behind one of the restaurants on a cell phone. The closer I approach, the clearer it is to see the agitation and stress on his face.

As usual, no one pays me any attention. It's a sunny but brisk day, and I've got my hoodie pulled up with my hands in my pockets. Living with the priest has granted me a much cleaner look although my beard still needs a good trim. It's getting out of hand, and the added growth makes it itch. Father James doesn't own a beard trimmer since he's got ladies from the parish who practically fight over who gets to trim his hair and beard. I know I could shave it all off, but the idea makes me squeamish. It serves as an added layer of protection for me.

"I'm sorry. I know. My car broke down, and I had to pay to get it fixed or else I wouldn't even have a way to… I know I was short three hundred for rent. I just thought that since I gave you the remainder, it would... Right. Well, I just need to work a few more shifts and—" The guy's shoulders slump. "Yes, I understand. Thanks." He ends the call and stares down at his shoes.

I continue walking past, and he doesn't even register my presence. The sound of someone exiting the restaurant's back door echoes through the alley. "Hey, Kev? They just sat your four-top."

He releases a long-drawn-out sigh. "I'm coming." His words are muted as he steps inside and disappears, the door slamming shut behind him.

I pause, hesitating. I'll be a few minutes late if I stop. I drag a hand down my face, my beard crinkling beneath my palm. With a sigh, I glance around to be sure I'm alone. Once I've withdrawn what I've never tapped into before, what I've deemed for a dire emergency in case I came across others who needed assistance right away, I head around the front of the building and tug open the front door to the restaurant.

It's still early, before the breakfast rush. The hostess looks up from the podium and does a double take.

I step up and lean close. "I need to drop something off for Kev, but I wanted to see if you had a piece of paper I could leave a quick note on?"

The petite young brunette's lips part, appearing a bit dazed, before she shakes it off. "Sure." Reaching down, she brings up a notebook and rips a sheet of paper from it. She hands it over, curiosity in her expression. "Need a pen, too?"

"Please."

She hands one over without a word. I turn and lean against the smooth glass window and hurriedly scribble my note before discreetly wrapping the paper around everything securely.

"Can you make sure he gets this right away? It's pretty important."

"Of…course." When she takes it from me, she purposely brushes her fingers against mine. Her smile turns a shade flirtatious. "Maybe you can leave your number for me…just to be sure?"

"Sorry. I've got a girlfriend."

I have no idea where that came from, but it spills from my lips just the same.

"Oh." Disappointment lines her face. "Well, hope to see you again, handsome."

Handsome. The word, meant to be a compliment, causes my hackles to rise in discomfort. It just feels… foreign to have someone take notice of me. Especially a woman.

She turns and heads off toward the back of the restaurant in search of Kev.

I exit the restaurant and pause, gazing through the large windows to ensure she's given it to him.

As soon as he has it in his hand, I dart away, not wanting another witness.

I only hope he respects my wishes in the note.

You need this more than I do. There's enough in there to cover what you owe for rent and a little extra just in case.

I only ask that you pay it forward if you're ever in the position to do so.

Back on track, I stride through the downtown area, hastening my steps to get to Pauline's in time. My shoulders are a little straighter, my gait a bit lighter.

"YOU GOT A SIDE PIECE NOW, don't you?"

I whip my head around to stare at Pauline. Of course she cackles, but she doesn't take her eagle eyes off me. I merely shake my head and return to changing the long overdue furnace filter.

"I can tell. You've been running behind a bit, putting this old lady on the backburner." She lets out a long, exaggerated sigh. *Jesus.* This woman never quits.

Still, I wouldn't have it any other way. She's a good soul. Spitfire? Definitely. But her heart is made of gold.

"I told you I was sick for a few days."

"Heard about that."

I stiffen, wondering what she means by it, but I can't give anything away. "You're all set now." I step away and return the screwdriver to the small toolkit she keeps handy.

"Thank you."

I nod and start toward the door.

"Can you wait for a moment?"

Her tone, and the fact that she's asking instead of her usual cackling demands, catches me off guard. Slowly, I turn around to face her.

Her eyes are fixed on me with an unusual intensity. "I thought that maybe by now you'd open up a bit." Her somber expression is one I've not seen since we met, and it's startling. "I worry about you."

"No need to worry."

She hobbles toward me, using her walker until she's right before me. Her fingers are gnarled, but she reaches out and presses the tip of her index finger to the center of my chest. "I know heartache when I see it. And you've been wrestling with it for too long."

I turn my head and clench my jaw because she doesn't understand my reasons.

A long sigh rushes from her lips, and there's no mistaking the disappointment in it.

"Fine. Be stubborn. Just know one thing." She waits for me to meet her eyes. "I'm here for you when the time comes. And it will. So you need to know that you're not alone."

She holds my gaze, and a beat of silence passes before I give a curt nod.

Instantly, her face transforms into a lighter, sassier

disposition. "Now, get outta here before I decide to pay you to fan me and feed me grapes. You'd be shirtless, and I'd objectify the hell out of you." She shuffles away in the direction of her kitchen, and her cackles tempt a smile from my lips.

Just as I pull the door closed behind me to head on my way, she hollers, "And you'd best treat that side piece of yours good!"

"HAVE YOU SEEN THE NEWS?"

I've just returned from walking Scout when Father James tosses the question out from where he sits at the small kitchen table. His small television sits a few feet away in the living room.

"Don't pay attention to the news." I hang up Scout's leash and stride over to Father. "I'm going to head out today. We both know I'm healed."

The older man swings his head around to peer at me. "I was just getting used to having a roommate." He frowns and mutters into his cereal bowl. "Never had one so neat and quiet before."

"Sure you'll be glad to get back to having the place to yourself." I head back to the small spare bedroom I've been occupying since I showed up on his doorstep a few weeks ago.

"Actually," he calls down the hall, "I was wondering how you'd manage to get groceries to the shelter if you can't get the key. It's a lot more difficult to track me down when we're not around each other here." There's a millisecond of a pause. "Hate to have your conscience heavy with being the cause of our shelter having a shortage of food."

I toss my head back and stare at the ceiling, cursing under my breath. "You sure know how to lay on the guilt."

He chuckles. "It's a gift. All Catholics are quite familiar with it."

The slight scraping of a chair sliding back along the kitchen tile and the clanking of a spoon in the bowl sound. I peer down at Scout. "What do you think?" I ask him quietly.

I sense his presence before he speaks, standing in the doorway. "I know you need to do other things, but I'm honestly getting older, Jude. And it's comforting to have you around…in case anything should happen."

Shit. I scrub a hand down my face with a silent groan. I can't conscionably leave him, especially if he's voicing concern over his well-being. Dammit. I'm between a rock and a hard place. Then again, living with him and his scheduled duties with the church and shelter have allowed me to come and go when necessary.

I'm torn. If I left and then something happened to Father James, I wouldn't be able to bear it.

But this wasn't part of the plan.

"Jude."

My gaze meets his, and I find myself wavering. "I understand if you need to leave, but I'd love it if you stayed a bit longer."

Staying in one place even longer will make me complacent. Lax. Ease me away from my responsibilities.

I draw in a deep breath while I war internally with my decision.

I give in, and I can only hope it's the last time I succumb.

"By the way, I need you to tag along with me tonight."

I fix a curious stare on him. "Where to?"

"Figure I should treat you to dinner since you've helped me out so much lately."

I part my lips to protest, and he waves me off. "I'm not taking no for an answer. Plus, it's a friendly place. All my buddies will be there."

I'll be surrounded by priests for dinner. Sounds like a blast.

"Don't look so enthusiastic." The older man chuckles before turning around to head in the direction of his bedroom. "I'm going to get cleaned up. Be ready at a quarter till six."

He doesn't wait for my response. I raise my eyes to the ceiling and mutter, "If you're up there, maybe you can help me out tonight, all right?"

Great. As if living with a priest isn't bizarre enough, now I'm talking to the big man upstairs, half expecting an answer.

I shake my head and drag a hand down my face with a groan. But I do it. Then I head to the bedroom to change.

And hell if it doesn't feel like an omen of some sort.

FRIDAY FEEL-GOOD STORIES

LOCAL SHELTER RECEIVES ANONYMOUS DONATION OF FOOD

An anonymous donor left dozens of bags of fresh produce, bread, and frozen foods just outside the door they use for large deliveries. The shelter's director said there was enough food to help feed more than two hundred people with a few additionally supplied items.

17

Faith

"Faith!" I'm greeted by the familiar chorus of voices in the Tavern. With a little wave, I slide onto a barstool, and once Harry finishes serving two patrons at the other end of the bar, he approaches me with a smile.

"Well, you're a sight for sore eyes." His smile grows wider as he takes me in. "Looking even better than ever." Without asking, he fills up a glass with my usual choice of beer and sets it on a coaster with the bar's name printed on it. His eyes flit to the door before settling on me. "Where's Father?"

"Probably at home." I check the time on my cell phone sitting on the well-worn lacquered bar top. "I called him earlier, but he didn't answer." I take a long sip of my beer and savor the pale ale.

"Speak of the devil."

I don't turn around because I know Father James will slide onto the stool beside me. When I finally notice the entire place has quieted, I raise my head, curious as to why he hasn't appeared at my side yet. Slowly, I turn around to face the entrance and immediately understand the reason for the ebb of conversation.

Oh, *shit.*

Jude stands beside him, looking a bit out of place. That's not saying much, considering we have a few undercover cops who look pretty rough. What's undeniable, though, is the vast difference when compared to Jude. He exudes this solitary vibe—a definitive "don't fuck with me" aura.

"Everyone," Father addresses the crowd, "this is my friend Jude." He rests a hand on Jude's shoulder. "Jude, welcome to the Tavern."

There's a beat of silence before Harry calls out, "Welcome, Jude! Grab a seat at the bar."

Everyone follows suit in shouting their welcoming, but I can tell it's more subdued than if Father were to introduce Max. My well-dressed roommate, ever so conservative in appearance, would get welcoming pats on the back as he entered the Tavern. Guaranteed.

The funny thing is, Max would shit himself silly in the midst of so many cops, which is why he avoids accompanying me to this place. He was arrested in his early teens for a few minor offenses, but to this day, he still steers clear of cops. He claims it scarred him for life.

Multiple Tavern patrons' eyes track Jude's movements as he and Father take a seat on either side of me. Flanked by two men, one I'm intrigued by and attracted to on such a visceral level, and the other who's been my saving grace for as long as I can recall. He brings a sense of rightness to the moment. As if this is meant to be.

Judging from the rigidness of Jude's spine, he doesn't feel the same.

I lean over and nudge his arm with mine, waiting for him to look at me. When his eyes meet mine, I wonder if

I'll always experience that little catch of my breath. His gaze is always so intense. Riveting.

Mentally shaking it off, I lower my voice. "The pale ale is really good. So are the fish and chips."

"Are those your favorite?" His eyes scan my features as though he's committing them to memory.

"Definitely." My response comes out a bit breathless.

Suddenly, he reaches up and drags the pad of his index finger along my temple near my right eyebrow. "How'd you get that?" I'd long forgotten about the tiny scar he was tracing with reverence.

"I was in the passenger seat leaning over to adjust my grandmother's radio when someone ran into us. The car was older and didn't have airbags, and the impact caused me to slam into one of the radio dials."

His lips part to say more, but we're interrupted by Father. "You two planning to chat all night and make a sad priest eat alone?" Jude's hand drops from my face.

I laugh and playfully shove at Father's shoulder. "Listen to your poor story of woe." With a glance at Jude, I smile, happier than I've been in some time. "We're definitely planning to eat dinner. I was telling Jude about the fish and chips."

"Oh, Jude." Father leans in toward the bar, and I lean back in my seat so I don't block their view. "You haven't seen this one"—he tosses a thumb in my direction—"eat, have you?"

Jude shakes his head, amusement filling his blue eyes.

Father continues, his voice filled with affectionate teasing. "Beware. She's been known to steal fries."

Jude's eyes land on me. "That so?"

I hold up my palms with a laugh. "I can't be held accountable for what the fries make me do."

"True story!" Ben, another cop, now off duty, volunteers before slipping an arm across the back of my barstool. "She's the biggest fry thief in Cleveland." He grins down at me, flashes a wink, and strolls over to the pool table in the far back corner.

"Three orders of fish and chips, Harry," Father calls out. "And two beers, please."

"You got it."

"Fry thief, huh?" Jude's so close I can feel his hot breath across my cheek. His husky voice sends shivers racing through me. I turn, and he draws back slowly.

"That's right." My own voice sounds hoarse.

He shifts and accepts the beer Harry slides in front of him with a softly spoken thanks. He stares down at the beer thoughtfully, and I can't help but ask, judging from his reaction.

"Do you not drink?"

His head whips around in surprise. "What?"

I'm trying to keep my voice hushed in case I'm right. I certainly don't want to cause him embarrassment. "Do you not drink alcohol?"

There it is. That edge of his lips tips up. "I drink alcohol, but…" He turns away to stare at the glass of beer. "It's just been a long time. I was actually trying to remember the last time."

"Do you remember?"

Slowly, he turns back to me. "I do."

"And is it a good memory?"

As if mulling it over for a beat, he nods, and his tone is tender with a hint of melancholy. "It was."

"Well"—I reach for my own beer and hold it out for him to clink his glass to mine—"here's to making more good memories."

Raising his glass, he touches it to mine, then we each

take a sip of beer. He carefully sets the glass back down on the bar coaster, his gaze never leaving mine.

"To memories."

Right now, Jude's allowing me to sneak in. To slip past his well-constructed walls, affording me a glimpse at what he keeps hidden from everyone else.

It's more of a baby step than a leap, yet it doesn't detract from the sweetness of this victory. It only makes me crave more. To see more of the real man underneath all these layers. To understand him, to know his pain, to help him soothe it.

I crave the bravery to confess my own pain.

"THANKS FOR A GREAT DINNER AS ALWAYS." I wave goodbye to Harry and everyone else as Father James, Jude, and I head toward the exit of the Tavern.

As soon as we step onto the sidewalk out front, a gust of wind barrels through, causing me to shiver.

"Here, take my jacket." Jude's already sliding one arm free when I stop him.

"I'll be fine." I tug my jacket collar closer. "My car's right over there anyway." I tip my head in the direction of where it's parked on the street about a block away.

"Mind seeing our fry thief home?" Father winks at me before glancing down at his cell phone. Then he flashes Jude an odd look. "I'm expecting a visitor in a bit, so I need to get going."

My eyes curiously volley back and forth between the men. Father's expecting a visitor? *Is that code for something?*

An odd expression suddenly washes over Jude's features as though he's about to refuse.

"I don't think she wants me babysitting her." The way

he says it makes me feel like I'm the last person on earth he wants to be around.

"Jude." Father's expression is pleading. "Please."

Jude hesitates. "Okay, sure," he answers in a noncommittal way. He sounds almost disappointed, as if he drew the short end of the stick and got saddled with babysitting hellion toddler twins or something.

Father drops a kiss on my cheek and says his goodbyes before heading in the opposite direction to his car.

I swivel around and start at a fast clip toward my car. I can try to blame it on the cold wind that feels like it blows right through me, or the beer I've had—even though I'm completely sober—but there's no mistaking it.

I'm pissed.

"Faith."

Oh? Now he wants to talk to me? Maybe he wants to pat me on the head and tell me to be a good girl and drive five below the speed limit.

"Faith." This time, his voice is louder, more demanding, but I don't stop until I'm beside my car. Before I can step down from the sidewalk to head around to the driver's side, my upper arm is caught in his strong grip. Instantly, I whirl around, wrench my arm away, and back away to put space between us.

"What is it with you?" My tone is ripe with exasperation, and I raise my voice as I continue. "Do you know that you make me crazy?" I gesture between us. "I feel this energy or something between us. And I'm trying to play it cool, but you have these moments when…" I falter, running out of steam, because his eyes darken, his features turn intense, and beneath the streetlights, I have no idea how to interpret his expression.

He takes a slow step toward me. "Moments when…?"

I swallow hard. "Moments when I think you might feel

it, too." I avert my eyes, instead focusing on the nearby shop window advertising a dry cleaning discount. "But obviously, I was wrong because you clearly don't want to be saddled with me." My lips twist, and I scoff. "Look, I don't want you to feel obligated to see me home. So"—I wave a hand dismissively, forcing myself to adopt a flippant tone—"let's just chalk it up to a stupid crush and a pint of beer getting the best of me and call it a night, okay?" I brave a glance at him.

He stands stock-still with that same fierce intensity and his attention locked on me. "You have a crush?"

I try to laugh it off, but it comes out sounding strangled. "I think it's pretty obvious."

He advances another step. "Because I helped you that night?"

"Ye—" I stop myself and shake my head slowly. "No," I breathe out. "It's more than that. It's because I feel safe with you; I feel as if I can be myself around you. Like you understand me somehow. Like you wouldn't judge me or look at me differently or think I'm ugly if I tell you…" *If I tell you I'm going deaf,* I silently finish.

His brow furrows, and he dips his chin, his eyes boring into mine. "If you tell me what?"

I pinch my eyes closed. This is it.

"I'm going deaf." The words rush out, falling from my lips, and float between us awkwardly.

When my confession is greeted with nothing but silence, my heart sinks. I heave out a heavy sigh of resignation, and my shoulders slump in defeat.

The second time isn't the charm as the saying claims. I'm proof of that.

I open my eyes and focus on a point above his shoulder. "Well, good talk. No worries. I'll steer clear of you. But please don't tell Father James, because no one else knows, aside from Max and—" I'm startled from my rambling when Jude suddenly advances and backs me up against my car. His mouth is fixed in a flat line, and he reaches for me, cradling my face in his large hands.

"Nothing about you could turn me off." His gaze never wavers from mine. "You're beautiful and brave." He dips his head slowly, his eyes regarding me carefully, as if silently asking permission, before placing a featherlight kiss to my forehead. A sensual shiver wracks my body as his soft lips skim across my temple and trail down along my jaw before veering to my earlobe. Arousal skitters down every inch of my spine when he nips lightly at my flesh and admits in a low, husky tone, "I can't fight this anymore."

When he leans back slightly, I peer up at him and ask, "Fight wh—" I suck in a startled breath when his mouth crashes down on mine, swallowing my words. My hands fly to his waist to fist in the thick fabric of his jacket as I surrender to his searing-hot yet tender kiss.

His teeth graze the sensitive skin of my lower lip before he angles his head to deepen the kiss, his tongue sliding inside my mouth. When I dart out my own to tangle and toy with his, a deep growl reverberates in his chest. Fingers thread through my hair, and his lips move over mine in a kiss that's hot and deliciously carnal, and the prodding hardness low against my stomach sends a rush of arousal fluttering through me. The rasp of his beard against my skin is decadent, and I can't help but wonder how it would feel in other places.

He breaks the kiss, and I'm partially afraid to open my eyes for fear of this being a dream. When I slowly open them to peer up at him, my breath catches in my throat at his expression. Fiery-hot desire mingled with fierce possessiveness tells me he's barely holding back.

I want nothing more than for him to let go. To unleash it with me.

"Come home with me?" I whisper and worry my lower lip with my teeth. I can count on one hand how many men I've slept with. In four years, there's only been one guy in my bed.

He drags in a harsh breath and rakes a hand through his hair, tucking the stray dark locks behind his ear. His hesitation makes my stomach churn with dread.

"You sure you know what you're getting yourself into?" His eyes are assessing.

I decide to go for it. All in. If I'm going to fail, I might as well risk it all.

"I know exactly what I'd like to get into with you." I mash my lips together as heat floods my face at the blatant insinuation in my words—at my forwardness—especially when he offers no response. With haste, I add flippantly, "In between deep conversations about fry theft and good beer, of course."

Jude's eyes darken before something incredible happens right before my eyes.

Both corners of his lips tilt up into what has to be the sexiest smirk I've ever witnessed. He reaches out to finger the strands of my hair, his eyes alight with humor. "You had me at fry theft."

"I CAN'T BELIEVE I had to bribe you with talk of fries." I shake my head as I unlock my door minutes later. "Such a blow to the ego," I muse as I enter the quiet and mostly darkened apartment. I pray that he can't detect the hint of nervousness threading my tone as I ramble.

"Where's Max?" Jude asks quietly, locking the door

behind him. There's hesitance in his movements as he unlaces his boots before setting them neatly on the mat beside the door.

I slip off my shoes beside his, toss my purse onto the nearby chair, and hang my keys on the hook. "He's out of tow—"

Jude spins me around and presses my back against the closed door, my legs parting to allow him to nestle between them. He braces his hands on either side of me, caging me in, and his mouth explores mine with an urgency that rips a moan from deep in my throat. My fingers fumble to unzip his jacket, and he shucks it without tearing his lips from mine. When I impatiently pull his shirt from where it's tucked into the waistband of his pants and finally touch the bare skin of his abdomen, he gasps against my mouth. He breaks the kiss and stares down at me while he reaches behind his neck to tug off his shirt.

Holy shit. I can't help but stare at him. My eyes slowly canvass the sight of the dark ink etched across his firm biceps and pectorals and rove along the ridges and indentations of his abdominals. I trace around the most recent scar on his side—from the injury he sustained because of me. Though Jude may not have a six-pack, it's evident he takes good care of his body.

"Please tell me you're Photoshopped. Because you're going to be so disappointed with this gross fat"—I shift to point at my lower abdomen—"right there, and no amount of gym time or crunches will make it go away."

His eyes crinkle at the corners, and he lowers his mouth to my ear. "I know for a fact I won't be disappointed. The only way I'd be disappointed is if you stopped touching me." His fingers wrap around my hand and bring the flat of my palm to the center of his chest.

Once he settles it there, the heat radiating from his body practically singes me.

He presses a gentle kiss to my temple, over the scar he'd noticed earlier, and leaves a trail along my jawline. "Rule is, if you get to touch, so do I."

My lips curve into a slow smile. "That so?"

"Mmmhmm." His affirmation vibrates against the column of my neck before I stiffen, realizing he's drawing closer to my more recent scar.

"Don't." He backs away slightly, eyes locked with mine. "Don't be afraid. Don't be ashamed." He returns his attention to the scar, and his thumb grazes it softly. "It's a testament to your strength. To what you've endured." Blue eyes are in rapt attention of me, and I close my eyes to savor this moment. "You're beautiful." He punctuates this with a kiss on the scar, and I feel it.

A part of my heart opens, blooming proudly like a flower flourishing in a well-tended garden.

His hands move to unzip my jacket, but when his fingers land on the zipper pull, his eyes flick to mine in question.

"May I?"

He's not simply asking permission to take off my jacket. He's asking me if this is okay, if I'm still on board.

If this man hadn't already claimed my heart, it would be gift wrapped and presented to him with a bow by now.

"Yes."

At my response, his eyes turn molten. He rids me of my jacket, tossing it onto the chair next to my purse. He glances at the closed door at the left and the other on the opposite end of the apartment. Then he dips his head, lips twitching in a sexy smirk. "Which way is your bedroom?"

Not trusting myself to speak, I point to the left.

Suddenly, I'm upended and staring at Jude's tight jeans-clad ass. "Hey!"

He swats at my backside playfully and stalks toward my closed bedroom door. In a moment, we're inside with the door closed behind us. He slides me down his front until I land softly on my feet with barely an inch of space between us. My stomach flips in nervous anticipation, and the realization suddenly hits me.

I've never been here before.

Sure, I've slept with a guy before, but I've never embarked on something that felt more like a journey. A discovery. Not simply of our bodies but also our souls. As hokey as it sounds even in my own mind, it's as though Jude and I connect on a much deeper level. We're both concealing something from the rest of the world, so afraid to be judged for it. I may not know his secret, but it's clear he's letting me see past the defenses he's erected to keep everyone else out.

And, for now, that's enough.

FRIDAY FEEL-GOOD STORIES

A young woman claims the notorious Good Samaritan saved her from a mugger. She preferred to remain anonymous but said an older teen ripped her purse strap from her shoulder, knocking her to the ground.

The Good Samaritan intercepted the teen and rescued her purse, all the contents intact. She tried to thank him and offered him money as a reward, but he politely refused.

18

Jude

Faith reaches up to slide her hands into the hair at my nape, tangling her fingers in the strands. My eyes fall closed, and a shudder rolls through me, radiating all the way to the marrow of my bones at the gentleness in her touch.

Her mouth hovers against the base of my neck, barely grazing my increasingly sensitive skin. Her hot breath washes against me, and there's an undeniable hint of humor in her whisper. "You smell fresh and clean, and I can't help but wonder…" She leans back to peer up at me, her eyes brimming with emotion. Her head tips to the side, and she smirks mischievously. "Did you plan to get lucky tonight?"

I arch an eyebrow, and deep within the recesses of my mind, I recognize that I've not felt this alive in years. Shoving the distracting thought aside, I can't resist the smirk that forms on my lips. I lower my head to close the distance, bringing our mouths so close yet barely grazing hers.

"I didn't plan this." With each word, my lips skim

against hers, and her sharp intake of breath at the simple touch sends shards of satisfaction rushing through me.

I lean back, and our eyes lock. "This wasn't part of my plan." *Finding you wasn't part of my plan.* A thick lump of emotion lodges itself in my throat, and I swallow hard. There's no way she can possibly understand the deeper meaning to my words or how much of an impact she's had on me. My voice is like sandpaper. "But there's no chance in hell I'll regret this."

I cup her cheek in my palm and skim my thumb along her full bottom lip. Without realizing it, I find myself whispering, "Without a doubt, this'll be the best memory I've had in years."

I'm not entirely certain my words are directed solely to her. Perhaps they're more for my benefit because I know I'll cherish this. The craving for human touch is something I suppressed for years. I don't want to delve into the meaning or the reasons I'm giving in now. With her. All I know is that when I'm around Faith, she sparks something deep within me I believed was dead. She's the only woman who's been able to reach beneath the surface, beyond all the armor, and get to the heart of me.

Her breath hitches, and I can't shake the feeling I'm embarking on something bigger than me. Bigger than either of us.

Her mouth slowly spreads, curving up at the corners in a smile I've not witnessed before. It's a private one reserved for me at this moment. A shade mischievous, a trace sensual, and knowing.

One hand slides from my nape and along my shoulder as her palm traces a path, leaving a heated awareness in its wake. Her touch slides over my chest, tracing the shaded ink on my right pectoral, and skims along the thin line of hair just below my belly button that disappears under the waistband of my jeans.

Something drives me to stop her. I encircle her roving wrist in my grip, drawing her to a halt and causing her startled eyes to fly up to mine. I need her to understand me before we go any further.

"If you change your mind at any time, just tell me." Her eyes widen a fraction, and I add, "We can talk. Or I can leave. Whatever you want, Faith."

I'm giving her an out. And I'd be lying if I said a deep part of me isn't scared shitless of what she might see once she burrows deeper beneath my skin and discovers more chinks in my armor.

When she'll finally realize I'm not worthy of her.

Her eyes form a bright sheen, and she tips her head to the side. Shifting her hand back up along the same path it descended, she stops, hovering over the center of my chest. Over the heart hammering so hard it practically threatens to burst free of the confines of my chest. It's almost as if it's trying to tell me something.

Something I'm not ready to hear.

"Whatever I want?" she questions softly, her voice barely a whisper.

I nod, all breath lodged in my chest, and wait for her response. She moves her hand away and, without breaking eye contact, leans forward to press a single kiss to my chest. Directly over my rapidly beating heart. The softness of her lips brushes against my skin when she speaks. "I want you."

Wordlessly, I tunnel my fingers in her long hair, tug her body flush against me, and bring her mouth to mine. The kiss is hard. Insistent. Raw. Needy. The moment it dawns on me how rough I'm handling her, I gentle my touch, my kiss, and draw away to apologize.

But she doesn't let me get that far.

"Don't you dare." Dainty but surprisingly strong fingers tuck into the waistband of my jeans and tug me back to her. Her eyes glow with heated arousal, mouth damp from our kiss. "I don't want you to hold back."

I trace the callused pad of my index finger around her lush lips, noting the faint redness beginning to bloom around her mouth. "My beard is—"

She presses her mouth to mine, cutting off my words, and when her tongue sweeps inside, a ragged groan is dragged from deep within my chest. She breaks contact and backs away. Her tongue darts out to slick her lips, savoring the taste of our kiss. "Your beard is perfect."

She reaches for the bottom hem of her long-sleeve shirt and tugs it off, tossing it to the floor. Her gaze never leaves mine. "I want to feel it here"—she drags her fingertips along the tops of her breasts, encased in a simple black bra, before reaching back to release the clasp and set them free—"and here." She traces the outer edge of each areola, nipples hardening even further like ripe berries begging for my mouth.

Her breathing quickens, but she doesn't stop there. Her hands drop to unfasten her jeans and kick them free to bare her underwear, simple and black like her bra, the sides consisting of a slim strip of fabric that could easily be snapped. The urge to do so has me clenching my fists and digging my nails into the skin of my palms. My nostrils flare, and I will myself to take my time with her.

"And here." Her husky whisper curls around me, and her motions entrance me. Her hands glide over her covered mound.

With hands that tremble slightly, I curl my fingers around the sides of her panties and tug them down over the flare of her hips. Her silky skin teases my fingertips, and I lower myself to my knees before her. She rests a hand on my bare shoulder and steps free of the fabric. I tug off each of her socks, leaving her completely bare before me.

I skim my hands languidly along her calves, then her thighs, and pause at her waist. My eyes lock with hers to find her watching me, lips parted as her breaths turn ragged the instant I bring my mouth between her thighs. I press a featherlight kiss to her mound, and goose bumps rise across her skin.

I lean back a fraction, and with my hands still on her hips, I guide her to lie back on the bed. Her hair fans out on the beige comforter, and I drink in the sight of her. I commit every curve, every sensual slope of her flesh to memory. The knowledge that I may never get another chance to savor her lingers at the dark edges of my mind. I need to show her how incredible she is, how much I cherish her secret, that I'm honored she chose me to confide in, and that her beauty could never fade.

"Jude." Her voice is a caress with arousal threaded through it. Regardless of the fact it's not my real name, a part of me wants to take advantage of this moment when I'm simply Jude. I'm a man who has nothing to offer, yet this woman—a woman whose soul is as breathtaking as her outer beauty—wants me.

My hands guide her thighs to open wider, and when her hands cover my own, it's as though she's the one guiding me. Ensuring me that she wants this. That I'm not taking but giving.

I wish circumstances were different. I wish *I* were different. Enough. Because I want so badly to give her everything.

I lower my mouth and press an openmouthed kiss to her entrance, and she draws in a sharp breath as her body bows instantly.

"*Jude.*"

The pleading desperation, the urging, is all wrapped up in that single word. My name. She wants me. The man weighed down by guilt.

The man who doesn't deserve anything, let alone affection from her.

The man who has no soul.

I drag my tongue along the crease of her entrance, gliding through her wet folds, and her taste alone causes a brief moan to escape my lips. My cock aches, and I press it against the mattress to stave off the urge to shoot my load in my pants like a damn virgin.

Shivers of arousal wrack her body, and her writhing urges me on as I feast on her. I taste her deeply, laving her wet, heated flesh with my tongue and lips before I thrust my tongue deeper inside her pussy. Her hands fly to my hair, burying her fingers in the strands moments before she comes undone. Her inner thighs tighten around me, and I brace my palms against them, pressing them wider while I devour her. When she floods my tongue with her release and my name falls breathlessly from her lips, my heart thunders within my chest.

Once I finally have the courage to share my secret with her, when she can't bear to look me in the eyes, when her view of me is tainted beyond repair, one thing will remain certain—I'll cherish this moment for the temporary miracle it is.

Faith single-handedly breathed life into a heart I thought was lifeless.

19

Faith

Half-dazed after shamelessly riding Jude's tongue, I lie on my bed like dead weight. My skin still tingles from the sensations of his beard chafing my inner thighs in its own decadent caress and the way the ends of his hair skittered across it. My arms spread across the bed, my entire body is limp in the best way.

I heave out a breathless sigh. "Whoa."

He huffs out a small laugh and rises from between my legs. A hand smooths down his dark beard, and he runs his tongue along his upper lip. "I love the way you taste." He reaches to unfasten his jeans but hesitates, his expression sobering, eyes questioning.

"Don't you dare stop now." My tone is commanding, and his eyes darken with heated lust. I scoot up farther on the bed, my head propped up on a pillow, and take in the sight before me.

His hard body is a work of art in itself, and I make a promise to myself to sketch him again, even with the knowledge that I could never do him justice. When he removes his jeans and boxer briefs before tugging off his socks, he pauses for a moment, as if allowing me to look my fill.

I rise to my knees and move to the edge, closer to him. I lightly trace over the scar he gained because of me, and I hate that I'm the reason his beautiful flesh was marred.

"Hey." Strong fingers beneath my chin tilt my face up to his. "I'd do it all again, Faith." His gaze is searching, blazing with intensity as if begging me to hear the vehement truth in his words. His vow.

I tip my head to the side. "I never got a chance to make it up to you." I skim my palm down his abs, and they tighten in response. I don't get very far before I encounter the jutting hardness of his cock, and when I wrap my hand around his steely length, his lips part on a harsh breath.

"You don't need to make it up to me, Faith," he grits out, his breathing becoming choppy.

"I know." I lean forward and press a kiss to his collarbone, hiding my face from him. As crazy as it is, I can't refrain from giving a voice to the words that have been floating around in my heart. "I just want to love you."

Every fiber in his body freezes, going impossibly rigid. My stomach immediately plummets. *Stupid, stupid, stupid!* It's What Not To Do 101. I rest my forehead against his chest, feeling his heart beating rapidly. He's probably preparing to run out of here. "I'm sorry," I whisper.

His fingers tangle in my hair, gently tugging me back. As he peers down at me, his gaze holds an indescribable intensity, and an array of emotions flits across his features. Pain. Hope. Vulnerability. And others I can't quite decipher.

"I don't deserve you." His voice is guttural as if drawing the words from the innermost part of his soul. He skims his thumbs along my cheekbones. "But hell if I can resist you."

"Then don't."

His mouth claims mine, lips feverishly working over me with a near desperation. The hands cradling my face tilt my head to deepen the kiss, and I whimper at the incessant ache between my thighs.

He guides me back on the bed and braces himself above me on his forearms, flexing his tattooed biceps. A shock of his dark hair falls forward, and I tenderly smooth it back behind his ear. His eyes fall closed, as if in reverence of my touch, while I lovingly trace his features. When I skim my thumb along his slightly parted lips, his eyes flare open, burning bright with heated affection, and he nips at the pad before soothing it with his tongue.

I arch instinctively as wetness pools between my thighs and drag a hand along his back to pull his body flush against mine. His hard cock nestles against my stomach, and I bend my knees on each side of his hips. He opens his mouth and takes my thumb inside, rasping his tongue against it. I never knew something like this could be so intensely arousing. He releases it only to envelop my middle finger in the hot cavern of his mouth again, creating suction. My hips move of their own accord, and I shift, whimpering, mindless to anything except the suction of his mouth and the need to have him ease the relentless ache between my thighs.

"I need you."

He releases my finger, then lifts his lower body away slightly, drawing an aggravated sound from my throat. He steers my hand down and presses my wet finger to my clit.

"Touch yourself."

I'm overwhelmed with a needy desperation to feel him. "Condoms." I tip my head in the direction of my bedside table. Amidst the heady arousal, I give thanks that I still have condoms stashed in the far back of the drawer.

Without a word, he reaches over, fumbling through the contents before finally withdrawing one. I notice his hands are unsteady when he rips it open. Rising slightly on his knees, he grips his cock and slowly rolls the latex over the flared head and down his thick length.

"Don't stop." His eyes burn bright with heat, flickering between where I've paused rubbing my clit and back up to meet my eyes. He wraps his hand around his cock and guides the tip to my entrance, nudging marginally, enough to have me holding my breath in anticipation. With aching slowness, he slides inside a fraction.

When he doesn't press farther, I practically growl. "Jude."

The corners of his lips tilt up in a sexy smirk. "Some things are meant to be savored."

I move my hands to his ass, tugging him closer to me while I arch into his touch. "We can do slow another time."

His chuckle transforms into a strangled groan as he sinks deeper, and our gasps mingle in the silent room. "I might not last long."

"I don't care. Now shut up and kiss me."

His mouth crashes down on mine, tongue invading my mouth while he simultaneously buries his cock inside me, and my inner muscles adjust around his girth.

He raises his head, eyes searching my features with concern. "Okay?" he murmurs softly.

"Okay."

He begins to move in and out in steady, thorough strokes, watching me with a curious mix of scorching heat and tenderness. His palm caresses along my shoulder and down to cup the weight of my breast. His thumb grazes my nipple, and I arch into his touch.

He shifts to his back suddenly and moves me with an

easy strength I can't help but admire. I readjust my position on top of him, and it drives him even deeper. I press my breasts into his callused palms, relishing the sensual abrasion against my hardened nipples. I shift my hips and begin moving over him while he toys with my nipples.

"That's it." Blue eyes turn molten. "Ride me, Faith. I'm yours."

I'm yours.

Frantic need claws at me, and I rest my palms on the hard wall of his chest as I increase my pace. To each of my movements, he responds with a deep upward thrust. I look at the juncture of our thighs, mesmerized by the sight of how slick and shiny he is from my arousal.

"So fucking beautiful."

His guttural words bring my eyes to his face. His gaze flickers up, briefly catching mine before returning his attention to where our bodies are joined. The clenching of his jaw and the heady glaze of lust in his eyes as he watches me work my pussy up and down his hard length urge me on.

He pinches his eyes closed, and a look of pain flickers across his features. His eyes dart up to me. "You just clenched around my cock." He captures my nipples between his thumbs and forefingers. When he tugs on my hardened peaks, a powerful surge of arousal rushes through me. "Can't wait to feel you come."

The lethal combination of his words and the perfect amount of pressure on my sensitive nipples sets me off. My release barrels through me, and my inner muscles tighten around him as I ride out the waves of my orgasm.

I slump, resting my forehead on his chest, my breathing ragged. "Holy shit."

His chest rumbles beneath me. "Holy shit, indeed."

I rise up to peer down at him, and he gently smooths my hair back from my face. "I'm sorry," I say with a wince.

His brows furrow, eyes glistening with amusement. "For what?"

Heat floods my cheeks, burning red hot, and I avert my eyes. "I totally went off the rails, without a care, and you're still…" I trail off, shifting over his still-hard cock.

"Hey." With a sigh, I drag my eyes up to his. His eyes trace my features with a heated affection that nearly robs me of breath. "You can go off the rails whenever you like."

"Yeah?" A hint of a smile plays at my lips.

"Oh, yeah." He guides me down for a tender kiss before he whispers against my lips in a tone laced with a hint of mischief, "Now it's my turn."

He shifts us, moving me to be beneath him, and drives deep, burying his cock to the hilt. His expression turns fierce, nostrils flared, and I lock my legs tighter around his hips. As if struggling to maintain control, he stills, his eyes drifting closed, jaw clenching tight.

But I don't want that.

"I want it all." The words spill from my lips, and his eyes flare open. "Don't hold back."

"Faith." My name comes out in a raspy groan.

I rock my hips, urging him on. "Please." My voice is needy, thin. "I need you." I grab his hips, the muscles tensing beneath my grip, and something makes me voice the challenge. "Make me come again."

"*Fuck.*" The expelled profanity is barely audible under his breath, but in the next moment, it's clear he's given himself over to baser needs.

He shifts to rest on his knees, settling with his lower legs beneath him, and lifts me so my lower half is braced on his upper thighs. I can't withhold the moan at the instant change, the deeper penetration, and his grip on my hips tightens as he holds me in place. He draws back before driving inside so deep it feels as if he hits every nerve ending, rocketing me back to the precipice of orgasm.

"Is that what you want?" he grits out, thrusting furiously, his hips pistoning.

"*Yes*," I manage. His steady, driving thrusts and the heat blazing in the depths of his gaze cause ribbons of arousal to enfold me tightly. Wetness seeps from me, and I watch entranced as his cock slides in and out, slick and shiny.

"You like watching me."

My eyes fly to his, and his clenched jaw indicates he's close to losing control. I flick my eyes back to where we're joined, where he's gliding in and out of me.

"Rub your clit for me."

Before he even finishes giving me the command, I have my fingers on my clit. I gently pluck at the sensitive bundle of nerves, toying with it between my thumb and forefinger. My inner muscles clench around him in response to my touch.

"*Faith*." The deep rasp of his voice skitters along my skin in a sensual caress.

I rub my clit in circles, and my eyes flicker between his own and down to where his cock disappears inside me. "I'm so close."

His grip on my hips tightens, and the power and speed of his thrusts intensify.

My voice shakes when my muscles tighten in anticipation of my release. "Jude…"

His eyes are a tumultuous sea of blue. "Come on my cock."

I arch into his thrusts, silently urging him to go deeper while I continue working my clit through my orgasm. My inner muscles clench around him like a vise, and my toes curl as I drench him in the flood of my release. He thrusts wildly before driving deep one final time and coming with a low grunt.

He grows still, our combined ragged breathing the only sound in the quiet room. Carefully, he lowers himself over me. With strong forearms braced on either side of me, he rests his damp forehead on my shoulder.

Our labored breathing is the only sound in the silence of the apartment. I feel limp in the best way possible.

"I like it when you go off the rails," I whisper softly.

He jerks his head off my shoulder, and when he peers down at me in surprise, I swear he's trying to decipher whether I'm serious.

I cant my hips, and the slight movement of his cock, still buried deep, elicits a groan from us both.

"You do, huh?" There's a slight upturn of his lips as if he's trying to fight a smile.

I don't bother trying to hide mine. "Uh-huh."

"Then maybe"—he dips his head to graze my mouth with his own—"I ought to do that."

Reveling in the sensation of his beard softly abrading my skin, I smile against his mouth and gently nip at his bottom lip. "You definitely should."

Needless to say, he doesn't disappoint.

"TELL ME MORE ABOUT YOU."

I'm curled up against his side as we lie in bed. My head rests on his chest, his fingers toying lazily with my hair, lulling me into a relaxed state.

Before I can answer, Jude lets out a grunt of dismay. "Fuck. I'm doing it all backward," he mutters under his breath.

This just makes him that much more endearing, which is a characteristic at odds with his intimidating appearance and the fact this man is well over six feet of lean muscle.

I mull over his response and realize he *is* accurate. We don't know each other's favorite color, food, movie, or book. Whether we're ticklish or not. We've gone about this a bit backward. We've still covered important facts, though maybe not directly. He's proven a great deal by not only his actions but also by his words—though they may be few.

With my chin propped on his chest, I gaze at him, and compelled to rid him of the unease and uncertainty etched on his features, I start with the basics.

"Favorite color is blue." I admire his eyes. "But not your run-of-the-mill blue," I add softly. "A stormy blue mixed with shades of gray."

Eyes locked with mine, I desperately wish I could see beneath the shutters and armor in place instead of merely catching occasional glimpses.

One edge of his mouth tips up, and his eyes take on a sparkle I'd like to say is reserved only for me. "I'd love a crash course in all things Faith."

The fact that he's asking, that he's this interested, gives me hope that there's more between us than simply a fierce attraction.

I tip my head to the side in thought. "I don't like spicy food, I love eighties music, I'm ridiculously ticklish, and I've always dreamed of living along the coast. Somewhere in the south where it's warmer." I shudder. "Without the bitter-cold winters like we have here."

His expression is thoughtful. "What's your ideal version of paradise?"

I don't answer immediately, gathering my thoughts. "It's probably different than most. I'd love to have someone amazing with me, have a special spot all to ourselves—

nothing fancy." I close my eyes, and I can see it in my mind. "A house with a large porch with one of those bench swings on it—wide enough we can both fit. Sometimes I'll have my head on his lap and he'll play with my hair. Or vice versa. We'll talk about whatever or nothing at all. We'll just…be. Simply enjoy one another's company." The image is so vivid. I imagine Jude is with me, and a relaxing pensiveness fills my entire body. I open my eyes with a satisfied smile. "To me, that would be paradise."

His eyes are locked on me, and a myriad of emotions flits across his face. Yearning. Envy. Sadness. "Sounds like a perfect version of paradise to me." His voice is husky, subdued, holding a hint of tenderness.

We fall silent for a beat before he prompts, "What else?"

"I strongly dislike Disney movies."

Surprise etches his features. "Really?"

I scrunch my face in distaste. "Most kids' movies have that whole happily ever after crap. They're like"—I change my voice to be higher pitched and slightly singsong—"'You're not smart enough to think for yourself or brave enough to be independent and have a career of your own. You need a man to save you and make you happy.' It's a terrible message. Telling girls everywhere that you'll suddenly find your Prince Charming, and then everyone will live happily ever after." I scoff. "Not how it works, people."

"And how would you have the stories be told?"

He appears truly interested in my answer, so I continue. "Honestly? I'd love to see a story featuring a woman who's smart, independent, makes hard choices about her life, and maybe even makes mistakes along the way. But she learns from her mistakes. Learns about herself as she goes. And when it comes to saving, she saves herself. I'd even be okay with her and the guy working together to solve whatever problem she's facing." A thought strikes me. "Or better yet, she helps save him." My lips curve up. "I kinda like that. A badass woman who helps save the man."

I realize he's fallen quiet, and his eyes have taken on a faraway look.

I clear my throat and avert my gaze, tracing my fingertip along the outline of the ink on his pectoral. "But of course, life isn't one big fairy tale." My tiny laugh is tinged with cynicism. "No way would they have a heroine who was going deaf." I fall silent for a beat, unable to shake off the cloud of defeat suddenly hanging over me.

20

Jude

"So it comes and goes?"

I know she's self-conscious about it, but I want to know more. I want to know everything that makes this woman tick. I lazily toy with the silky strands of her hair while she explains more about her hearing loss.

"Yeah," she replies softly. One word. So simple yet chock-full of pain and disappointment. "Except it's gotten even worse. More going." There's a brief pause. "It's genetic. Certain bones in my ear formed incorrectly, and there's no treatment or cure for it. I didn't have noticeable symptoms until the past few years." She shifts to place a hand on my chest and prop her chin on top. "And as awful as it sounds, I don't want the typical cochlear implant devices that are bulky and so obvious. I don't want to be visibly different like that." Her downcast eyes and the way her voice grows smaller and weaker gut me. "I've just tried to get better at lip reading."

"That's why you pay such close attention to my lips when I speak," I murmur more to myself than to her. It makes so much more sense now, but I can't resist teasing her. "And here I thought you were taken by me."

She lifts her gaze, a soft smile forming on her lips. "That, too."

I shift slightly and focus on the ceiling, deep in thought. "So, explain to me what the procedure entails."

She snuggles closer, resting her head on my shoulder. "Well, my doctor told me about a new implant that's smaller and not so obvious. Less to fuss with. They insert the implant beneath the skin, and the electrode part is inserted into the cochlea—part of my inner ear—so it sends impulses to the hearing nerve. It all works with an external sound processor, and this newest one is the size of a quarter and fits against the skull." Faith smooths back her hair and taps a finger a few inches above the shell of her ear. "Right there. And it's waterproof and heavy duty. Pretty much everything you could ask for."

She falls silent, and I prompt gently, "But?"

A sigh ripples through her. "It's expensive. Even with what my insurance partially covers." Another sigh. "Want to hear the real kicker?"

"What's that?"

"The whole reason I went into journalism was because my gran lectured me day and night that my art would get me nowhere, and I'd be without a job with no health insurance—nothing. Yet I found out at my last doctor's visit that if I had no job and no insurance, I'd qualify for aid to help defer the costs. *Greatly*."

"Do you mind if I ask how much it costs?"

"With my insurance, I'll still owe sixty-four thousand."

Holy fuck. "You have to be shitting me," I breathe out.

"Yeah. Exactly." Her dejected tone makes me tighten my arm that's wrapped around her. "And I don't want to take out a loan—assuming I'd even be approved—but I'm not sure I have a choice. Especially if I plan to keep my job." Her laughter is subdued and humorless. "It helps to actually *hear* people's answers when I interview them."

"It'll happen." *Dammit.* There has to be a way.

We lie in comfortable silence. With her body flush against mine and her arm draped over me as if she's holding something precious, I take a moment to store this in my memory bank. To ensure I have this glimpse of what it would be like to have someone cherish simply being with me.

"Thanks for not spooking."

Her words are spoken so faintly that I strain to hear her, and it takes a solid sixty seconds for me to grasp what she's getting at.

"Why would that spook me?"

She turns her head to face me, and the muscles in her arm tense beneath my hand. Her eyes meet mine. "I was engaged and…" She averts her gaze and traces an invisible pattern along my chest. "When we learned of my diagnosis and what it meant, my ex-fiancé, Todd, told me it changed things for him."

Lips flattening into a thin line, I force myself to draw in slow, steady breaths to suppress the sudden rage that rolls through me. *What kind of asshole breaks up with a woman because of that?*

"Jesus, Faith." I furrow my brow. "He's a damn idiot."

Her smile is laced with sadness. "Well, I can't entirely blame him. It's a big adjustment." She lifts one shoulder in a slight shrug. "The implants aren't guaranteed to work." Her eyes are so wide and unapologetically honest. "None of us really ever thinks ahead like that. We have stars in our eyes when we're in love. I mean, he asked a woman to marry him who had all her senses." There's another partial shrug as though she's physically trying to shrug off the lingering pain caused by the rejection. "He didn't sign up to have a wife with major hearing loss."

I pinch my eyes closed and tug her closer. "This might piss you off," I murmur softly, "but if I could beat the shit out of him right now, I'd do it in a heartbeat."

Her tiny giggle eases the tightness in my chest. "It doesn't piss me off." She lifts up to dust a soft kiss on my lips. "I appreciate the thought, but it's over and done with. And honestly?" She wrinkles her nose. "I dodged a bullet because now that I've seen him for who he really is, he's definitely lost all appeal."

She smooths her fingers over my beard, wearing a thoughtful expression on her face. I close my eyes to her touch, relishing in how something so simple can bring me a sense of peace.

"I need to trim this damn thing," I mumble. "And cut my hair." It's grown far too long, now touching my collar.

"I can do it."

My mouth curves into a slow smile, and I open my eyes. "Really?"

"I sometimes do it for Max when he's in a bind."

I narrow my eyes on her. "You two were never—"

"*Never*," she interrupts with a shudder. "So gross."

"Good."

Her expression morphs into one of mischief, and she arches an eyebrow. "Already throwing your weight around, huh?"

I thread a hand through the hair at her nape and lower my lips to hers. "Something like that," I murmur.

"Well, then." As Faith sits up and climbs off the bed, I admire her curvy, lithe body. Legs that seem to go on forever. Breasts that are a perfect fit in my hand. Hair that cascades past her shoulders in a slightly mussed curtain. But more than that, all these parts pale compared to the one thing that's managed to slay me. Because it's obvious she puts it in every single thing she does.

Her heart.

"Quit checking me out and put on some clothes so I can beautify your rugged self." She tugs a camisole and some pajama pants from her dresser and drags them over her body.

"Slave driver." I groan and roll over to retrieve my boxer briefs and have to tuck my still semi-hard dick inside. After being celibate for so long and just now indulging in smoking-hot sex with this gorgeous woman, it's to be expected, I guess.

Moments later, I'm sitting on the wide top step of a folding three-step stool in her bathroom, waiting on Faith. She enters with a small handful of newspapers and electric clippers in her other hand.

"Let me spread these out to catch the hair." She bends down to layer a few around where I'm sitting. I catch sight of one of the headlines, and my muscles immediately go rigid. *The Good Samaritan strikes again! Local woman and son receive help when they needed it most.*

"Have you heard anything lately?"

My eyes snap up to meet hers, and she gestures to the headline on the newspaper. I merely shake my head and avert my gaze, my jaw tight.

"I haven't."

If she detects the odd facet to my tone, she must dismiss it. Thankfully.

Refocusing on my hair, she drapes a towel over my shoulders. She runs her fingers through the length of my hair. "How much do you want off?" I close my eyes, relaxing into her touch.

"As much as it takes so it's not getting in my eyes."

"Okay." She alternates between combing and cutting,

the only noise between us is the sound of the clippers as they make quick work of my hair. The difference is instant, the length of my hair no longer weighing me down as it falls soundlessly to rest on the newspapers spread out beneath me.

She shuts off the clippers, and I open my eyes. "How does it feel?"

I drag my hands through the shorter strands, now probably about two inches in length, and raise my eyes to hers. "Feels amazing."

She gestures to my beard. "Ready for me to attack that, or would you rather do it?"

"Actually, I think I might do it, if you don't mind. Then I'll help clean this mess up." I dip my chin in the direction of where my hair now litters the newspapers.

"I can get it."

I stand. "Faith, I've got it. Promise." I press a kiss to her forehead and move around her to the sink. Accepting the clippers from her, I trim the length off my beard and clean it up considerably. It had been getting itchy with so much growth, so this'll be a nice reprieve.

I attempt to dust any stray hairs from my beard into the plugged sink so I don't leave a trail through her apartment.

"Wow."

I meet her startled eyes in the mirror. "Wow in a good way?"

She steps closer, still watching me in the mirror. "Most definitely." With our eyes locked, she runs her hands over my shoulders and trails them down along my stomach. "Just dusting away a few stray hairs." The corners of her lips twitch, trying to restrain a smile. "In fact"—she dips a hand inside the front of my boxer briefs, and my breath hitches in surprise—"I might need to check and make sure there aren't any more strays." Her fingertips graze over my tip, tracing the moisture gathering there, and I can't resist pressing into her touch.

"I appreciate you being thorough."

Her smile takes my breath away. She turns me, guiding me to lean back against the counter. Her fingers tug the fabric down as she lowers to her knees before she grips my hard length. She runs her thumb over the tip, gathering the moisture there before bringing her thumb to her lips. My hips buck instinctively the moment the tip of her pink tongue darts out to lap it up. When she guides me to her lips, enveloping my cock in her hot, wet mouth, it takes everything in my power to resist the urge to thrust deeper.

Bewitched by her, I watch her lips glide up and down my length and grow impossibly hard at the sight of my cock disappearing in her mouth. I tangle my fingers in her hair, and when she opens her eyes, flecks of gold and green shimmer amidst the brown.

I can barely manage to draw air into my lungs when she tongues the slit of my cock before dipping to trace along the underside. Her wet mouth slides up and down my shaft, creating a strong suction with each stroke, catapulting me to the precipice. My breathing is labored, choppy, and I'm so damn close.

"Faith." I force the words out, attempting to warn her. "If you don't want—" She suddenly hollows out her cheeks, and I wrench my hands from her hair and slam my palms against the vanity, gripping it with violent desperation. "*Fuck.*"

A groan is ripped from my throat as I arch instinctively and shoot my release in long, hot spurts. She swallows every drop and drags her tongue along the slit to ensure nothing remains. With a satisfied smile, she carefully slides my boxer briefs back into place. As soon as she rises to her feet, I tug her close and rest my forehead against hers. "You're gonna be the death of me, woman."

I can hear the smile in her voice when she ducks her face to whisper against my neck. "Ah, but what a great way to go." Her hot breath fans against my skin, and much like weeds bursting through the cracks of a sidewalk, Faith penetrates the deepest, darkest recesses of my heart.

ELDERLY MAN CLAIMS A "GOOD SAMARITAN" REPLACED HIS GROCERIES

"I slipped on the ice and spilled everything on the sidewalk. This man just told me to hang on and came back with everything that had gotten damaged or ruined. With my meager Social Security check, money is tight. He was a real angel in disguise, saving me from another expense."

21

Faith

MAY

"What a wonderful surprise!" Terri looks up when William escorts me inside before the shelter opens for the day. She sets an enormous bag of potatoes on the counter before rounding it to enfold me in a hug. "So good to see you."

"You, too."

"William said you wanted to interview me for a story?" She hustles back to her spot and begins peeling the potatoes in quick, confident motions.

I withdraw my notepad and pen. "Yes, I was informed that someone was dropping off food recovered from dumpsters outside grocery stores, and this was indicated as one of the places the food was delivered to."

Her head is down, eyes concentrating on her task, but I still notice the slightest stutter in her motions. Without looking up, she asks, "Now, what's this story you're covering?"

Something odd is intertwined with her overly casual tone. I edge a bit closer to her workstation.

"I'm trying to determine who this Good Samaritan actually is."

This time, Terri's hands pause for a full beat before she looks up at me. Head tilted to the side, she frowns. "And why is that so important to people?"

I falter for a moment because honestly, it wouldn't be that vital for me, aside from what I've been promised if I successfully reveal the person's identity. But I have to maintain professionalism, so I offer up, "It's a feel-good story, and Lord knows everyone needs that these days."

It's a copout, pure and simple. I know it, and judging by the way Terri's features cloud, she does, too.

She resumes peeling the potatoes with extreme concentration on her task. "I honestly don't know what to tell you, sweetie. We've received donations, yes, but it's come from the local stores like usual."

"And a few months back when I was here, you mentioned there was a shortage of food donations…" I trail off suggestively, trying to pinpoint what exactly it is I'm missing here. I distinctly recall her telling me many of the local businesses didn't renew their donation agreement.

Her head snaps up, and for a split second, I swear there's a tinge of panic in her expression before it's wiped clean. A surprised smile spreads across her face. "Ohhh, that." She waves the potato peeler dismissively. "That was a misunderstanding. We got it all straightened out." With a thumb tossed in the direction of the stacks of loaves of bread and other overflowing items, she winks at me. "As you can see, we're well stocked."

I nod slowly. "So, you haven't come across anyone who's been doing these good deeds or bringing food to those in need?"

"Nope. Can't say that I have." Flashing me an apologetic look, she shakes her head. "Sorry I can't be of more help."

"No problem at all. I appreciate your time, Terri."

"Of course, sweetheart." This time, her smile is less forced and more genuine.

"I'll see you soon."

"Look forward to it!" She waves, her hands dripping with potato starch, and quickly gets back to work.

After thanking William on my way out, I hit up another lead which turns out to be a dead end.

The entire drive home, I can't shake the feeling that Terri is hiding something.

THE KNOCK at the apartment door is unexpected. One of his admirers probably pseudo-stalked him and discovered where he lived.

The sound of male voices surprises me. I can't decipher exactly what they're saying, so I step around the corner from the small kitchen to get a better look.

As soon as I do, alarm floods me, because Max is speaking to Monroe and Parris, two detectives I've met a few times through Father James. They don't frequent the Tavern, which is understandable since Father mentioned Detective Monroe is a recovering alcoholic and prefers to steer clear of temptation as much as possible.

The men are dressed in polo shirts and slacks with police badges affixed at the waist. Their sober expressions make it evident this isn't a social call. "Is something wrong?"

Max turns. "They said they found something they wanted to ask you about."

"Okay," I say slowly.

"Faith, we're sorry to interrupt."

"No, it's fine."

Both detectives had spoken with me after I'd gained

consciousness in the hospital following the attack. They were the ones who informed me that the man who'd assaulted me was also hospitalized with severe, life-threatening injuries. They'd exchanged one of those skeptical looks when I'd told them I had no idea how he'd been injured.

It was the truth. I was unconscious when the altercation happened. And, frankly, I didn't—and *still* don't—care what happened to him.

Detective Monroe offers one of those smiles meant to put the other person at ease. I'm familiar with that tactic since I've used it when interviewing people. "May we come in for a minute?"

"Of course." I wave toward the small dining room table. "Please have a seat."

"Something smells delicious," Detective Monroe remarks with a smile.

I offer a polite smile. "I'm waiting on dinner in the oven."

He and his partner take their seats. "We thought it might be easier to recall details from that night now that you're home and more comfortable."

Max locks the door and flashes me a look of concern. We join them at the table.

"We're trying to find the identity of the man who rescued you that night."

I frown in confusion. "But I already told you at the hospital that I had no idea who he was. Someone off the streets quite literally found me." It's partially true. I don't know his full name. But something deep within me is screaming for me to withhold this information.

The weight of Max's eyes is unsettling, and I know he'll lay into me after they leave.

As casually as possible, I ask, "Is that person in some sort of trouble?"

The detectives glance at one another, and it doesn't take a genius to decipher it.

"We'd just like to talk with him."

Detective Parris chimes in. "The family of your assailant wants charges to be pressed against him."

I stare incredulously, back and forth between the two of them. "The man who attacked me and tried to rape me —*his* family wants the prosecutor to press charges against the man who stopped him from doing so? Are you *kidding* me?" I toss a glance at Max, and he looks just as shocked. Returning my attention to the detectives, I protest, "But he saved my life!"

Detective Monroe's lips press thin, and he shakes his head slowly. "I understand where you're coming from. We're working to identify the person who saved you so we can get their side of the story." He exchanges a look with his partner, who appears just as frustrated with the news.

I shake my head in disgust. "I can't believe this is happening."

The two men don't respond for a beat, but then Detective Parris withdraws a business card from his billfold and slides it across our table. "I know we gave you a card last time, but just in case... If you remember anything at all, don't hesitate to let us know."

"Yes, sir." Dazed, I slide the card closer and stare at it. Vaguely, I hear Max usher them out, saying their goodbyes. I trace my index finger over the simplistic business card.

I sense his presence behind me before he slides onto the chair he vacated moments before.

Tentatively, I raise my eyes to meet his.

"You lied." Max's voice is subdued yet confused.

"I didn't actually—"

He throws up a hand to stop me, his brows slanting together. "You know exactly what I mean."

Dropping my chin to my chest, I murmur, "I can't let a man get into trouble for that. Not after he was the one who brought me to the hospital." I raise my head and stare back at him. A fierce possessiveness barrels through my veins at the thought of Jude being in trouble because of me. "He found me and brought me in. He'd covered—" My voice breaks as raw emotion rushes to the forefront. "He covered me with his own jacket and carried me four blocks to the hospital, Max. You and I both know that these days, most people would—and, in my case, they probably did—pass me by." A tear finally manages to break free, trickling down my cheek. "But he didn't."

Max leans forward, resting his elbows on the table, and runs his hand over his jaw. "I don't like the idea of you withholding information." His eyes are pleading. "It's the *police*, Faith."

"I know. But"—I reach over and lay my hand on his—"please, just…trust me on this."

Releasing a long sigh, he nods reluctantly. "For now."

"Thank you."

He leans back and stretches his arms out to the sides, eyeing me. "So what's the latest? How's your story coming along?"

I slump and rest my chin on my palm. "I've got some leads to follow up on, but…it's odd."

"How so?"

I blow out a long breath. "What I've uncovered so far alludes to the fact that this person has been on the scene and doing these"—I break off to hook my fingers in air quotes—"'good deeds' for the past five years or so."

Max cocks his head to the side. "Seems like a long time to keep at it. The only reason I'd stick with something like that is if—"

"There was really strong motivation behind it."

We sit in thoughtful silence until the oven timer beeps, alerting me that the pesto chicken I'm cooking is done.

"Smells so damn good," Max groans. "Remind me again why we aren't married?"

I huff out a laugh as I open the oven door and withdraw the casserole dish using hot pads. "Because we don't love each other like that."

"To drive home that point, you also found time this past weekend to get it on with someone new, huh?"

The casserole dish clatters loudly onto the trivet on the counter, and I whip around to stare at him. "How do you…?"

A smug grin stretches his face. "I can tell when a woman's blissed out." He runs a hand down his chest before dusting invisible lint off each shoulder. "I've been known to do that many a time."

I make a gagging sound and turn back to grab a large serving spoon for the roasted carrots. He laughs before sobering.

"Is it who I think it is?"

I slowly turn my head to look at him quizzically. "And who do you think it is?"

"Well…" He leans back in the chair, eyeing me curiously. "I hope like hell it's not Asswipe." He refuses to say my ex-fiancé's name, which is fine. Asswipe is an accurate substitution as far as I'm concerned.

I scrunch my face in disgust. "God, no."

"That's a relief." He continues to study me, and I grow antsy, so I turn to start plating the food. "Is it a certain someone who works that dark and dangerous vibe like it's nobody's business?"

I can't restrain my snicker. "Interesting observation."

"So you're not denying it…"

Carrying a plate in each hand, I slide one in front of him before placing one at my spot and take a seat. "Nothing to deny."

"Look, I may have judged him a little too harshly." At my sarcastic *You think so?* expression, he merely rolls his eyes and continues. "I'm still cautious. Because, well…it's you."

I get it. He's protective of me. And I love him for it even when he's a pain in my ass.

He eyes me with curiosity and leans his forearms on the table. "So, what's his story?"

I part my lips only to snap them shut because, well… *Shit.* Every time I'd attempted to steer the conversation his way, it somehow ended up in my lap. But I let it go because he'd appeared genuinely interested in my answers and wanted to learn more about me. And when Jude listened, he actually *listened.* He didn't simply wait for me to finish talking so he could take his turn as many people do. He listened and asked for more. And his follow-up questions proved he was listening.

Max's expression transforms to one of exasperated disbelief. "Faith…" There's a lecture coming, so I deflect in the only way I can guarantee he'll drop the subject…for now.

"It wasn't like we made a ton of time for pillow talk." I lift my eyebrows suggestively.

He throws up a palm with a grimace. "Enough. I have to maintain some appetite."

With a laugh, I pick up my fork, and we both dig in. As soon as Max tastes the first bite of the pesto chicken, he moans around his mouthful of food. Once he's swallowed, he compliments me.

"This is so damn good. Too bad you won't quit your job and just cook for me all the time."

I shake my head with a chuckle. "You know I can't quit my job."

Silence immediately descends upon the room, and I hate it. I didn't even think about it when I spoke, but I hate that it's gotten like this. Where even the slightest mention sends a cloud of melancholy over us.

My eyes lock with his. "I didn't mean to—"

He waves me off with a forced smile. "I know. I get it." Releasing a long sigh, he scrubs a hand over his face. "I still wish you'd let me help you. It's not like I don't have the mon—"

"Max." My tone is stern. "We've already talked about it." I refuse to borrow money from him, especially for something this expensive.

"If only you weren't so damn headstrong." The affection in his eyes softens the blow of his words.

"If only you'd find a damn girlfriend," I shoot back.

He puffs out his chest, stretching his plain white T-shirt across his broad chest. "It's tough to find a woman who can handle this much goodness long term."

I shake my head with a laugh. "Get up and grab us some drinks."

I'm focused on cutting a piece of chicken on my plate when I look up to find Max looking at me with concern.

A fierce knot forms in the pit of my stomach. "Sorry."

There's that crease of worry between his brows, but he gentles his expression. "No worries. You just tuned me out." His laugh sounds forced. "Women usually do."

I laugh it off, but we both know we're masking the

issue. Covering up the fact he'd been speaking to me, and I didn't even hear him.

If I don't figure something out soon—if I don't manage to nab this story—it means I won't get that raise. Which means the solution to my problems will be further out of reach.

And I can't let anything get in the way of that.

22

Jude

MAY

"Well, hello there, handsome!"

Margie, the owner and sole employee of a small shop called Muffin Top, waves me over as she darts around the counter to hug me. Not once has she allowed my gruff and quiet demeanor to deter her from hugging me. She didn't even blink when I'd never offered up my name and just accepted it like it was no big deal.

With always perfectly coiffed dark gray hair, a friendly smile, and normally dressed in jeans that hug her larger figure paired with a Muffin Top T-shirt, she wraps her arms around me.

I haven't wanted to admit it, but something's been hanging over me. Like a sense of dread as though the sky's preparing to fall in on me. For the first time since meeting her, I feel like I actually need one of Margie's hugs.

"You've been away." I've been worried about her. It's not usual for her to miss more than a day or so if she's come down with a nasty cold here and there.

But I've noticed her absence for the past few weeks. As well as the new accessory on her right arm.

Margie holds up her cast with a chuckle. "Would you believe I tripped and fell?" She shakes her head in dismay. "My knees and those darn back steps got me."

I frown in concern. "Your back steps here?" My mind's already racing on how to fix this.

"Yes. I was just taking out the trash. Nothing extreme." Her tone is a mixture of embarrassment and disgust. "But my daughter is trying to price ramps." She wrinkles her nose. "They're just so expensive."

"Let me know if I can help you with anything around here." I nod toward the cases holding a variety of muffins. "Least I can do since you always sneak me a muffin."

She swats at my arm playfully, her eyes dancing with laughter. "Oh, you! I can hardly tell you indulge in them." A customer enters the small shop, and she rushes behind the counter to assist them while I step aside.

Something about Margie has always made me open up more and feel a little lighter when I'm around her. It's probably because she reminds me a lot of my own mother before she passed away.

Once she finishes helping the customer, I tell her I'll take her trash out back for her. She fusses. "You don't have to do that." I wave off her protests and gather up the large plastic bag from the waist-high Rubbermaid trash can in the back.

I saunter out the heavy steel-enforced door, which sticks before it finally creaks open on the hinges. Stepping out, I draw to a stop at the sight of the steep steps leading down from the landing. I toss the bag into the large dumpster sitting about a few feet away designated for each of the nearby shops.

Re-entering, I scan the back area of the shop until I find what I'm looking for. Grabbing the small can of lubricant, I spray a good coat on the hinges of the door, testing it out to ensure it opens and closes smoothly.

"Oh, you didn't have to do that." Margie's rushing over to me.

"No big deal. It took less than a minute to fix." I replace the lubricant on the shelf and toss my thumb in the direction of the back door. "Those steps are a death trap. It's a wonder you didn't take a spill earlier."

She shakes her head. "My daughter and I will have to figure something out."

Once I'm finished helping her with a few other odd jobs and, of course, after another goodbye hug from Margie, I head on my way.

Even though I know it'll put everything at risk, I have to do it.

After a stop in an internet café, it takes me about twenty minutes to ensure everything is in order, and I walk out knowing it was worth it.

I've been off the radar for so long, the average person wouldn't be able to find me.

But I know better. Especially now that I'd tapped into funds I haven't touched since I left. I just need to have faith they'll leave me be and respect my wishes.

That I won't need to prepare myself for the repercussions.

I NEVER LOOK, never glance, and sure as hell never read the headlines of the newspapers in the boxes situated along the business section of the downtown area.

But today, something—an inkling in the back of my mind—made me look.

As if he has an uncanny sense of things, Scout draws to a stop in front of one of the newspaper boxes. With the odd sensation as though I'm preparing for an impending blow, I draw in a deep breath and exhale slowly before allowing my eyes to lower to the headlines.

Tremors immediately radiate through my body, and my breathing hastens because I don't believe the words printed on the headline, let alone connect them to the mugshots below it.

Guilty Verdicts Receive Applause from Residents of El Paso

Three sentenced to life in prison for murdering food bank coordinator of El Paso

I barely manage to bite back a growl filled with disgusted fury at the fact that the murderers' faces are larger while the victim's photo is reduced to a small square off to the side of the article, as though just an afterthought.

A fucking afterthought.

I continue to scan the article like a fucking sadist.

"Riddled with mistrials"

"Was esteemed by the community for her service to those in need and in feeding the homeless"

"Burglary gone awry"

"Pregnant"

"Shot multiple times and left for dead"

There's no telling how long I stare down at the newspaper. This is why I've avoided news in any form. It's not surprising the story's reach would be this extensive—from El Paso, Texas, to Cleveland, Ohio. A pregnant woman being gunned down in her own home is enough to warrant an article in newspapers. Throw in the fact that she was dedicated to her job of serving those in need within a large city, and it's easy to understand how this would land on the front page.

I'm so lost in my thoughts that it takes a moment for the awareness to sink in. *I'm being watched.*

As casually as possible, I tug my hat down over my eyes before turning with the excuse of lowering myself to murmur to Scout. "Hey, boy. You ready to head back?" I pet his soft fur and slowly raise my eyes to scan my surroundings. I don't have to look far. Across the street, my eyes clash with the man's seconds before he hurriedly sets down the cell phone he'd had aimed in my direction.

Fucker took a picture of me, and I can't have that.

He nods at me with a smug grin, and he must think all is well between us. As though he wasn't just fucking around with my life—or what's left of it.

I glance both ways and guide Scout to cross to where the man's sitting outside the Cleveland Bread Company. Drawing to a stop barely a foot away from where he sits with a suited leg casually resting atop one knee, I enjoy the flicker of unease that settles over his features.

"Why…what can I do for you?" He quickly recovers and makes a show of patting down his pockets with a grimace of mock disappointment. "Sorry, but I don't carry any cash."

"Not looking for cash." I reach over and grab the phone he's set on the newspaper.

The newspaper that's upside down.

"Hey!" I ignore his protest and notice it requires a password. I turn the face of it toward him and lower my face to his. "Enter the fucking password."

"Why should I?" Wary stubbornness laces his tone.

Between clenched teeth, I practically growl, "Because you'll be eating through a fucking straw if you don't."

He goes rigid and hurriedly types in the code. I immediately find the photos he's taken of me and delete them. With my lethal stare centered on him, I lean in closer. "What's with you wanting my picture?" I curve my lips into a grin that I know is cold and dangerous and allow my eyes to flick over him in a quick once-over. "Need some spank bank material, huh?"

The horrified expression on his face would be laughable if I weren't so damn worried about his motivations. "No!"

"Then, why?"

He clamps his lips tight, but the look in his eyes tells me everything I need to know. He's onto me. Don't know how, but I can tell.

"Who do you work for?"

He eyes me for a beat as if wavering on his decision of whether to answer. Finally, he says, "*The Vindicate.*"

Fuck. Unease reverberates through me. *Why is he photographing me? Is it related to Faith's story?*

I've got to watch my back and cover my trail even more carefully.

"Can I have my damn phone back, now?"

The smugness in his tone grates on my nerves, and for that, on top of everything else, I make a decision right then and there.

A few swipes here, a few taps there, and it's done. Passcode reprogrammed.

"Wait, what are you…?" he sputters when I toss the phone down on the table.

Spinning around, I toss over my shoulder, "Enjoy cracking that code, asshole," as Scout and I head back to the parsonage.

A FEW DAYS LATER...

The large commercial truck pulls up along the street, and the men quickly emerge to unload the cargo from the back. Sliding up the back door, they settle the heavy ramp onto the road and disappear into the back. Moments later, they emerge, carrying the aluminum ramp, ready to install it for Margie.

From my perch in the shadows, I watch the men work to secure it to the back, and when they're nearly finished, Margie opens the door in surprise.

"What's all this?" Confusion laces her tone.

"We're installing a ramp as ordered, ma'am." The man who answers doesn't look up from where he's finishing up the installation.

"But I..." She trails off, likely worried about the cost. "I didn't order this."

The other man straightens, withdraws thick tri-folded papers from his pocket, and holds it out for her to accept. "It's been paid for."

Stunned, she accepts the receipt and reads it over.

"Warranty is included."

"And...who paid for this?"

The two men collect their tools, and one shrugs. "Not sure. It just said it was already paid in full, and the warranty information was to be in your name." He hesitates. "If there's nothing else you need, we'll be going."

"Thank you." Her voice is but a faint whisper, filled to the brim with emotion. Margie's face crumples. "God bless you both."

The men retreat to their truck. She remains rooted to the spot after they've left, staring at the ramp in awe and swiping at her now tear-stained cheeks.

Before I sneak around the corner to make my escape, I allow myself a brief second to recognize the sensation in my chest. The satisfaction is brief and all too fleeting, but I know I've done some good.

And I won't stop. I can't.

It's my eternal penance.

23

Jude

JUNE

"Never thought I'd see you in here willingly."

Father lowers himself to the space beside me in the pew.

I release a quiet huff of breath. "Wonders will never cease."

"A lot on your mind?"

"You could say that." I glance around to ensure we're alone in the cathedral even though I'd witnessed the final person file out the doors at the end of the mass more than ten minutes ago. I've been on high alert, paranoia setting in ever since that day I discovered the reporter watching me. I'd mentioned it to Father James once I'd returned from walking Scout, and he agreed we needed to be more careful, discreet.

"Tomorrow night is the usual day for produce, and I don't want to risk the shelter not having enough..." I mention the designated day when the nearby grocery store disposes fresh produce—still perfectly edible but past the sell-by dates they're made to follow.

He lays a hand on my shoulder and levels me with a

stern look. "Jude, it's not your responsibility. You know that, right?"

I don't reply because he could repeat those words until he's blue in the face, and I don't think I could ever believe him. I feel a responsibility, but for reasons he can't possibly understand.

"I've got meetings coming up with a few big names, and they're promising some great donations."

"Well, until then…"

He regards me thoughtfully, and I can't sustain the weight of his eyes, so I turn my attention to the front of the church again.

"I need you to know how much your help means to us, Jude."

His words wash over me, and for the first time, they elicit a sense of pride.

I simply nod.

We sit in companionable silence before he finally broaches the subject I know he's been dying to ask me about.

"I noticed you and—"

One of the large church doors creaks open, and I stiffen but resist the urge to turn around. Father rises to welcome the person, moving out of the pew.

"I'm Father James. Welcome to St. Michael's. I'm afraid you just missed our final mass, but if you'd like to pray a while, you're certainly welcome to do so."

"I appreciate that, sir, but I'm actually plannin' to slide on in that same pew you just left." The familiar Southern Texas accent has me mentally uttering cuss words I have no business thinking in a damn church. "Figured I'd find a tall, grouchy man much like that one." I can already imagine his damn blue eyes shine with that incessant humor.

"You two know one another?" I hear the unspoken question in Father's tone, asking me if it's safe.

Without turning around, I heave out a long breath. "Quit yammering off the poor priest's ear."

"He's so dang delightful, isn't he?"

I detect the soft footfalls approaching me while Father calls out to me, "I'll be in my office if you need me."

"Thanks."

I turn to see the visitor stop at the end of the wooden pew. Tall and muscular with broad shoulders, his easy grin combined with his dark blond hair and blue eyes has always made him a chick magnet as long as I've known him.

Kane Windham. Former Green Beret who now works in the private security consulting sector.

He also happens to be my cousin.

He drops himself onto the wooden seat of the pew with a long, melodramatic sigh. "Not quite the welcomin' I was expectin'. No hugs. No goodhearted slaps on the a—butt. No gleeful whoops of delight." He shakes his head in mock sadness. "So disappointin'."

I ignore his comment and instead get right down to it. "Part of me wonders how you found me." With a humorless chuckle, I add, "The other part wonders why it took you so long."

"Why, darlin'." His accent thickens, mouth curving into his trademark grin. "Who says I didn't know all along?" Kane glances around. "Though I must say, I never thought I'd see the day you'd hang out in a church." He eyes his surroundings appreciatively. "Can't say you didn't choose well, though. This is one spectacular place. Just gives off that heavenly vibe, doesn't it?"

"You never did need anyone to help you carry on a conversation," I reply drily.

"And you never used to hide from people who care about you."

Damn, that jab hurt. I pinch my eyes shut because that hit where it counts, which is exactly what he'd intended.

"How'd you find me?" My voice sounds weary, and I realize with dismay that I feel the same way. Been feeling it more and more.

Since Faith.

Kane glances around to ensure we're alone. He drapes an arm along the back of the pew. "Boss has a guy. Lives off the grid but still has fingers in all the pies. Gets all sorts of intel." He shrugs, and his tone is casual and nonchalant, as though we're talking about sports or the damn weather. "It helped I knew where to look after that few grand came out of your checkin' account for a ramp installation. But you almost made it too easy with this whole Good Samaritan racket you got goin' on."

I groan. "Not you, too."

There's a beat of silence before his voice softens. "Did you find out about the—"

"Yeah." I cut him off because I don't think I have it in me to actually hear him say it.

"Nobody blames you, man."

I clench my jaw and swallow hard past the thick lump of emotion. "You might not, but that doesn't mean I don't."

Kane exhales loudly. "What's it gonna take? How many years until you get it through your head that it wasn't your fault?"

I stare straight ahead at the altar, unseeing, and shake my head. "I don't know."

Silence surrounds us for a few moments until he finally speaks. "Well, I'll tell you a couple of things right off the bat that I know for sure."

I turn and eye him with hesitance.

"One, the story's gonna break." He tips his head to the side. "It's inevitable."

"And two?" I prompt tonelessly.

"Two, I expect you to show me around this fine place called Cleveland. Especially since I flew all the way from where it's a delightful ninety degrees." He raises his eyebrows pointedly. "And has the ocean."

I don't bother holding back a derisive sound.

"And three—"

"You said a couple. That means two."

He grins. "Nothin' gets past you, does it?"

I pinch the bridge of my nose between my thumb and forefinger. "Why me?"

"Because I love you." His quick answer, spoken with such nonchalance, has me jerking my head around to stare at him. Without acknowledging his words further, he continues. "And three, I'd like to meet this lovely lady you've taken a fancy to."

I stare at him coolly. His grin merely widens. "I can already tell it's gonna be the"—he holds up his hands, fingers spread apart, and wiggles them—"best. Weekend. Ev-er."

I drag a hand down my face with a groan. "Awesome."

He looks around the church. "Well, now that I've seen the inside of this place, what do you say you get me outta here and wine and dine me like the smooth-talkin' man you once were?"

Before I can shut him down, he grins and looks past me. "Care to join us, Father?"

"I'd love to."

Kane claps his hands together with glee. "Well, hot dang. I've got myself a date with a grouchy homeless dude and a priest." Putting his palms together, he closes his eyes and utters with over-the-top reverence, "Lord Jesus, I knew you were listenin' to my prayers all along."

Rolling my eyes, I rise from the pew and stop beside a grinning Father James, who says, "I like him."

Kane preens and walks over to join us. "I'm honored. Although, I do feel it pertinent to mention I'm"—he winces dramatically—"a Southern Baptist."

Father's mouth widens into a smile, and he pats Kane on the arm with a wink. "I promise I won't hold it against you."

In response, Kane's booming laughter echoes throughout the cathedral.

And that's how a nosy former Green Beret, a priest, and a homeless man end up hanging out in a bar.

Claims of the notorious Good Samaritan taking action to help a local bakery owner have spread throughout the city.

The owner of Muffin Top says she's still recuperating from a fall that occurred while walking down the dilapidated set of steps at the back of her shop that resulted in a fractured wrist.

A company came shortly after to install a ramp and were quick to inform her it was paid in full.

24

Faith

JUNE

"Father James said he was running behind." Harry sets my beer on the bar. "Something about a surprise out-of-town guest."

I shrug. "Okay, well, I'll wait for him to get here before I order. Thanks for this." I raise my glass of beer, toasting him. "Been a hell of a week at work."

"Don't work too hard, now." He winks at me before turning to refill some beers for others.

I take a grateful sip of beer, and for a moment, I think my hearing is doing that wonky thing again because the bar suddenly falls oddly hushed. The clue that it's not my hearing, and it's the actual patrons of the bar peering curiously in the direction of the entrance behind me is when a deep male voice says, "Is this seat taken?"

A smile spreads across my face, and I turn to find Jude along with an unfamiliar man who eyes both me and Jude with interest. Jude slides onto the barstool beside me while Father James takes the one on the other side of him. This leaves the empty seat on my opposite side open to…

"Kane Windham." After sliding onto the barstool, the

tall man with dark blond hair and the broadest shoulders I've ever seen holds out a hand to me.

"Faith Connors." I accept his hand, expecting a handshake. He turns my hand over and places a kiss on the top. His aquamarine eyes, filled with merriment, flick over my shoulder, and his grin widens.

"That's enough," Jude practically growls.

Kane releases my hand and laughs. "He's so easy."

"And how do you two know each other?" I dart a look back and forth between the two men.

"Would you believe that delightful man wrapped up in layers of extreme joy is my cousin?" Kane asks in a mock whisper.

I can't help but snicker. "Really?"

"Really."

"Did you grow up together?" Though I'm surprised by Kane's visit, I'm hoping this means Jude might start to finally open up to me.

Kane shakes his head. "Sadly, no. I only saw him when he and his mama would come down to Texas for family reunions. They were the only Yankees of the bunch."

I frown curiously and turn toward Jude. "So, where did you grow up?"

Jude's eyes are locked on Kane but quickly veer to me. He shrugs. "Not far from here."

"Ready to order?" Father interrupts and leans on the bar to address Kane. "Pretty much everything here is good. Especially the fish and chips. And the pale ale."

"Well, then, that's what I'll have." Kane leans his thick forearms on the well-worn bar top and raises his eyebrows pointedly at Father James. "And the bill comes to me tonight."

Father nods. "I appreciate that." He flags down Harry and places the orders.

"After all," Kane continues, his words directed at me, "it's not every day I get to meet such a lovely lady like Faith." He nudges my arm with his. "Tell me, darlin'. Are you seein' anyone or are you single?"

So caught off guard, I don't answer initially. "I, uh…" I stammer because I don't actually know. Jude and I never actually discussed anything, so…

"Windham." Jude's voice is low, lethal sounding, and the warning is distinct. "She's not interested in you."

I whip my head around to stare at him. Something flickers in the depths of his gaze, almost like uncertainty. His eyes search my features as he adds softly, "Unless you are…"

"I'm not."

There's a millisecond pause before the edges of his mouth turn upward ever so slightly. His eyes appear less cloudy, a lightness in them that wasn't there before. Without looking away, he raises his voice slightly. "Hear that, Windham?"

"Loud and clear, Destroyer of Hopes and Dreams."

I laugh at Kane's deadpan tone. "You two are something else."

"Believe it or not"—Kane leans toward me and lifts his chin in Jude's direction—"he was quite the charmer back in the day."

I can't restrain my smile. "Is that so?"

"Oh, darlin', you have no idea. He'd have to beat the women off with a stick. He perfected the art of workin' the tall, dark, and handsome vibe." He gestures with his hand at Jude. "Those blue eyes? Those lashes? Pffff. Hook, line, and sinker."

Harry slides the beers in front of the guys, and they each thank him. I reach for my own and take another sip.

"So, I have to know." At Kane's hushed words, I turn

to him in question. His somber expression makes me uneasy. "What was it that drew you to him?" He discreetly gestures to encompass Jude from head to toe. "I mean, especially looking like that."

I mull over the question and sit back to allow my eyes to trail over Jude thoughtfully before I turn back to Kane.

"Honestly?"

"Honestly," he says without any hesitation.

I lean in closer and lower my voice. "Because even though he doesn't see it, he's a good man with an amazing heart."

Kane appears to digest my words, nodding slowly before his eyes crinkle at the corners and his mouth widens in a pleased smile. "Good to know I'm not the only one who can see it." He pats the top of the hand I have resting on the bar and reaches for his beer.

MY PHONE LIGHTS up with a text message when we've finished our dinner and are nearly done with our beers.

Max: Feel like coming out and meeting us at The Ritz?

I hesitate because if things were normal, I'd just turn and ask the guy I was dating if he'd like to come with me to a bar or club. No big deal.

Except I feel weird asking because there's an unspoken dress code since the place is a bit ritzy—hence the name.

"You'll give yourself a migraine if you overthink that any more."

I jerk my head around to find Jude watching me. I worry my bottom lip and finally throw caution to the wind. He's going to say no, but I'll ask anyway.

"Would you like to go with me to The Ritz?" I barely

resist the urge to wince when I pose my question. "No worries if you don't because—"

"Okay."

"It's no b—" I stop and lean closer with a startled frown. "I'm sorry, what?"

His eyes are watchful. "I said okay."

"Oh."

He turns to peer into his empty beer glass. "Unless you'd rather me not."

Dammit, I'm screwing this up. "No." I lay a hand on his forearm; the tense muscles flex beneath my fingers. "I do want you to come along. I just… There's a bit of a dress code."

"What she's sayin' is you need to get outta your ugly-ass clothes if you wanna have her brand of arm candy."

We both turn to stare at Kane, who merely shrugs. "Am I right?"

"Yes, but that was a little harsh."

He makes a face. "Trust me, darlin'. He faced much harsher criticism back in the day when—"

"*Windham.*"

At Jude's warning, Kane merely smirks. "Lovebug? How excited are you to get a makeover?"

"About to do backflips in glee," Jude responds drily.

"See." Kane leans in toward me and says in a loud whisper, "He pretends to be this hard, crusty, overbaked roll, but when you get inside, it's like the ooey gooey center of a s'more."

"If you keep running your mouth, I'll tell you what you'll be getting s'more of."

I whip around to stare at Jude, gaping. "Did you just…?"

Straight-faced, Jude winks at me and slides off his

barstool. "He's not the only one who can be witty. Wait for you outside."

I'm still staring after Jude in a daze after he exits when Kane mutters, "Well, darlin', I do believe you just caught a glimpse of him."

He withdraws his wallet and tosses down the cash to cover the bill that sits beside his empty beer glass. With a wave to Harry, who's serving customers seated in a few booths toward the back, Kane slides off his stool. He offers a smile and nods at Father James, who's deep in conversation with another cop friend, murmuring something about someone "nagging him for an interview and leaving multiple voicemails," but I don't give it another thought.

"If you stick with it"—Kane offers his crooked elbow, and I slide my hand through—"you might just be able to reveal the whole man and not just glimpses."

We head toward the door, leisurely. "And *should* I stick with it?" I peer up at him.

"You ever put together a puzzle? I mean, a real challenging one that took you days to complete?"

"Yes," I answer slowly.

"Well, my cousin is one of those three-thousand-piece ocean puzzles. So many damn shades of blue, it makes your eyes cross. But the photo on the front of the box showing you the result is breathtaking, so you stick with it. You spend hours putting that sucker together but have trouble in a few different spots. It gets frustrating. There are other people around, but they're not interested in puzzles, or they're just no good at problem solving. So you give up."

I wait for him to continue. When we draw to a stop at the door, he finally resumes. "He's a lot like that puzzle. He can't put himself back together. But you? You're good at puzzles. You're the one who can help him see where the pieces go."

I purse my lips in thought. "But"—I hesitate—"does he still have all the pieces?"

Kane shakes his head, and his brow creases with concern. "That's what I'm not entirely sure of. But what I will tell you…" He tosses a thumb in the direction of where Jude waits outside on the sidewalk. "That man out there is a puzzle that's more complete than he's been in quite a while."

He offers a half smile. "And that, darlin', is because of you."

25

Jude

"I don't know about this." I scrub a hand down my face as apprehension rolls through me.

Father James said he had to head home after we finished dinner at the Tavern. I figure he'd received a message from someone needing some medical attention back at his place. He shook Kane's hand and told me he'd walk Scout, and to enjoy an evening out.

And I'm questioning for the millionth time why I'd agreed—hell, why I'd practically *jumped* at the chance to go to the bar with Faith. Not to mention, letting Kane use me as his makeover muse is equally, if not more, delusional. I think his presence made me miss that old part of me. The part that would've kicked my own ass before turning down a beautiful woman's request. And it's undeniable that Faith makes me want to be…*more.*

Now, Kane and Faith have led me to one of the downtown clothing stores—more boutique style than anything—that even pre-homeless me would have rather died than entered.

Kane playfully slaps me on the back. "Never known

you to back down from a challenge." He tugs open the door and gestures for Faith and me to precede him. As soon as we enter the store, Faith's cell phone rings from within her purse. She reaches to withdraw it and glances at the display before flashing me an apologetic look.

"Sorry. It's a work call. I need to take it."

As soon as she exits, I spin around to Kane, already dreading what he's planning to make me endure in here.

"Let's get this done."

My cousin winks. "I love when you bring your go-get-'em attitude."

Two well-dressed female employees look up, weariness plain to see in their expressions since we've walked in with barely twenty minutes to spare before closing. And it's a Friday night, to top things off.

I'm about to tell Kane to scrap this idea when he strolls past me and sidles up to the counter.

Of course, within sixty seconds of Southern-accented sweet-talking and a plethora of darlin's, they're practically tripping over themselves to help us. Moments later, he steers me in the direction of the dressing room with a couple of shirts and two sports coat options.

Fifteen minutes later, he's gotten one of the ladies to steam some of the wrinkles out of the shirt and sports coat we'd finally agreed on.

"I feel ridiculous." I grimace and glance down at my clothes for the hundredth time, feeling self-conscious as hell.

"You look handsome," the redheaded saleslady claims.

"I'd do ya."

I level a squinty-eyed stare on Kane. "God knows I'll sleep like a baby tonight knowing that."

I'm dressed in a blue (because Kane deemed it "matches his eyes") button-down shirt that costs far too much—probably could've fed at least three dozen or more at the shelter for that price—and a gray sports coat to accompany my already well-worn jeans for the "stylish wear vibe."

"You have that rugged hipster look." Kane circles me in the store, inspecting me from all angles.

"Just what I was going for," I deadpan before I wince with a grimace. "I feel like a douche."

"Well, you don't look like one, and that's what counts." He waves toward the doors. "Go test it out on your woman and see for yourself." My old shirt is folded and in his grip. "I'll pay for this stuff and be out in a minute." He walks over to the counter, and the two ladies practically trip over one another in their haste to help him.

I draw in a deep breath and head outside to see Faith. She stands a few feet away from the store's entrance, her small notepad and pen in hand, cell phone braced between her ear and shoulder. She has that crease between her eyebrows, and she's deep in thought as she listens to whoever is on the other end of the call. She jots something down on her notepad, and when she ends the call, I expect her to look up. Still in stern concentration, she slides her phone in her purse and jots a few more notes.

I step closer. "Hey."

She spares me a partial glance, obviously distracted. "Hey." But then she goes right back to writing down notes.

She's concentrating so hard, I figure I'll wait until she finishes. A beat later, she visibly stiffens and makes a disgruntled sound. Her eyes close, and she reaches up to pinch the bridge of her nose between her thumb and forefinger. With closed eyes, she mutters tiredly, "Look, I'm flattered, but I'm just not interested…" Her words trail off when she finally settles her gaze on me. Almost comically, her eyes widen as she takes in my appearance. "Oh, wow," she breathes out.

Her perusal causes a rush of uncertainty to overwhelm me. "So, uh…" I avert my eyes and shove my hands in the pockets of my jeans. "Do I look passable?"

Fuck, I hate how nervous I feel.

"No."

Her immediate answer makes my eyes jerk to hers in both panic and dismay. She shoves her pad and pen in her purse and steps forward. "You look"—she smooths down the lapels on my coat, and it's as though she needs a minute to regain her composure—"incredibly handsome." Her eyes canvas my form appreciatively.

Kane steps out onto the sidewalk, holding a bag. "I vote we toss this old shirt in the trash."

I release a pained groan without bothering to respond.

"Kidding." He smirks. "I'll drop it off with Father James."

"You're not coming with us?" Faith asks.

My cousin's expression is laced with regret. "Sadly, I can't. I've been traveling much of the day, and if I don't get my allotted eight hours of beauty sleep…" He trails off with an exaggerated wince.

No way I can refrain from an eye roll after hearing that garbage. "When do you head out?"

He shrugs. "Figured I'd stick around and see what Cleveland has to offer for a day or so. Not long since I've got work waiting for me."

I tip my head curiously. "Short trip."

His blue eyes meet mine. "Had to check up on you. But I think if you know what's good for you, you'll figure things out soon." He opens his arms to Faith. "Can Uncle Kane get a hug goodbye?"

She laughs and steps into his arms. He enfolds her in

his arms, grinning over her head at me. And he holds the embrace longer than he should. Taunting me.

Damn fucker.

"That's enough." My words are curt, and I glare at him.

Of course, he simply tips his head back on a laugh and releases a curious Faith.

He winks at her. "Keep at the puzzle, Faith." Then he holds out a hand to me. When I accept it, he catches me by surprise, tugging me toward him in a quick hug.

I back away, and he holds my gaze. "Be safe." He points his index finger at me. "And don't be a stranger."

I nod.

With a final wave, he heads off to his rental car, leaving Faith and me standing on the sidewalk. I turn my attention to her, appreciating the way her lips look in the lipstick she reapplied while I'd been trying on clothes. She also twisted her hair up in a clip. As much as I love her hair down, this accentuates the slim column of her neck.

Still dressed in work clothes, she's wearing a long-sleeved black shirt that has cutouts baring her shoulders, paired with gray dress pants that cup her hips and ass just as I've been dying to. Her simple black heels bring her nearly eye to eye with me.

She steps closer and smooths a hand down the front of my shirt before tugging the lapels of my coat playfully. "This is a good look for you."

I snake an arm around her waist, drawing her flush against me. "Think so?"

"Absolutely." Her eyes are bright, happy, and they hold an emotion in their depths I'm afraid to give mention to.

I duck my head a fraction and skim my lips across hers. "Ready to go?"

She sighs against my mouth. "A part of me wants to

keep you all to myself, but I haven't gone out with Max and the others in forever."

The hand I have at her waist drops to graze the curve of her ass, and then I lower my lips to her earlobe and nip at it gently. "You can have me to yourself later."

She shivers, and a soft sigh escapes before she takes a step back. "Shall we?"

I offer my upturned palm, and hazel eyes blink at me in surprise. There's the slightest hesitation before her mouth transforms into the widest smile I've witnessed and her eyebrows arch. "Making a statement tonight, huh?"

She slides her hand in mine, and I thread our fingers together. With a tug on our joined hands, I cup her nape with my other palm and bring our lips together. I mean for it to be quick, but when she shifts to slide her hands around my waist and pull me closer, it all goes out the window.

I deepen the kiss and explore her mouth, my tongue darting inside to toy with hers, and I'm mindless to anything around us.

A cell phone ringtone jars us apart, and when it takes a moment for Faith's eyes to flutter open, combined with the slightly dazed expression on her face, it sends a rush of satisfaction through me.

"Your phone."

"What?"

"Your phone's ringing." I gesture to her small black purse that slid from her shoulder to the crook of her elbow.

"Oh!" Hurriedly, she unzips it to retrieve her phone, swiping a thumb across the screen and putting it to her ear. Immediately, the noise on the other end is jarring, and I can hear everything Max says.

"Are you on your way or what?"

"Yes, of course." Faith's eyes crinkle when she smiles at me. "We got a little held up after dinner."

"Is that code for you went back to the apartment and fucked each other's brains out?"

A rush of color paints her cheeks, and she ducks her head. "*Max*."

"Just hurry up and get here, all right? I have a surprise for you."

"We'll be there in a few."

She ends the call and avoids my eyes as she slips her phone back inside her purse. "Sorry about that."

"Don't be."

She gestures in the direction we need to walk in, and as we stroll along the sidewalk in easy silence, I take her hand in mine as nonchalantly as possible.

I feel lighter tonight. It might be a combination of Kane's visit and having this time with Faith. But right now, at this moment, I can honestly say I'm experiencing something I've not had in far too long.

Holding Faith's hand in mine while strolling along the sidewalk like an average young couple out on the town resonates to my core.

I feel alive.

26

Faith

As we stroll hand in hand along the sidewalk, I can't stop stealing glances at the ridiculously hot guy whose thumb continues to lazily caress the top of my hand. I mean, there was always that *something* about Jude before that well-worn and dull clothes could never disguise. Regardless of his hair and beard before the trim, I could see beneath it all to the man with the sharp jawline and long, dark lashes who would make the average woman weep in jealousy, captivating blue eyes you can lose yourself in.

Now, with that well-fitted button-down shirt tucked into his jeans showcasing his trim waist and flat stomach, it's more evident he's got a hard body beneath the fabric. Broad shoulders are accentuated further by his sports coat. Those jeans still hug him in all the right places, encasing powerfully muscular thighs and the ass I know firsthand you can bounce quarters off.

Even as my eyes skim him from head to toe, I keep coming back to his face. The tension that's usually present has dissipated. More so, his eyes appear brighter as though the shadows have subsided a bit.

I can only hope that maybe, just maybe, a little of that is because of me. That I'm getting through to him and making him realize he's more than just his circumstances. He's so more than just a homeless man.

The number of people navigating the streets and sidewalks increases dramatically when we reach the area known as "yuppie-ville." Most of the buildings have been renovated, and the four-block radius got a major facelift. Occupied by mostly microbreweries, wine shops, and eclectic bars and clubs, it's a fun place to hang out, but it's evident a majority of the people who head down here are…a certain "type." Metrosexual men who care more about their hair than the average guy, and women normally dressed in skinny jeans and tiny tops, if not in thin strips of fabric that barely pass for a dress, are the usual patrons. Jude fits in far better than I do, and I can't bring myself to mind so much that my attire stands out among the other women. Not when I'm this happy.

I draw to a stop at the entrance of The Ritz and hesitate, suddenly self-conscious as I notice the overabundance of low-cut dresses and tops on other women. Music continues to spill around us from the other bars featuring live music.

"Hey." I turn to find Jude watching me intently. "You okay?"

I exhale slowly with a wince and avert my gaze. "I just realized how overdressed I am compared to the other women."

He gently tugs me to him and places a finger beneath my chin, forcing me to meet his eyes. "You're beautiful." The corner of his lips hitches upward in the faintest fraction. "You could wear a trash bag, and you'd still be the most beautiful woman here."

I squint at him. "A trash bag *might* be pushing it."

He pretends to consider it, his eyes sparkling with mischief. "Maybe if it were the white one instead of the plain black…"

I practically gape. I can't help it. "Who are you?" I say with a little laugh.

Sobering, his eyes gloss over my features. His voice drops to something low and husky, seductively wrapping itself around me. "The guy who can't keep his eyes off you."

My mouth parts on my sharp intake of breath. "Jude…"

He skims his lips over my forehead. "Let's go see your friends."

I nod, attempting to regain my composure, and we take one step toward the entrance of The Ritz. Suddenly, Max comes rushing out the doors, barely paying any attention to where he's walking, his thumb working his phone before he puts it to his ear. My phone starts ringing inside my purse. Max's head snaps up at the sound, and he stops short at the sight of us. It's almost comical the way his jaw drops. The hand holding his phone falls to his side as he gapes at Jude.

"Wow." As if finally realizing he's staring, he recovers. "Nice shirt."

Jude nods. "Thanks. I was told it matched my eyes."

Max's eyebrows shoot up, nearly hitting his hairline. "Did Mr. Serious just crack a joke?"

I glance over at Jude before smiling at Max. "Ready to head inside?"

"Uh, sure. I was just coming out to check on your ETA." He winces. "And to give you a heads-up that Parker's here."

I groan. Jude tosses us a questioning glance, and Max supplies, "Co-worker who always tags along." He tosses up a hand in a *What can you do?* kind of way, and adds, "Pretty much an asshole, but we put up with it because he's one level higher than me, so I have to play nice for now." Max grins at me. "Just until Monday."

I nearly squeal at the excitement on my friend's face. "You're getting the promotion?"

He nods but darts a quick glance around before lowering his voice. "It's not official yet, though. My boss pulled me in his office. He's planning to announce it first thing next week." He beams with pride.

I step forward and hug him tight. "I'm so happy for you."

"Thanks, sweets."

"Congrats." Jude offers his hand. Max accepts it, and the two men exchange a quick handshake.

"Thanks."

Jude's attention settles on Max. Or, more importantly, on what Max is wearing. "Nice sweater vest."

My friend is at a momentary loss for words. "Thank you?" There's a questioning lilt at the end as if he's not entirely sure how to take Jude's comment. Then, leaning toward me, he whispers, "Was that sarcastic or an actual compliment?"

My lips quiver as I try to restrain a smile. Offering a shrug, I say, "Up for interpretation."

"Huh." Max appears torn as he runs a hand down his vest. "The lady at the Express store in the mall told me I looked hot."

I pat his cheek. "Totally spot-on."

With a satisfied grin, Max tips his head in the direction of the entrance. "All set?"

"You did mention a surprise of some sort," I prompt.

His smile widens, and I wonder what the heck he's got up his sleeve. "You'll see."

As soon as we enter the bar, Jude's grasp on my hand tightens a fraction as if he's worried about me misstepping. I'm grateful for his hold since this place is extremely dark, and even the strip lighting in certain places is dim. The band on stage is currently performing a cover of "Fast Car" by Tracy Chapman.

We continue weaving our way through until we draw to a stop at the bar, where Jude and I each order a bottle of water. As we wait our turn with the bartender, I focus on the band—they're well-known around town and perform a variety of songs—and can't resist singing along.

When Jude's hand moves to the small of my lower back as he hands me the water, I thank him and wonder if he realizes how comfortable he's gotten when it comes to touching me.

The other bartender serves Max his usual request of vodka and Red Bull, and after accepting it gratefully, he gestures for me and Jude to follow him. He leads us toward the far right of the bar and over to a round table. Surrounded by wide leather bench-style seats, a few of Max's work friends chat animatedly.

I slide onto the bench, and Jude follows suit. After waving hello to everyone, I wait until there's a lull once the band finishes a song to introduce Jude to Tyler, Scott, Dean, Parker, and the woman snuggled up to him by the name of Tina. It's been so long since I've hung out with these guys, and she's definitely Parker's flavor of the month since he's a notorious ladies' man, according to Max. There's another drink sitting unattended at the table beside a sleek black clutch purse, and I assume it belongs to one of the other guys' dates.

The band begins to play a slow song, and the volume is not nearly as amplified. I didn't anticipate this as being a bad thing until Parker leans in over the table and, in an effort to be heard over the music, says to Jude, "So, what kind of work do you do?"

I choke on my sip of water, and everyone's eyes volley to me as I flash a horrified look at Max, who's gone pale.

"Mostly volunteer work lately."

Oh shit. It's like a shark that's picked up the scent of blood in the water because, out of Max's three co-workers, Parker has always been my least favorite. He's the most pretentious, the one who always plants one of those zinger comments in the conversation when you least expect it. The ones that toe the line between being a flat-out insult and a joke.

Parker's face scrunches up as though he's tasted something sour. "Volunteer work?" His gaze inspects Jude—at least what is visible to him since the table hides anything mid-chest downward. "Can't be easy making ends meet doing that."

"I make do." Jude casually takes a drink of water.

Parker narrows his eyes with a smug smirk. "Obviously. Because water is pretty damn expensive these days."

My spine goes stiff, and I part my lips, ready to lay into him. The strong palm on my back stops me.

Jude shrugs as if he doesn't have a care in the world and swirls the water in his cup, the slice of lemon floating in a circle. "Just don't feel the need to prove my worth by drinking overpriced, watered-down alcohol."

"So, what do you do when you're not volunteering?"

"What's with the interrogation?" Max interrupts Parker. "Jesus, dude. It's Friday night. I came to chill."

Parker pastes on a tight smile. "Just making conversation with Faith's date." Focusing on me, he cocks his head to the side with interest. "How's the newspaper business?"

"Fine, thanks."

Parker waits for me to elaborate, and when I don't, he

gestures between me and Jude. "So, tell me. How did you two meet?"

"I ran out of gas one night on the way home from work. And Jude was kind enough to help me out." I look over at Jude and smile. His eyes meet mine, and his features soften. "I knew he was a good guy from that moment on."

"That's so sweet," Tina coos.

Something draws my attention, and I glance up to see someone striding our way. The dimness of the bar makes it difficult to decipher much, but I can't deny there's an oddly familiar air about her. It's not until she's within two feet of our table that I get a better look, and my jaw drops.

"*Reece?*"

The woman gives a happy little squeal, and I jump up from my seat to hug Max's sister.

"Oh my gosh! This is the best surprise ever!"

She draws back with a wide smile. "It's so good to see you."

"Max didn't tell me you were coming into town! How long are you here?"

She makes a face. "This was an impromptu trip." She lifts a shoulder in a half shrug. "I'm in the process of a major change job-wise and needed to get away for the weekend." I sense there's more to it, but now's not the time to pry.

I reach for her hand and give it a comforting squeeze. "Well, regardless of the reason behind it, I'm glad you're here." Scanning her from head to toe, I take in her seemingly effortless beauty and the way she always looks put together. Right now is no different. In a silver camisole with sleek black dress pants paired with heels of the same color that further accentuate her long legs, she's one of the few women who seem to embrace her height rather than try to mask it or tone it down, and I've always admired her for it. She's beautiful, inside and out, but judging from what I picked up on, even she's experiencing some challenges.

Reece leans to the side to inspect something behind me before her grin widens. Her attention on me with eyes sparkling in excitement, she raises her eyebrows. "Who's the hottie you're with?"

I fight the smile that itches to form. "That's Jude."

"Jude." She repeats his name slowly, thoughtfully, as if testing out how it sounds. Her eyes flicker back to him. "That name suits him."

"How so?"

"He just looks like…" She cocks her head to the side analytically. "Like he makes his own rules. Doesn't let anyone's expectations interfere. Paves his own way." There's a brief pause. "There's a lot to be said for a person like that." Something in her tone strikes me as odd, but in the blink of an eye, she's fixed a bright smile on me. "Ready to dance and show that man of yours how things are done?"

He's not my man, I internally protest.

But I'd give anything for him to be.

The band starts playing a hit from the eighties that I love, and Reece's eyes light up knowingly. She and I share an ardent appreciation for all music from that time.

"Girls Just Wanna Have Fun" by Cyndi Lauper has us practically squealing like two kids on Christmas morning. She grabs me by my hand, tugging me back over to Jude. "Mind if I steal your woman away for a bit?"

I swear he's fighting a smile as we rush to the dance floor. And it's at this moment that it hits me.

I've been absorbed with the weight of consequences and subsequent needs pertaining to my hearing loss and still dealing with the remnants from the blow Todd dealt me when he broke our engagement because of it that I entrenched myself in a world much darker, drearier, and less lively.

I haven't been actually living, aside from little snippets here and there.

Not until Jude. He's dragged me from the darkness and thrust me into the light again. He's shown me what I've been missing. That not every man out there is unable to deal with the painful blows that life often brings. That I'm not a lesser woman or unappealing because of it.

That I still have so much to offer.

I lose myself, a freer sense about me, as Reece and I go heavy on the dramatic singing to one another while busting into laughter intermittently. We're not alone on the dance floor, but it's obvious we're the only two out here who don't care about what others think about our dance moves—or lack of gracefulness or elegance. We're genuinely having fun.

Like a magnetic pull, my attention is drawn back to the table where I'd left Jude.

Then it happens. All noise becomes subdued, as though someone's lowered the sound on the radio until it becomes barely audible. Jude must notice something in my expression because he mouths, *You okay?*

As discreetly as possible, I tip my hand to gesture *so-so*. With a nod of understanding, he sets down his drink before rising from his seat. He approaches the dance floor and extends a hand to me. I slide my hand in his and let him guide us to a spot closer to the stage where the band performs, and with one hand at my waist, he speaks slowly to ensure I read his lips.

Feel the vibrations. The music.

I nod, and he draws me close, and in my heels, we're

nearly cheek to cheek as we sway. His trimmed beard brushes lightly against my skin in a tantalizing dance all its own. The hand at my back shifts, and his thumb slips beneath the bottom edge of my shirt to lazily caress my skin. Distractedly, I notice my hearing has returned, the band now playing a cover of "Wicked Game," but my senses focus on Jude's touch. His simple caress of my back sets my body aflame, and I edge even closer, feathering my fingers through the hair at his nape.

He shifts, lowering his head, and his lips graze my earlobe. His hot breath washes over my sensitive skin, sending a jolt radiating through my body. Arousal pools between my thighs, and when he leans back slightly to peer at me with a gaze filled with yearning, my breathing becomes ragged.

I'm jostled as an influx of people spill onto the dance floor when the band begins playing a softer acoustic version of Mazzy Star's "Fade into You," but I'm unable to drag my eyes from Jude's. We're surrounded, and I can't spot the others from here due to the crowd. It's perceived seclusion, in a sense, but it feels like Jude and I are the only ones here. Everything fades away as we dance; our eyes locked.

He watches me, heat simmering in the depths of the blue, which is at odds with the hint of concern displayed in his features.

This man is at war with himself, and I sense his inner turmoil. I want so desperately to calm him. To soothe him.

In a painfully languid motion, he gently cradles my cheek in his palm. His thumb skims along my cheekbone, and his eyes track the movements.

"What is it that draws me to you when I know I should stay away?"

The hint of torment in his words causes emotions to war in my chest.

"I don't know. But what I do know is, I don't want you to stay away." I wait a beat, willing him to see the truth on my face. The truth that I'm not yet brave enough to admit aloud.

That he already owns my heart.

That I don't need to know his past to know that I want him to be a part of my future.

I lift up, intent on pressing a soft, quick kiss to his lips. Before I can draw back, the hand at my back presses me closer, and he tugs, gently nipping at my bottom lip with his teeth. I suck in a startled breath a second before he deepens the kiss, his tongue darting inside to tangle with mine. A groan is ripped from my throat, and I can't seem to get enough of him, of his taste intermixed with the tartness of the lemon from the water he drank earlier, of the way his hard body presses against my softer one.

A loud and piercing wolf whistle has us breaking the kiss, both our chests rising and falling with heavy breaths. Delicious shivers skitter along the length of my spine at the sight of the blistering heat in his eyes.

"Wanna blow this popsicle stand?"

The corners of his eyes crinkle slightly, and he nods, dropping his hand from my cheek to link his fingers with mine. "Let me use the restroom real quick."

"Okay." I glance over at the table where Max and the others sit. "I'll say goodbye to them and wait for you outside."

He dusts a kiss to the top of my hand before releasing it. He heads in the direction of the restrooms while I return to the table to tell Max and Reece I'll see them at home later. I wave at the others, noting Parker's empty seat beside Tina, and head outside to wait for Jude.

As soon as I step onto the sidewalk, I breathe a sigh of relief and hitch my purse strap on my shoulder. About three feet away from the doors to The Ritz stands one of the large ornate streetlights, and I walk over and lean against it to people watch while I wait for Jude.

I'm so lost in my thoughts that the sudden commotion doesn't immediately register. What does have me whipping around is the sound of Parker's annoying voice.

"You just gonna walk away?" Parker taunts, following in Jude's wake. And *whoa.* Although Jude exudes an outwardly calm demeanor, it's the little nuances I pick up on that clue me in on the angry storm brewing within him.

The tic of his jaw as he clenches and unclenches it, his lips pressed in a thin, flat line, and the slight broadening of his shoulders allude to the effects from whatever Parker's said to him.

I step away from my perch and start walking toward Jude, and as soon as his eyes find me, Parker follows his line of sight. When he settles his narrowed gaze on me, I get a sudden rush of foreboding.

I quicken my pace to reach them, wondering what the hell Parker's up to—besides being an asshole, of course.

"Ah, there she is." Parker's smile is so nasty it sends shivers down my spine. "Guess your next volunteer project is 'volunteering' to finally tap the prude, huh?"

Jude stops dead in his tracks, but before he can whip around, I stop him with a hand on his arm and step in front of him.

With a dark glare leveled on Parker, I grit out each word. "What's that supposed to mean?"

Parker lets loose a hearty laugh, and I'm pretty sure he has no idea he's sealing his fate tonight. "You know what it means. No one's gotten in those panties since, what?" He cocks his head to the side, and his eyes dance with the delight of someone who knows a secret. "Since your ex dropped your deaf ass."

I feel like I've just been sucker-punched in the solar plexus. *How does he know?*

"*Faith.*" Jude's entire body radiates a tenseness as if he's ready to pounce at any second. He gently grips my upper arm and tries to steer me behind him protectively, but something inside me snaps. Perhaps being around him has encouraged me. Who knows? Whatever it is has instigated the fighter who's been buried within to finally take charge.

I place my hand over Jude's and give it a little squeeze while attempting to tell him with a look that I've got this. Then I turn my attention to a smug Parker.

"And you found this out how?" I have no idea how my voice sounds so calm.

Parker shrugs as though he's merely dropped word of the clothing store having a half-off sale and not my freaking personal business. "I overheard a conversation Max had with you one day."

"Huh. Interesting."

"Faith." Jude's practically vibrating with energy, and I know he wants to knock this asshole out, but this is my fight. And it's a long time coming.

With a look of faux seriousness, I furrow my brow. "Hey, Parker? I just have one quick thing to tell you." I clench my right hand into a tight fist.

His cocky face scrunches in disbelief. "And what might that be?"

"I might be going deaf, but at least I'm not an asshole with a broken nose."

He scrunches his face in confusion. "Wha—"

I swing as hard as I can and connect with his perfectly straight nose. "Fuck!" he yells as blood gushes from beneath the hands cupped over his face. "Fucking *bitch*." He runs toward the doors like the pansy he really is.

"*Shit!*" I exclaim, bending at the waist and cradling my hand. "Fuck me, fuck me, fuck meeeeee." Dammit, that hurt a hell of a lot more than I imagined. Through my teary-eyed wincing, I peer up at Jude. "They make it look so easy in the movies."

He rubs my back in soothing strokes. "We need to get ice on that." There's a pause when I whimper again at the pain radiating through my hand. "Can I take a look and just make sure it's not broken?"

I force myself upright, and still cradling my hand, I allow him to inspect it. I hiss when he gently straightens my fingers, the busted knuckles protesting angrily.

"Just some bruising. Nothing appears to be broken." His eyes lock with mine. "You'll be sore for a little while."

"Hurts like hell."

Blue eyes sparkle with amusement. "You *did* just hit a guy and bust his nose."

I can't help the satisfied smirk that toys at the edges of my lips. "I did, didn't I?"

He slides an arm around my waist and kisses my temple. "Come on, Slugger. Let's get some ice for that hand."

COMMUNITY HIGHLIGHTS

Figure Eight, the women's clothing store located downtown on Market Street, reports that customers are regularly purchasing gift cards specifically for anyone in need. The manager has hung a sign in the window to alert possible individuals trying to re-establish themselves who may need clothing for job interviews. Individuals can come into the store to redeem the gift cards.

Thus far, many women who have experienced extreme hardships and are currently residing in a shelter have benefitted from this generous act of kindness.

27

Jude

"Take these, and it should help." I hand Faith two ibuprofen capsules, and after she pops them in her mouth, I hand over the glass of water.

I'd snagged her cell phone on the way back to the apartment and called Father James just to play it safe. Thankfully, he'd agreed that she wasn't showing any signs of a fracture in her hand and had given a few instructions to help ease the pain and swelling.

Once she swallows the capsules, she hands me the glass of water to set on the coffee table. I take a seat beside her on the couch.

Propped up on two throw pillows, I've sandwiched her bruised hand between two ice packs and carefully bandaged her split knuckles. She's stretched out on one end of the sectional.

I hold up the television remote. "Want to watch anything in particular?"

Head resting against the back of the couch, she turns tired eyes my way. "Not really."

"Tell me if I hit on something." I flip over to the guide

and scroll through what's playing. My thumb hesitates as I hover over a channel that's due to start playing a marathon featuring the *Twilight* movies.

"Can we watch that, please?" I look over, and she flashes me a smile etched with a tinge of embarrassment. "You'll probably roll your eyes, but I've read the books and love the movies."

"Then this is what we'll watch." I hit the select button and set the remote down on the coffee table.

The beginning credits and music start, prompting me to ask, "So, are you Team Jacob or Team Edward?"

She laughs softly. "Honestly, I wavered for a while there. But I'm Team Edward."

I tsk playfully. "I don't know how anyone can't root for Jacob, especially when he spends so much time with her and helps her restore that bike."

My response is greeted with heavy silence. So thick that I turn to her and discover her gaping at me in surprise.

"You've seen these before?"

I studiously fix my attention back on the TV as I feel the heat rush to my face. "I, uh, read the books, too."

More silence. Shit. *Why did I admit that?*

"I think I just totally fell in love with you," she jokes with a laugh.

I join her, but my laughter is a bit forced and brittle sounding. Not because I'm embarrassed, but because of what she just said and how it made me feel.

The idea of her loving me is both insanely terrifying and exhilarating.

"Jude?" Her tone is muted, tentative.

"Yeah?"

"Thanks for tonight."

"For what?" I look at her in confusion.

Her gaze settles over me in what feels like a caress. "For

doing something outside your comfort zone tonight. For me."

I reach for her good hand and bring it to my lips to press a kiss to it. "Anytime."

As we both direct our attention to the movie starting, I wonder if she knows that I'd do just about anything for her.

Hours later, I manage to successfully carry Faith to her bed without waking her. After carefully tucking her in beneath the covers, I take advantage of the moment to admire her, allowing my eyes to skim over her serene expression and the way her hair fans against the pillow. Just then, the sound of the apartment door opening and muted voices alert me to the fact that Max and his sister have returned. For whatever reason, I feel like I should leave. As I shift to leave a sleeping Faith and head back to the parsonage, she stirs and her eyes flutter open.

"Jude?"

"Shh." I bend and dust a light kiss to her forehead. "Go back to sleep."

"You're not leaving, are you?" Though groggy sounding, I detect the worry in her tone. "Please stay."

I hesitate, but when she reaches out her uninjured hand to me in invitation to get in bed with her, I relent.

There's not much I could deny this woman.

Quickly shucking my jeans, shirt, and socks, I slide in beside her, and she promptly curls up to my side. With her head on my shoulder and right hand gently resting on my chest, I murmur in the darkness of the bedroom, "How's your hand?"

"Still sore but better now." She drops a soft kiss to the side of my neck and releases a tiny sigh of contentment. "I'm always better when you're with me."

She has no way of knowing how much of an impact her words have.

She has no way of knowing that I feel the same.

Faith splays the fingers of her injured hand flat over the center of my chest, and I know, regardless of how this ends, this woman has branded my heart.

"BUSTED SNEAKIN' in well past curfew."

The low murmur would've caught me off guard if I hadn't already spotted his rental car parked out front of the parsonage this morning.

I pocket my key and squat down to greet Scout, who's happy to see me if his wagging tail and wet kisses are any indication. I stride quietly around the couch where Kane's sprawled and take a seat in the nearby chair.

"Nice to see you're making yourself at home."

He doesn't even bother opening his eyes. "Father's a good guy. Hospitable. Doesn't ditch me for a woman."

My glare must be fierce enough to sense because my cousin grins. "You know I'm just bustin' your balls." There's a brief pause, and his expression sobers. "She's a good one." He turns his head and opens his eyes to peer at me in the dimly lit living room. "Sees through a lot of your layers."

I jerk my eyes away and focus on petting Scout, who's seated on the floor by my feet.

"What are your next steps?"

I lean back in the chair and tip my head back, training my eyes on the ceiling. "Don't know."

With a sigh, Kane swings his legs off the couch and plants his feet on the floor. Forearms resting on his jeans-clad knees, he links his fingers and eyes me with a seriousness that's at odds with his Southern Texan's easygoing, humor-at-the-ready personality.

"Look, you've met Kavanaugh. Bossman is a good guy. We're takin' on more and more work and could use a good addition—"

"No, thanks."

His mouth flattens in a thin line. "What's it gonna take for you to get your shit together?" he hisses angrily but quietly, mindful of Father James, who's still asleep in his bedroom down the hall.

I jerk forward in my chair, fury rushing through my veins. "I never asked you to come here." My words are forced from between clenched teeth. "I don't need anyone."

His eyebrows fly up. "Really?" He waves in the direction of Father's closed bedroom door. "What about him? You needed him, didn't you? He probably saved your ass from dyin' of a damn infection on the streets. And don't get me started on all the people out there who you're helpin'."

"What the hell's that supposed to mean?"

He flashes me a look of disbelief. "Don't try to tell me you don't need all those people you're helpin'. Because you do. They might need you, sure. But you need them as much. More, actually. They're givin' you the affirmation you're dyin' for." He shakes his head sadly. "But you just don't get it. You can't expect these people to hold the power to put you back together again." Jabbing his index finger in my direction, he adds, "You need to do that yourself."

He falls silent, and we glare at one another for a beat. "And don't get me started on Faith."

I release a groan and run a hand down the back of my

neck to grip the tense muscles. "I don't want to hear any more."

"Too damn bad." Kane's intense stare bores into me. "That woman is a keeper. She may be the key to gettin' you back to normal, but she *isn't* the cure."

I should've fucking stayed at Faith's instead of heading back here, dammit. A weary sigh spills past my lips. "Kane. Let it go."

"Not happenin'. I may have only met her briefly, but it doesn't take a genius to realize she's the real deal. And I won't have you use her as a crutch."

I jump up from my chair, startling Scout. "You need to back. The. Fuck. Off."

He slowly rises from the couch as though he doesn't have a care in the world and acting as if I'm not a breath away from ripping him apart.

"I won't." He steps so we're practically toe-to-toe. "Because that's what you do when you care about people." He matches my dark glare with one of his own. "You don't let them piss away their lives. If you have a problem with that, too damn bad."

The faint sound of a bedroom door opening drifts down the hallway a split second before we hear, "Morning, gentlemen."

"Morning, Father," Kane and I say in unison, stepping back to put distance between us.

He makes his way past us to the small kitchen. "I have to facilitate the Rosary this morning. Perhaps you two would like to attend." He withdraws a glass from a cabinet and fills it with water. "Might help with some of those anger issues." He turns and takes a long drink while eyeing us pointedly.

"Sorry about that," I breathe out on a sigh.

"I apologize, sir. Just tryin' to"—Kane tosses a thumb in my direction—"knock some sense into him."

Father walks around the couch and grabs the TV remote before taking a seat on one end of the couch. "Have a seat and relax a bit. Just want to check the news before I leave."

I sit back down in the chair, and Kane takes a seat on the couch. My shoulders begin to relax slightly, and I hope Kane will let things drop now that he's had his say.

The channel Father chooses is currently running a commercial, so he turns to Kane. "If you're not rushing back home, maybe Jude can show you around the shelter. He's been an incredible help to us."

"I'd like that." Kane's eyes meet mine, and I get the feeling this is a bit of an olive branch. For now.

Father continues. "Jude's managed to…" He trails off when he glances at the television screen, his eyes going wide.

Oh, fuck.

"Timothy Altman, who also goes by Timmy Shanks, has been pronounced dead early this morning at Erie North Hospital. His mother has confirmed they are confident the man responsible for causing the injuries that led to the death of their son will be found, and they are prepared to do anything to bring him to justice.

"Katherine is live at Erie North." The screen splits to show a thin blonde holding a microphone and standing in front of the main entrance of the hospital. *"Katherine, what else can you tell us about this situation?"*

"Mrs. Altman is adamant about justice being served. She said she is angry that the man has managed to evade authorities this long."

"But did she also acknowledge that her son has quite the criminal record? And that he was in the process of sexually assaulting an employee from The Vindicate*?"*

Katherine refers to a notepad in her hand. *"Well,*

Hannah, when I brought this up, she simply claimed that her son had made some mistakes but was still a good man."

Hannah responds carefully. *"I'm not entirely certain everyone would agree with that assessment, but I can understand it's heartbreaking that she's lost her son."*

"Indeed, Hannah. It's an unfortunate situation all around."

"Thanks, Katherine. That's Katherine reporting from Erie North Hospital.

"In other news, the editor-in-chief of the city's very own newspaper, The Vindicate, *announced earlier this week that one of his reporters will feature an exclusive on Sunday revealing the identity of the Good Samaritan.*

"The reporter slated to write the feature is none other than Faith Connors. Many will recall Connors's interview a short time ago which featured the superintendent of schools. He had been accused of siphoning school monies into his personal accounts and utilizing it for lavish gifts and trips received nationwide attention. Connors's feature on Sunday is expected to…"

My ears start buzzing, the voice on the television fading as panic settles through my bones. This isn't what I wanted —to be known, identified. It depreciates every single act I've done. I need to give back unselfishly, untainted, anonymously in order to even come close to making it up to her. To both of them.

Now I've been revoked of that ability.

As if that's not enough, betrayal churns within the pit of my stomach.

I never expected Faith would sell me out for a story.

28

Faith

A FEW HOURS BEFORE THE NEWS BREAKS...

The sun spearing through the tiny slats of my window blinds rouses me, and I discover I'm alone in my bed. Thankfully, my hand isn't throbbing nearly as much as it was last night. But it'll slow me down when it comes to writing or sketching, that's for sure. When I reach for the pillow that still has a slight indentation from Jude, I notice a piece of paper lying on it.

Hey, Slugger,

Had to go check on some things. Keep ice on that hand.

J

Typical Jude. Short and to the point. His little nickname for me brings a smile to my lips, and warmth unfurls in my chest. *Slugger.*

I roll out of bed and find my phone on the bedside table. Jude must have anticipated me needing it and set it there last night. Plodding over to my small desk in the corner, I open my laptop and note the time in the top right corner. Just enough time to put any finishing touches on my article before I head into work to catch Anthony. My workaholic boss will be in his office like usual on a Saturday morning, and I need to figure out a way to make him see that this article is worth running instead of the original idea.

The more I learned about the individual deemed the Good Samaritan and mulled over the notes and remarks from those who had information or interactions with him, the more I realized this person is doing these acts anonymously because he truly wants to help others. It's definitely not for notoriety or for money. But that isn't what's most striking.

More and more people I spoke with, including many shop owners, have reported witnessing people—complete strangers—helping one another. It's as though this Good Samaritan has struck a chord with them, and they feel compelled to give a helping hand to someone else in need.

Don Bullard, owner of Fiore Pizzeria, which offers jumbo slices of pizza with one topping for a dollar, claimed people began coming in and paying ahead for anyone in need. Some confessed to be homeless and desperately trying to get back on their feet and told him that slice of pizza had been their first hot meal in a long while.

The manager of the nearby women's clothing store, Figure Eight, reported customers purchasing gift cards specifically for those in need. She stuck a sign in the window to alert anyone fitting that profile to inquire inside. The manager claimed she helped three women find and purchase clothing for job interviews.

It hasn't stopped there, though. Nearby schools have reported anonymous donations submitted with the request to pay off lunch accounts for struggling families. Restaurants are reporting frequent pay-it-forwards when the individuals have offered as much as one hundred dollars for as many meals as it would cover for others.

It's undeniable: The Good Samaritan has changed attitudes in this city. Normally, tragedy is the only time people will band together to help one another, much like 9/11 had done not only for New York City but also everywhere throughout the country. This, however, is different. It's far more powerful. This man has managed to reach the hearts of people and inspire them to help those who have fallen on rough times. For that, I believe this city owes him the respect to maintain his anonymous identity.

Once I'm showered and dressed, I head to work with the printed copy of my article in hand. I've already submitted it via email to Anthony, but I included a message that I'd like to discuss it with him once I arrive.

The serene sense of calmness that settles over me as I approach the door tells me I've made the right choice.

"Connors?" Anthony barks at me and waves me in impatiently.

I perch on one of the chairs facing his desk. "Thank you for meeting with me. I know you planned something different for this story, but I—"

"Choked on the story?" His expression is one of disgusted exasperation. "Evan told me." He points at a folder on his desk. "Already got it. He took up your slack."

I can't tear my eyes away from the folder Evan gave him, clearly marked with *The Good Samaritan*. The room feels like it's closing in on me.

"What? But it was my assignment," I sputter. "How long has he been working on this?"

He waves me off, dismissing my question. "Connors, this"—he taps a finger on the file folder—"story is solid gold. Our ratings will be through the roof, guaranteed."

My chest grows tight with unease. "But I have an alternative story I know will—"

"You don't get it." He stares a hole through me. "You had your chance, and it's gone now." He flashes me a look of pity when I begin to protest. "Scandal sells. Drama. Not some bleeding-heart piece you want us to run." He slides on his glasses and returns his focus on whatever task he'd been working on, effectively dismissing me. "That bonus is a non-issue for you. Get to work on that piece I just emailed you regarding the threat of lawsuits against the mayor."

I've been dismissed. Just like that.

In a daze, I leave his office and decide to forgo the elevator in favor of the stairs. I race down each step, desperate to escape this building and the threatening suffocation.

Once I escape to the safety of my car, I promptly lock the doors. I toss my article on the passenger seat along with my purse and buckle my seat belt. Resting my head on the seat back, I can't help but think of how much things have changed. I used to enjoy this job and the thrill of reporting on stories that needed to be revealed, to make people aware of what was going on around them. But now I'm overcome by the sick feeling I've just assisted in damaging someone who has no nefarious intentions and only wants to help.

My cell phone starts ringing, muffled slightly from inside my purse. Grumbling, I reach for it.

"Hello?"

"Hello, Faith. It's Detective Monroe. Sorry if I caught you at a bad time, but I wanted to see if you could come down to the station and look at some video footage we discovered."

I bite back a groan. "What is this pertaining to?"

"A nearby store owner had some cameras installed after a break-in late last year. His manager recently realized one of them faced one end of the alley where you…" He falters for a beat, then clears his throat. "Although it's a little late, he discovered some footage that might be of interest, and it contains a glimpse of an unidentified man. We're trying to determine if he was involved in your incident. And just today, another shop owner turned in their footage of the large alley space that opens up behind multiple stores, because he noticed a man—possibly the same one spotted in the other footage—lingering nearby suspiciously. We're trying to determine if these are related in any way and would like you to take a look and see if you recognize anything."

I pinch my eyes shut in resignation. "I already told you I don't know anything."

"It would just be a big help if you could look. Just so I could check it off my list, and we can move on with things."

I expel a sigh. "I'm leaving work now, so I'll be there in about ten minutes."

"Thanks, Faith. See you in a few."

I SLIDE onto the uncomfortably stiff chair with resignation, wishing I could just head home and vent to Max and Reece. Maybe Jude will come over later. He always tends to make me feel better about things.

"Thanks again for coming in, Faith."

A weak smile and a nod are all I can muster for Detective Monroe. We sit at a small table with a laptop in front of us. There's a legal pad and a pen on his opposite side.

"Remember, if there's anything that jogs your memory,

let me know." He taps a key on the laptop, and the video footage comes to life. The one from the night of my attack is grainy and doesn't trigger anything. I don't notice anything out of the ordinary and expect the second will be much the same.

"Now, this one was taken late one afternoon." He starts the second clip for me and uses his capped pen to point at one section of the screen. "Ignore the two men there. They're installing a ramp for the nearby cupcake shop owner. That's her." Monroe gestures to the woman with a cast on one arm, who watches over the men as they work. He taps the far left side of the screen, bringing my attention to a third man standing in the shadows. "I'm interested in this guy right here."

I watch closely as an unnerving sensation washes over me. Something about this man seems familiar.

I lean forward, peering closer. Once the two workers leave and the woman goes back inside her shop, the man, well disguised within the shadows, slides his hands in his pockets and adjusts the hood over his face. He darts around the corner and out of sight, but the way he walks, that stride…

Oh my God.

"Recognize anything?"

I never thought I'd be grateful he and his partner don't frequent the Tavern. Otherwise, I'm sure there's a good chance they would've put two and two together. Hell, I'm kicking myself for not picking up on it before now. I feel like an absolute fool. It's as though I've had blinders on; I've been so close to the situation that I was oblivious to the signs—to what was right in front of me.

To the fact that Jude—*my* Jude—is the Good Samaritan.

I mash my lips together and shake my head. "I don't

know…" With a wince, I massage my temples, noting the signs of an impending headache. "Sorry. I had a rough night."

"What happened to your hand?"

Startled, I glance down at the knuckles that now have freshly dried scabs, though the bruising is still pretty bad. "I, uh…" I hesitate, realizing I'll be admitting to assaulting someone—to a police detective, no less.

"Faith?" he probes gently, but the underlying worry is easy to detect.

I heave out a resigned breath. "I punched an asshole last night."

He rears back in surprise. "That so?"

My shoulders slump. "Are you going to arrest me now?"

He barks out a short laugh. "Not unless someone's pressing charges against you."

"Doubtful. He's a misogynistic jerk. There's no way he'd admit to anyone that a woman busted his nose."

"Remind me never to get on your bad side."

I smile weakly. "Is that all you needed?"

"That's it." He hesitates. "If anything comes to mind, let me know."

"I will."

Detective Monroe thanks me, and we say goodbye at the exit. By the time I'm inside my car, I'm hell-bent on finding out exactly what Jude's story is.

29

Faith

"What in the fresh hell..."

Max and Reece continue to stare at me with dumbfounded expressions after I stumbled inside, plopped down on the couch, and told them what had transpired today at work and with Detective Monroe.

I can only offer a weak shrug. As if recognizing Jude in the footage wasn't enough, things have turned even crazier.

I tracked down Father James, but he was in a church meeting and couldn't talk. On top of that, my search for any sign of Jude or Kane has been fruitless.

"Wow," Reece breathes, a myriad of shock and worry etched on her pretty features. After she and Max noticed my bruised knuckles, I finally divulged my secret to Reece and filled them in on what had happened with Parker last night.

Max's expression transforms from shock to worry. "Uh, Faith? You haven't heard the news today, have you?"

I eye him warily. *What the hell else has happened?* "No, why?"

He releases an expletive under his breath and darts a

quick glance at his sister before wincing. "The news just broke that Timothy Altman died, and his family sounds like they're on the warpath to find the person responsible for putting him in the hospital and make him pay."

"We figured that would happen." I frown when he hesitates. "There's something else?"

"They said *The Vindicate* claimed they were releasing a feature in tomorrow's paper revealing the identity of the Good Samaritan. And"—the concern etched on his features has my spine stiffening in alarm—"they named you as the reporter."

All blood drains from my face. *This can't be happening.*

I cover my face with my hands and groan. "He'll think the worst of me."

"Faith." Max's gentle tone has me raising my eyes to his. "I might not understand the two of you together, but the fact that you've been happier than I've seen you in years says it all." His gaze is pleading as if urging me to remain positive. He darts up from the couch and begins pacing. "Okay, let's think about this for a minute. He's homeless and has been doing all these things for other people. But strictly anonymously. You were assigned the story to find his identity, but you didn't do it. You changed your mind in the end." His expression hints on hopeful. "That has to count for something."

"But…he still lied to me."

"Did he?" Reece finally speaks up. When I toss her a sharp look, she holds up her hands in surrender. "I'm just saying. Did he ever actually lie to you?"

"I asked him if he'd heard anything about the Good Samaritan, and he…said no." I purse my lips.

"I mean, he was probably telling the truth, Faith. He hadn't heard anything."

I toss up my hands in frustration. "But he could have

told *me*!" I stare down at the floor, and my words sound hollow. "After everything, I really thought…" *That maybe he loved me.*

But I don't dare say it out loud. It'll just make this entire situation more pathetic.

I clear my throat, vying for composure but fail as my eyes fill with tears. "As if all that isn't shitty enough, I'm back to square one." My eyes lock with Max's, and I watch as it dawns on him what I'm referring to. "No bonus to help pay for the cochlear implant."

Max and Reece converge on either side of the couch and hold me as I give in to tears. And I can't help but recall how, by simply being with Jude, my hearing loss hadn't seemed so daunting, and having a job I wasn't in love with hadn't been quite as bad. Being around him had lifted me up much like he'd done for this city.

I grasp at a miniscule shred of hope that he'll realize I wasn't planning to sell him out for a story. But even that's not the biggest concern. He hasn't been one hundred percent truthful with me, and it's not just pertaining to him being the Good Samaritan—it's that I've fallen in love with him, and I don't really know him at all.

I'm not even sure anything between us was real.

I entrusted him with my secret only to discover he doesn't trust me—or love me enough—to share his own.

THE KNOCK COMES a few hours later after Reece has rescheduled her flight so she could stay a little longer. Max ran to the store to get us the proper pity party necessity: chocolate peanut butter ice cream.

I know panic is written all over my face when I look over at Reece. She mutes the TV and walks over to the apartment door before looking through the peephole. Her shoulders relax before she pulls it open.

"Could I speak with Faith, please?"

Reece steps back. "Sure, Father." When he comes into view, I can tell by his resigned expression that he's heard everything.

He takes a seat in the chair across from where I sit on the couch. "I can tell by your face that you're upset."

I snort derisively and stare down at the tissue in my hand. "To put it lightly."

"Are you still running that article tomorrow?"

My head snaps up, and I gape at him. "I'm not running any article. I told my boss it wasn't right and offered an alternative article, but he refused."

Father shakes his head, features drawn. "I'm afraid Jude's under the impression you are. Especially since that's what the news station claimed." He releases a long, slow breath. "He doesn't do these things for others because he wants recognition. He does them because—"

I hold up my hand and stare at him with narrowed eyes. "Wait a minute. You knew all along?"

He shifts in his seat uncomfortably. "I had my suspicions, and he all but confirmed them when he had me help him get the unspoiled food from the dumpsters in order to supply the shelter."

"I can't believe this." With a humorless laugh, I shake my head. "Was I the only moron who didn't pick up on it?"

"Faith, don't—"

"I trusted him!" Another rush of tears burns my eyes, and I avert my gaze to my lap. "And I…" I falter as tears trail down my cheeks, and my voice fades, sounding so small, fragile. "I fell in love with him."

I hear Father rise from the chair seconds before the

cushion shifts beside me as he takes a seat on the couch. He places his hand over mine. "I can't imagine what you're feeling right now, but you have to know that Jude *is* a good man. He wasn't doing anything to hurt you. I know he cares for you."

I huff out a breath. "Well, I'm sure that's over and done with since he believes I'm about to reveal his identity. Evan's feature is due to run in tomorrow's paper."

He shakes his head and expels a dejected sigh. "I should have known that reporter was trouble. He just wouldn't give up."

I whip my head around to stare at him. "What?"

"Evan Phillips left so many messages it filled my voice-mail box. He showed up at the church and tried to corner me, peppering me with all sorts of questions. I brushed it off, but obviously, I should have taken it much more seriously."

"He's nothing if not persistent." Then I add quietly, "And a world-class jerk."

Father's laughter is stilted. "That much is evident." He pauses before gently asking, "So, what's next?"

Absently, I trace the pad of my index finger along the arm of the couch. "I'm not sure."

Father James tsks. "It's not good to lie to a man of the cloth." There's a brief pause. "So you haven't figured it out, then."

I can only stare at him. "Figured out what?"

"The fact that you've never enjoyed your job? That your real passion is your art?"

I expel a long sigh. "It's no secret the term 'starving artist' obviously came from somewhere."

"Maybe so, but you'll never know if you don't try." He shrugs. "Not to mention, there's nothing carved in stone that says you have to stay at this job. Even if you need backup income, there has to be something better that you'd actually enjoy."

"It's just a hobby," I say dismissively.

"I know what your gran told you, but you *are* a talented artist, Faith."

I part my lips to protest, but he waves me off knowingly. "I'm not saying it just to say it. I'm saying it because it's true." He reaches for his pocket and pulls out his wallet. Pinched between his index and middle finger is a cream-colored business card. "She's a parishioner who owns Expressionista Art Gallery. I've spoken with her about you and your work." He flashes me a sheepish look. "I showed her the sketch you drew for me."

My jaw slackens in horror. "I did that years ago." I bury my face in my hands with a groan. "And it was horrible."

"She loved it." My head snaps up, and I stare at him. "She's interested in setting up an appointment to look at your other sketches." Father toys with the card between his fingers, his expression turning solemn. "You've always been the daughter I never had. I'm proud of you—don't get me wrong, but…" He hesitates.

"But?" I prompt.

His smile is tainted with sadness. "But when you stopped believing in yourself, in your gift, and didn't at least give it a shot, I wished you wouldn't have let your gran snuff out that hope." He sighs and extends the card to me. "At least consider this. But if you do it, give it your all—one hundred percent. Because then, if it doesn't work out, at least you'll know, and you won't be haunted by any what-ifs."

We fall silent for a long moment as I mull over his words, but my mind is still overrun by Jude and what will happen tomorrow.

"They're going to run the story. Front page." I pinch the bridge of my nose with my thumb and forefinger and close my eyes. "And he'll hate me."

"He can't hate you for what someone else revealed."

I spear him with a sharp look. "You really believe that? I doubt it'll matter in the end."

Father falls silent for a beat, his gaze flitting over my face inquisitively. "Are you more upset over his reaction?" He lowers his chin and peers at me with that all-knowing look. "Or because *he* didn't tell you his story?"

My lips part to answer, but I stop, faltering, because… well, I don't know. I drop my chin to my chest and mutter, "Maybe both."

"Just tell him the truth." He lays a hand on my shoulder and gives it a comforting squeeze. "Just like your namesake, have faith."

MAX AND REECE drag me out of the house, citing the fresh air might do me some good. We drop Reece at the airport, and it strikes me when we hug goodbye that I've put a damper on her brief visit here.

"I'm sorry," I whisper.

She merely tightens the embrace. "Nothing to be sorry for." When she releases me and backs away, I widen my eyes and blink rapidly to stem the threatening flow of tears. I've cried more than enough tears today. The last thing I need is to break down in public.

Reece gives my arm a quick squeeze. "Hang in there. It'll all work out."

"You need to get going if you're going to make it through security in time." Max steps forward to hug his sister. "Let me know when you get home."

"I will. Love you."

"Love you, too."

We watch her hurry away, toting her small suitcase on rollers behind her, until she disappears in the flurry of travelers.

"Let's head home."

I don't argue since I'm still reeling from the emotional toll of this.

Once Max drives us back home and parks the car, we start up the sidewalk leading to our apartment building. I turn the corner to enter the breezeway only to draw to an abrupt stop at the sight of the man leaning against the wall beside our door. I'm unable to shake off the sensation that my feet are trudging through wet cement as I warily approach him. The baseball cap tugged low shadows his face, and I can't decide whether I'm relieved or disappointed I can't see his eyes.

Max lays a comforting hand on my shoulder before unlocking the door and leading us inside. He kicks off his shoes. "I'll be in my room if you need me."

I painstakingly remove my shoes and set them neatly on the mat by the door. Jude enters behind me, closing the door with a soft click.

I straighten and attempt to draw in a fortifying breath before I speak, but he dives right in.

"You sold me out for a story."

I jolt, startled by the way his words cut right through me. His voice is low, lethally quiet, but the underlying hurt is what curls around my chest and tightens like a fist.

"I didn't!" I protest. "I was assigned the story, but I told him I couldn't go through with it and—"

"When?" Although I know he's asking me a question, his words come out biting and flat, his eyes cool, demanding.

"I—"

"*When*?" He stares at me and speaks between clenched teeth. "When did you finally decide you couldn't go through with it?"

I pinch my eyes closed, already knowing the damage has been done. That I waited far too long. That I should've fought harder. That I could've made the choice in the early stages not to write the story. I could've refused to expose the Good Samaritan's identity.

My answer comes out on a ragged whisper as waves of defeat wash over me. "Today."

I brave a look only to see his features become shuttered, closed off. All the warmth I've become accustomed to is gone. He backs away as if to avoid coming into contact with something toxic.

Me.

I step toward him, hand outstretched, pleading. "I was torn because the bonus I'd get for the story would mean I could get my procedure!"

He backs away, shaking his head. "I should've known better."

Anger surges to the forefront, and I stomp toward him, my feet eating up the distance. I toss my hands up in heated exasperation. "You never even told me your real name, for God's sake!" I falter, my throat closing off, welling up with emotion. Now my voice is softer, more faint. "I fell in love with you, and you never opened up to me."

His hard stare chills me from the inside out. "Yet you were ready to sell my story."

"You lied to me!" I jab a finger into his chest, punctuating my words. "I asked you about the Good Samaritan, and you told me you"—I break off and use air quotes, my tone sarcastic—"'hadn't heard anything.'" I narrow my eyes on him, fiery fury racing through my veins. "You lied right to my face."

"I never lied. You asked me if I'd heard anything." His words are clipped. "I told you I hadn't. That was the truth."

My shoulders slump because I know it's over. There's no coming back from it. He won't see past this.

I drop my chin to my chest and close my eyes, fighting desperately against the pain radiating deep in my chest. My heart feels like it's been shattered and only shards remain.

"I'm sorry. I tried to fix things, but someone else submitted the story on you. They're running it tomorrow."

My words are greeted by silence until I finally detect the barest sound of movement.

I don't have it in me to look up because I can't bear for the last sight of him in my memory to be the one of his back.

Of him walking away. Leaving me.

When he pauses at the door, I can't restrain that seed of hope that unfurls. Maybe he's going to say he understands. That he—

"Goodbye, Faith."

The door closes behind him, and only now do I allow the raggedly whispered words to spill past my lips as my heart screams for his own to hear it. I simultaneously crumple to the floor, wrap my arms tightly around my knees, and give way to sobs that wrack my body.

"I love you."

THE GOOD SAMARITAN'S IDENTITY REVEALED!

But is he really what this city needs?

By Evan Phillips

The rash of "good deeds" occurring around downtown Cleveland has become rampant, spurring talk of a Good Samaritan, an anonymous individual who has done such things as delivering mass amounts of food to homeless shelters and helping those less fortunate. But the burning and ever so pertinent question arose: Who is this person? That answer requires us to return to September, a little over five and a half years ago.

In a small home on the outskirts of Fort Bliss, Texas, lived a young couple, Simon and Katie Sullivan. Katie was well known within the community of nearby El Paso, Texas, as the director of the El Paso Mission, which served much of the homeless population. Simon was approaching his eight-year mark as a medic in the military and facing the decision whether to pass the torch to another brave soldier. He had no way of knowing

his final deployment would also bring tragedy tenfold.

Katie became the victim of a burglary gone awry. Three young men, sixteen-year-old Marty Faulkner and seventeen-year-olds Danny Miller and Sam Enger, broke into the Sullivan home at two thirty in the morning on September 7, 2012.

According to the police report and confessions obtained from the three intruders, Katie awoke and made her way to the kitchen, presumably to get a drink of water. She happened upon the three men in the process of removing the flat-screen television from the wall, and Faulkner was the first to act.

Faulkner chased a fleeing Sullivan down the hall and tackled her to the floor. He then proceeded to repeatedly strike her face. Miller and Enger claim they panicked, and when Miller pulled the gun he had in his waistband, he shot Sullivan at point-blank range three times, firing two bullets at her chest and one at her face. They left Sullivan in a pool of her own blood, unaware that she was also five months pregnant.

Her husband was deployed to an unspecified overseas location, and by the time word reached him, Katie Sullivan and her unborn child had died. Neighbors of the Sullivans reported that the couple were friendly people, always ready to help others, but they'd sensed tension leading up to Sullivan's final deployment. This proves true as I discovered Katie had filed for divorce just two weeks before her death.

Shortly following the funeral, Simon Sullivan's time in the Army was up, and he chose to not re-

enlist. Upon his discharge, he seemed to disappear. It wasn't very long until the anonymous acts of goodwill began occurring in our beloved city, which, coincidentally, is also not far from where Simon lived and was raised by his single mother until he joined the Army at the age of seventeen.

Before we hail this man a hero or refer to him as an angel, as many have declared, I would be remiss if I didn't address the more recent grievances against Mr. Sullivan. He is solely responsible for the injuries that led to the eventual death of Timothy Altman. Altman, also known on the streets as Timmy Shanks, reportedly attacked Faith Connors in an alley near *The Vindicate* headquarters, but Sullivan intervened.

Altman, discovered much later, was unresponsive but alive and rushed to the hospital. He suffered severe brain trauma and was subsequently placed on a ventilator. His organs shut down shortly thereafter, and he was pronounced dead at Erie North Hospital. Altman's family is currently in the process of not only grieving the loss of their son, but are planning to make sure justice is served against Sullivan, who has also been reportedly going by the alias "Jude."

According to a separate police report, Darrel Bodner was found dead from multiple stab wounds in the woods of Erie Park earlier this March. Bodner also had quite the rap sheet, citing numerous arrests for theft and assault, and sources claim he wasn't welcomed by most of the homeless population. Sullivan is wanted for questioning as reports indicate the two were involved in an altercation prior to Bodner's death.

Sullivan has been living among the homeless in downtown Cleveland for much of his time here, prior to being taken in by Father Joseph James of St. Michael's Parish. It is unclear if the priest is aware of Sullivan's past or the impending questioning for the manslaughter charge. James was unavailable for comment.

Some claim Sullivan is a man haunted by the memories of his deceased family and living out his penance for not being able to protect them, perhaps by living among the homeless to feel closer to his wife. Arguably, it can also be claimed that Sullivan has taken situations into his own hands and is enforcing his own twisted form of justice, which is a frightening prospect for this city. One can only hope the authorities find him and put him away where he will no longer pose a threat.

If anyone has any information regarding Simon "Jude" Sullivan's whereabouts, please contact the Cleveland Police Department and ask to speak with Detective Monroe or Detective Parris.

30

Jude

Funny that when things go sideways, sometimes you end up where you least expect.

"Thought I might find you here." Father takes a seat beside me. "Although it seems you're getting braver now, moving closer to the altar." His attempt to inject some lightheartedness falls flat, but I know he means well.

"You're lucky. I threatened a few of the reporters lurking around here by acting like some sort of wacky religious zealot. Told them if they wanted in here, they'd have to go to confession with me first and then publicly ask for forgiveness at the next mass." His laughter is weak. "Last time I witnessed people stuttering and running away was when the topic of tithing was brought up during the recession."

I'm unable to force a laugh or a smile right now. I know I shouldn't be here. I'm only putting him in the line of fire, especially now with the article out. I had to practically threaten Kane to head back home and let me take care of things on my own. He'd given me shit about it but finally gave in.

"I'm sorry." The words burn a path as they rise from my heart and pass through my lips. The bitter taste of regret lingers in their wake. I shouldn't have stayed. I should have ensured he wouldn't be involved in any way.

"For what?" The weight of Father's stare is heavy, but I maintain my gaze on the ornate altar in front of us. "For being flawed? Son, we're all that way. But don't you dare let that idiot from the newspaper fool you into believing you haven't done good for this city. You've changed people. Opened their hearts."

"But I made a lot of mistakes along the way."

He falls silent for a beat. "You know many mistakes were made in the Bible. Paul is a prime example."

I don't acknowledge his words, merely remaining quiet as he continues.

"Beforehand, he was known as Saul, and let me tell you, he was quite the character. Not very likable. Hell-bent on destroying anything related to Christianity. Until God revealed himself to him, and it changed him. He became the Apostle Paul and dedicated his life to spreading the message of salvation to the world."

He lays a hand on my shoulder and gives it a brief squeeze. "All is never lost. Dig deep, and you'll find the way. Do I have all the answers? No. Are all the answers in the big book?"

I glance at him, and he leans in. "Between you and me, I don't think so either. I believe He wanted us to have guidelines, but the rest is up to us." He pauses for a beat. "It doesn't matter what you have faith in, Jude, as long as you have it."

He lets me mull over his words, leaning back in the pew to gaze thoughtfully at the ornate ceiling. "Know why I still manage to fill these pews on Sundays? Because I remind them of this. We all need to be reminded sometimes—even me—that as long as we have faith, we're on the right track."

Father pats my shoulder and rises. "Same goes for you. Don't let anyone strip you of it." He exits the pew and pauses. "Whatever you do from here, know that I have faith in you." He curls his fingers into a fist and taps the wood pew lightly. "I always have and always will. The rest is up to you."

He starts walking away, but I call out to him, and he pauses, half-turning back to me. "Father, would you…" I hesitate, hating to ask someone else for help. "Would you take care of Scout for me for a little while?"

With a wan smile, the priest nods. "Of course. Oh, and you might want to slip out the back, just to be safe and avoid any nosy reporters." He stops at the doors and hesitates. "Just remember, Jude. Have faith."

Have faith. It's far easier said than done.

I'VE NEVER BEEN to the big cities where famous stars are often hounded by paparazzi, but this scene makes me wonder how they put up with the questions and accusations hurled at them, not to mention the unnerving awareness of the cameras trained on their every move.

This is when I'm grateful my mother isn't around, because there's no way in hell I'd want her to witness this.

"Do you feel remorse for Timothy Altman's death?"

"Did you stab Darrel Bodner?"

"Were you jealous of Altman because you wanted to be with Ms. Connors?"

"Is it true you've been living with a priest? Are the two of you in a relationship?"

I pause mid-step on my way to the door of the police

precinct, every muscle in my body taut with anger. How dare they bring Father James into this? How dare they taint his name in any way?

I turn slowly toward the person who spouted off that nonsense, and the fury must be evident in my features because those reporters all visibly rear back.

"Don't." I grind out the word from between my clenched teeth. "Don't bring him into this."

I hold the man's eyes, watch as he swallows hard, his pallor pale, before I take the steps two at a time, rushing to escape the sharks. As soon as I enter, it seems like everyone stops and stares at me as if fearful or expecting my next move to be one of violence. I pause and slowly raise my hands, fingers splayed to show I don't hold any weapons.

"I'm Ju—" I shake my head, more at myself than anything. "Simon Sullivan. I've come to turn myself in."

31

Faith

It's all over the news. You can't breathe, walk, or live without hearing or seeing Jude's story plastered everywhere. The man who'd seemed so isolated yet oddly confident in his solitude and destitute life had run from tragedy.

Why? That word—that question is on a continuous loop in my brain. Why didn't he tell me? Why didn't he trust me enough? Why didn't he share his past with me?

Why didn't he love me enough to let me in? This is the one that hurts the most, that shakes me to my core.

Again, I wasn't enough. *Again.* Before, it was because of my hearing loss. Now…now I don't even know how I'm lacking, but it's clear, in his eyes, that I am.

Regardless, I refuse to stand by and allow anyone else to taint his name or mar what he did for the city of Cleveland. Refuse to allow a pathetic excuse for a journalist to drag his name through the mud. Jude helped us believe in the good in people again. In a sense, he restored our faith in humanity.

He made me believe in myself a little more, too.

I'd been busy, taking the necessary steps and reaching out to key players. Emails have been sent, phone calls have been made, and every time I placed a checkmark next to an item on my to-do list, I felt a little more whole.

All except for my heart, that is. That sucker has been hollowed out, and Jude stole the contents with his unassuming charm and gruff sweetness.

The problem with heartbreak is two things. It's not heartbreaking at all. It's worse. It's the shattering, the evisceration…an incineration of every single particle of your beating heart. As though hot volcanic lava has demolished the organ, leaving only ash behind.

The other thing is, the world doesn't stop just because your heart's broken. You still have to report to work. You still need to pay your bills. You're still expected to be a fully functioning human. So, I do what I need to do. I pretend I'm not dying on the inside and focus on righting my life. On fixing it to be the life *I* want it to be.

"Thank you for being so accommodating and meeting with me." I will away the urge to smooth down my pencil skirt and keep my hands in my lap to exude calmness.

"Of course, Faith." Madeline, the owner of Expresionista, flashes me a warm smile. Their art gallery is not necessarily large, but the layout creates the illusion of it having a wider, more expansive feel. The art they display varies and includes sculptures, paintings, sketches, and photography.

Madeline is seated on the other side of the table beside her partner, Auggie. She had introduced him, explaining he was in charge of new inventory and handling the bulk of acquisitions. "It's a pleasure to meet you. Father James speaks so highly of you."

Her eyes flit to the array of sketches on display that I

brought with me. I included a few different landscapes; one of Reece from her recent visit, with the unmistakable worry in her eyes and etched in her features; Max when he smiled at me across the dinner table the night I'd announced I was planning to make some changes in my life; Father James when he had consoled a woman at the end of mass who was still grieving the loss of her husband; and one of Jude from the first time I'd brought him home with me. In the sketch, I'd captured the lighter look in his eyes, a hint of what I swore was affection in the depths when I'd been curled up against his side in my bed.

The final sketch is one I still can't bring myself to look at. Depicting the day Jude had confronted me was the hardest one to sketch…and to finish. Jude's face is mottled with anger and hurt, his lips in a flat line, the lines bracketing his mouth more pronounced. His eyes hadn't held any hint of affection; instead, I was faced with a cold, dark blue abyss that chilled me to the bone.

Madeline reaches for that particular sketch, and I flinch when her fingers grasp the outer edge of it. "My eyes keep coming back to this one." She studies it so intently, nervousness courses through me in powerful waves.

"I agree." Auggie points in the direction of the sketch with his pen. "But I also need to say this. You manage to somehow pull off landscapes in a way that has the viewer feeling the emotion of the weather. The rainy, soaked downtown area makes me nearly shiver because you convey the wind blowing the rain sideways. And the puddles and dripping water in various areas make it come to life even more. The same goes for your fall leaves. They appear crisp, as though I could reach into the sketch and touch a dried leaf for myself.

"But like Madeline said," he continues, "that right there is the piece that elicits such a visceral reaction. It portrays so much heartache and pain, the emotions on such clear display, it makes me want to hug him." He pauses briefly before turning back to me. "Or you."

Auggie eyes me inquisitively, and it makes me wonder if he has the uncanny ability to see right through me—right through my art—and realize the truth.

Madeline returns to her seat and folds her hands on the table. "Can I be honest with you, Faith?"

This can't be good.

"Yes." My answer has a slight questioning lilt to it.

She exchanges a look with Auggie before addressing me again. "We were a bit hesitant to meet with you, especially since your name has been in the news. But after seeing this"—she waves a hand to encompass my displayed work—"it's evident you have talent. Normally, we keep Friday and Saturday showings for established artists, but your talent ranks up there already, and we'd love to feature your work…"

She pauses, and my stomach lurches as I wait for the other shoe to drop. "But we'd prefer to do it once everything dies down a bit and your name has a better chance of being recognized for your art instead of anything else."

I nod. "I understand." And I do. It makes sense. I don't want to wonder if people flocked to my art or purchased anything simply so they could claim they have a piece done by "that reporter who was involved with the homeless guy."

"However"—Auggie leans forward and links his fingers together—"I'd love to display a few pieces in the gallery to start with. If you'd like to move forward, we can work out the pricing and discuss the contractual terms."

I find myself smiling wider than I have since my world imploded days before.

"That sounds great."

AS SOON AS I step off the elevator, he must have sensed it because he instantly swarms.

A heavy palm settles on my shoulder. "Tough break, Connors."

Evan's practiced expression of concern makes my stomach churn sickly. I shrug off his touch and continue walking toward Anthony's office. He scrambles to stay beside me.

"Nothing personal, you know? Just doing the job. Had to put your name in there to really get the story to take on a life of its own." His smug tone has me itching to slap it out of him. "That guy tried to screw with my phone, but I got the last laugh because everything saves in my online storage automatically." He pauses briefly before proudly adding, "After I overheard part of your conversation with him in the hospital, I knew there was something fishy about him. Turns out facial recognition and a few contacts helped me get to the bottom of things."

I draw up short a few feet away from my boss's door and school my expression. With a sweet smile plastered on my face, I peer at him. "Evan?"

"Yeah?" His wary expression has my smile stretching wider. I'm making him nervous? *Perfect.*

"I submitted my resignation to HR, effective immediately." Before his features can fully turn smug, I lean closer. "And I've already submitted a story to *USA Today* that is due to run tomorrow, *and* I've secured a freelance deal to cover the story if it goes to trial." I pat his chest, and my tone is dripping with faux pity. "Have fun running around writing the equivalent of tabloid articles. Nothing personal, you know?"

He sputters angrily in my wake as I approach Anthony's office. My boss glances up and does a double take.

"Connors," he barks and gestures for me to have a seat.

I step inside, but I don't sit. Instead, I carefully set the paper on his desk. "I'm providing a hard copy, but this has already been filed with HR this morning."

His eyes jerk up, and he stares at me incredulously. "What the hell is this?"

"It's my r—"

"I know what it is." He tosses his pen down with a huff. "You're one of the favorite reporters. If this is because you're pissy over Evan—"

"*No.*" I steel my spine and stare into the eyes of a man who is on the fast track to turning this place into a cheap gossip rag. "I'm resigning because I can't hold a position where my morals or integrity aren't valued."

He sneers angrily. "You've got your head in the clouds, Connors. No one wants to read—"

"I appreciate your concern." My smile is tight as I interrupt, my tone icy. "But it turns out *USA Today does* believe others want to read what I write." I take a step back and offer a curt nod before striding out of his office, ignoring his angry retort.

For the first time in years, I hold my head higher, feeling lighter and less weighed down.

A cynical part of me wonders why it took getting my heart broken to be the driving force behind me making a change.

AFTER PARKING ALONGSIDE THE CURB, I stride toward the Tavern to meet Father for dinner. Before I reach the doors, a man in an expensive-looking suit approaches me with a large manila envelope in hand.

"Ms. Connors."

My steps slow as I try to place the man but promptly fail. "Yes?" I reply hesitantly.

He advances and draws to a stop before me, extending the envelope. "This is for you."

Cautiously, I accept it. He simply nods and offers, "Have a good day," before he turns and strides down the sidewalk. I inspect the envelope and realize the name of a local law firm is printed in one corner.

With it firmly in my grasp, I tug open the door to the Tavern and head inside. Instantly spotting Father James, I slide onto a barstool beside him and set the envelope on the lacquered surface of the bar.

His brows furrow at the sight of it, his eyes lifting to mine in question. I shrug. "No clue. A guy outside just handed it to me."

He peers closer at the envelope. "Cartwright, Donohue, & Leland, Attorneys at Law." His eyes flick to mine. "Might want to open this." He pushes it toward me. "Just to make sure you're not…"

I wince because I know what he's not voicing. *Just to make sure you're not involved in any legal mess connected to the Altman family.*

I inhale what I hope is a fortifying breath before I open the envelope and slide out a thin sheaf of paper-clipped papers. A few brief sentences are typed on the cover sheet, and when I read them, I'm instantly grateful I'm sitting down.

Ms. Connors,

You will find all necessary paperwork,

including the receipt verifying services yet to be performed, have been paid in full by Pauline Cartwright-Donohue, Esq. The offices of Dr. Emerson and Associates have record of this and will be awaiting your call to schedule the procedure.

Sincerely,

Donald Leland

Sure enough, as I page through, a receipt for full payment for my cochlear implant procedure stares me in the face. There's a reminder card from the doctor's office to call and schedule it. But it's the final page that catches me off guard.

Dear Faith,

I almost wrote Miss Connors, but I feel like I've come to know you over the years. First, through your articles and, later, through our mutual friend.

I must admit to being nosy and meddlesome and hiring someone to dig into your background. That day at the coffee shop was planned because I'd hoped to be able to sit down and chat with you and see for myself that you're good enough for him. With as broken as he was when I first met him, I've noticed a change since he met you. You're good for each other, but more so, you're both simply good people. That's becoming more and more rare in this world.

He never gave me his name, but I think "Jude" is quite fitting. He continuously battles his past and his guilt, but I witnessed the weight lessen from his burden because of you. You somehow helped him, giving him that little nudge he desperately needed.

That doctor of mine says my heart is close to giving up on me, and I'm not going to be around much longer, so I decided it would be prudent to get everything situated.

You and I both know that Jude isn't a bad person, and that co-worker of yours is intent on smearing his name. I know you won't stand for this, but I don't want you to lose yourself in a man who cannot or isn't willing to give you his all. You deserve better. Please promise you'll find your way and find a job that truly makes you happy.

You're extremely gifted, Faith, and I know once others witness your immense talent, it will finally afford you the opportunities you haven't granted yourself. (When you're an old woman who has nothing but time and money, you can find many things out about people. As I said before, I had to be sure you were the right person for him.) Have your procedure done, heal fully, both physically and emotionally (as much as you possibly can), but don't let a man stop you from living your life and finding happiness. As much as I hold him dear in my heart, I don't want him hampering you and your healing.

By the time you read this, I'll likely be gone, and if they paid any attention to my last wishes, my ashes will have been spread along the flowering shrubs bordering my house. If there's any sort of afterlife, I think I'd find great joy in messing with the new owners of the place.

Find your happiness and zest for life. You deserve it.

Sincerely,

Pauline Cartwright-Donohue

P.S.

Tell that handsome priest I said hello, and that I always had a taboo crush on him. Something about that grayish-white beard of his always got my engine running.

I can't resist a surprised snicker as I finish reading the letter. Turning to Father, I hand him the paper-clipped stack. "Apparently, you've been lusted over."

His brow furrows as he reads it. When he gets to the end, he throws his head back with a laugh. "Oh, Pauline." Then he skims the other papers.

"You know her?" My voice is laced with surprise.

"I met her a few times at community events. Quite the character." He chuckles before his expression turns somber. "Heard she passed away a few days ago." His eyes meet mine. "She was a good woman and a phenomenal attorney." He hands the papers back to me.

"Pauline was a spitfire, but even in her old age, she had a sharp mind. Always generous and thoughtful. She made anonymous donations to the shelter." The corners of his mouth tilt up thoughtfully. "Only way I discovered it was when the bank had some sort of snafu and informed me of the donor." He shakes his head with a small laugh. "She was livid when I called to thank her. Said she didn't like people finding out because it took away from her joy and people looked at her differently. She liked doing it anonymously and watching people smile again, liked being able to ease the burden."

"She certainly eased mine." I let out a slow exhale before I brave a look at him. "I'm sorry I didn't tell you about my hearing…"

His mouth forms a wan smile. "I had an inkling but figured you'd tell me when you were ready. You know I love you, regardless." He settles a hand over mine. "But I see the path you're on now, and I'm certain there are great things ahead for you."

I nod slowly, returning my attention to Pauline's letter. *Find your happiness and zest for life,* she'd written.

If only part of my zest for life didn't lie with a certain man currently sitting in jail.

32

Jude

"You have a delivery."

My head jerks up at the announcement and the clinking sound as the cell is unlocked. One of the two uniformed men waiting on the other side tosses a thick, folded newspaper my way. I catch it in the nick of time.

The clinking of metal is muted as I unfold the paper and stare down at it in a stupor. Shock *and* pride. Pride that my—I immediately shut down that errant mistake and mentally rephrase it—that Faith managed to land a front-page article on *USA Today*.

It's probably wishful thinking, but I swear the unmistakable coconut scent of her shampoo and body wash lingers with the newspaper.

A note is taped to the very top, and I trace my thumb over her neatly printed words, the mere sight of them serving as a loose connection to her.

Jude,

This article is gaining attention and is even being discussed outside the US. The number of

people willing to come forward and testify to your character speaks volumes.

Not sure you care, but I wanted you to know I'm having my procedure done next week. I also showed my sketches to a gallery owner, who is placing a few on display. And I'm strictly freelance now with my writing.

It drives home the fact that she's already doing better without me around to drag her down. I scrub a hand over my face, my beard crinkling beneath my palm, as I work to drag deep breaths into my burning lungs. It physically hurts to know that I can't be with her. Not if I want what's best for her.

As if she's trying to gut me, the final two lines carry out that mission with flying colors.

I'm not sure if you realize it, but I've always been yours, Jude. And you're already everything I want.

Love always,

Faith

While I'm damn proud of her for landing a freelance job with *USA Today*, I'm not sure I have it in me to read the article.

I hate that my last words to her were spoken in anger. Forced solitude has helped me realize how badly I'd reacted to her that day in her apartment. I'd lashed out, feeling exposed and vulnerable. Afraid.

I suck in a deep breath before letting it out in a slow whoosh. Tracing my finger over the newspaper, I stare down at the fleshy pad, now tinged and slightly discolored from the ink of the newsprint.

Not like you have much else to keep you occupied these days.

Then I focus on the article before me.

THE GOOD SAMARITAN: What you don't know about the man behind the deeds

By Faith Connors

Homeless people hide in plain sight. Society doesn't always "see" them. Oftentimes, the reason we're numb to it is because it's so prevalent. Or perhaps we have strong preconceived notions about these individuals. We assume they're all drug addicts, alcoholics, or prostitutes who are nothing but a drain on society. That may be true in some instances, but it's not always the case.

Picture this: Your spouse just passed away, and now you're reeling from all the debt they accumulated. Perhaps you weren't aware of the credit cards they'd maxed out to satisfy their gambling addiction. Now bill collectors are hounding you, your car gets repossessed, you lose your home, and on top of caring for two small children (one of whom is special needs), you have nowhere to go nor any family or friends who are able to take you in. What happens now?

Your only refuge is living on the streets.

Kimberly Blakely, mother of two sons, one of whom has severe autism, found herself in this exact situation. She was brave enough to share her story with me.

Kimberly and her children scavenged for food each day. They even resorted to begging for food or money to buy food but were never very successful. The St. Michael's shelter was a godsend, but only if they could manage to secure a spot there each night. This proved challenging when

Kimberly needed to work late cleaning offices after hours. She had to sneak in her kids after school because she didn't have anyone to watch them.

Kimberly is not an addict. She's a woman who was dealt a vicious hand in the card game of life, if you will. Even in the worst of times, the days when she didn't think she would make it, when she was sure she was the utmost failure of a mother, she didn't give up. She sacrificed everything to make sure her children were fed, albeit meager portions at times. She went to bed with a stomach grumbling loudly because she'd only eaten an apple all day, but she never thought twice because her kids had been fed.

Kimberly is the face of the homeless.

Reagan (who kindly requested we not publish her last name) fell on extremely difficult times after her divorce. From the time she and her husband married, he'd insisted she stay at home, and when their son was born, she truly embraced it. However, when her husband filed for divorce and had the financial means to hire a "cutthroat" lawyer, she was left with the clothes on her back and little child support.

Reagan ended up getting a job as a waitress and a second job as a part-time housekeeper in a desperate attempt to make ends meet.

Reagan is the face of the homeless.

Kevin is a waiter at a local downtown restaurant (who also requested we not publish his last name or his workplace). His car broke down almost immediately after he'd scrounged up the money to pay for his next semester of college, and he'd found himself unable to pay his rent in full—he was three hundred dollars short. His landlord, even though it was the first time Kevin had ever been late or had an issue paying his rent on time, refused to give him more time to supply payment. Kevin is an orphan who grew up in the foster system until he "aged out," so he has no one to fall back on.

Kevin is the face of the homeless.

I could elaborate even more with these narratives—I have more than fifty accounts—but I don't want to forget the most important part of these stories, one commonality they all share: Jude. The city's Good Samaritan.

Kimberly informed me that a man (now identified as Jude) saw them huddled beneath an awning of an old, dilapidated, and abandoned factory building. Minutes later, he returned with still edible and unspoiled food he'd gathered from a nearby dumpster behind the grocery store, as well as extra money she'd later discovered stuffed into her jacket pocket. "He told us to head over to the Salvation Army because they'd just put out a bunch of new clothes that were donated. When I told him we didn't have any money, he turned and started to walk away. When he got nearly to the corner of the building, he called out over his shoulder, 'Check your right pocket.' And then he disappeared."

They followed his instructions and purchased warm clothing and gathered insulated sleeping bags. It wasn't until a few days later that the man stumbled upon them again. "He told us to go ask for Father James at St. Michael's shelter, and he promised they would have a place to stay as long as we asked for the priest," Kimberly said. That was the last time they saw the man, but when they arrived at the shelter and did as the man had instructed, it allowed them to cut through some red tape since there had been a vacancy. They gained a room in the section of the shelter for women and children with accommodations for up to three months. Kimberly was able to acquire gainful employment, and they recently celebrated her nine-month milestone with the company. Her son is at a school that can accommodate his needs, and they are grateful to be where they are and have an apartment they can call home.

All thanks to Jude.

Reagan was unable to share her story without breaking down into tears. So moved still, many months later, she told me her son had begged her for the light-up superhero shoes that other kids had at school. At that moment, she confessed, "I felt like the world's biggest failure. He wanted a pair of shoes, and I couldn't afford the ones he wanted. They were only ten dollars more, but I needed that remaining ten dollars to pay for food to feed him. As a growing boy, he's always hungry." When the clerk at the shoe store handed her the gifts cards for both that store and the grocery store nearby, she thought it was a joke. "I'd honestly thought someone was playing a trick on me." And when the clerk confirmed it was indeed "for real," Reagan barely made it out of the store before she broke down. "I couldn't believe that someone would do that for us. It was like an angel had finally answered my prayers."

All thanks to Jude.

And Kevin, the full-time waiter and student who was between a rock and a hard place in fear of losing his apartment? Someone had hand delivered the money necessary for him to pay his rent, with a little extra just in case.

"Our hostess walked up to me with a piece of paper wrapped around something thick and handed it to me. Said some guy dropped it off, asking for me. I opened it up, and it was five hundred dollars. The note said, 'You need this more than I do. There's enough in there to cover what you owe for rent and a little extra just in case. I only ask that you pay it forward if you're ever in the position to do so.'"

Kevin said, "I paid my rent and started looking for a new place. I moved in just last week. I hope to pay it forward once I graduate at the end of the semester. To think that a stranger did that for me... It's powerful, you know?"

All thanks to Jude.

I have to stop reading because this…these people are painting me like I'm some sort of savior. But I'm not even close. With a flick of my wrist, I toss the paper to the floor, the *thwap* of the thick newspaper echoing on the cement. I flip around on the paper-thin mattress and link my fingers before sliding them behind my head. Instead of staring up at the ceiling, I close my eyes and give in to temptation.

I've heard it's telling who or what you think of in your last moments on earth or when you think your life will end. Neither are currently the case for me, but while I'm here and my only companion is solitude, there's only one person in particular who's a continuous visitor in my memory.

Faith.

I didn't expect her to reach out to me. Especially after the way we left off when I'd last seen her. Deep down, I think I knew she would never stoop so low as to divulge my story, but I couldn't see past the overwhelming panic and fear that had its talons deep under my skin.

I'm not sure if you realize it, but I've always been yours, Jude. And you're already everything I want.

"Fuck," I whisper into the muted quiet of my confines. I move a hand to my chest and rub the center, over the spot that burns deep within and singes my heart.

COVERAGE OF THE GOOD SAMARITAN CONTINUES...

One of the most highly publicized stories to hit the city of Cleveland, Ohio, is the death of Timothy Altman, also known as Timmy Shanks, the infamous gang member and drug dealer who was injured while in the act of sexually assaulting local news reporter, Faith Connors.

Altman was interrupted by Simon Sullivan, who fought Altman to protect Connors. The impact from Sullivan's punch resulted in Altman's head snapping back and hitting the hard brick building. Doctors we interviewed explained that the blow to Altman's head likely caused his brain to ricochet against the skull and subsequently hemorrhage.

Sullivan then covered a nearly naked Connors and proceeded to carry her to the hospital, where she was treated for multiple lacerations, a concussion, and brain swelling. She fully recovered.

We await word whether the Altman family will be granted their wish to try Sullivan for murder charges. Sources say one prestigious and established law firm in the area has claimed that

anyone who takes on the Altman's "poor excuse" of a legal case will "single-handedly ruin their reputation among the legal community."

It's clear there will be more to come from this trending story. To stay up to date, follow *#Good-Samaritan* on social media.

33

Jude

"Sullivan, you have visitors." A guard escorts me from my cell and leads me down the hall to a small meeting room. I have no idea who the hell might be here to see me.

He escorts me to a small square room and ushers me to the chair sitting opposite a woman and man, both dressed in expensive suits with briefcases sitting on the table to the side. The guard removes my handcuffs before I settle into my seat and rest my forearms on the table.

"You have twenty minutes with your client," he tosses over his shoulder before closing the door behind him.

I barely register his words. I'm far too busy trying to figure out who the hell this woman is with the elegant updo and sleek business suit, and the man with the perfectly styled hair wearing a three-piece equivalent. Especially since I didn't contact a lawyer of my own. I don't deserve that privilege and certainly have zero intent on allotting any money for this—for myself—since I did what they were accusing me of.

As soon as the click of the door sounds, the woman withdraws a thick file folder from her briefcase and sets it in front of her. Reaching out a hand to me, she introduces herself.

"I'm Margo Leland, and this is Eric Conroy. We're with Cartwright, Donohue, & Leland. We'll be representing you."

Confusion settles through me, and I part my lips to ask just as much but stop when Eric leans back in the chair, gaze assessing.

"We've been supplied funds for your legal needs by Pauline Cartwright-Donohue. She specified in a notarized letter, prior to her death, that should you require such services, they were to be provided to you with no cap."

Pauline...Donohue? "She's dead?" Shock reverberates through me.

Eric offers a curt nod, but I detect the flash of remorse in his eyes before it's gone.

I huff out a breath that's filled with both surprise and anguish. Should've known she'd figure out a way to not only shock the hell out of me but to be involved in my life even after her death. I blink back the sudden moisture gathering in my eyes.

"Numerous individuals have volunteered to come forward and testify to your character. And I think"—Margo leans forward, one eyebrow arched—"you'll be interested to know a certain judge was assigned to your case."

"A certain judge?" I repeat slowly, not fully understanding what she's alluding to.

"A judge you happened to rescue from a car in that horrible pileup that happened the same night Altman attacked Ms. Connors." She pauses. "Judge Veronica Thomasino."

My eyebrows nearly hit my hairline as it dawns on me. "Is that even allowed?"

Margo crosses her arms, leveling me with a pointed look. "Why wouldn't it be?" Her expression challenges me as if to say *Don't look a gift horse in the mouth.* The judge must not realize who I am or how we're connected from that night.

I raise my hands in surrender. "I'm not privy to how this all works."

She leans forward, resting on her forearms, and looks me in the eyes. "You need to keep your mouth shut. Let us do our job, and everything will work out." She withdraws a white envelope from her briefcase and slides it across the table to me.

I eye the envelope warily. "What's this?"

All I get in return is a slightly exasperated, "Just read it."

I flip it over and lift the unsealed flap to withdraw a handwritten letter as apprehension rushes through my veins. As soon as my eyes zero in on the cursive handwriting, the slightly unsteady loops every so often as though the person struggled to control the pen, an invisible fist clenches my chest.

If you're reading this, then I'm off tormenting my heinous excuse for a mother. Well, aside from reuniting with my dear husband, Albert. This means no ice melt and no more chats over iced tea or hot cocoa, I'm sorry to say.

Recognition hits me like a tsunami, and I force myself to continue reading.

You may not have known this about me, but I was pretty sharp back in the day. When we started our law practice, I knew I could make a difference. As the years passed, though, I became jaded. Life can often do that. But you made me believe again. You made me believe in the good still on this earth.

I hope you'll forgive me, but I had to know more about you. I had a trusted friend dig deep, and what he discovered simultaneously surprised me and broke my heart.

It wasn't your fault. I need you to repeat that until you finally begin to believe it. It wasn't your fault. It could have happened to anyone. You must understand this. As trying as it may be, some things are simply out of our hands.

I also learned of the reporter you're sweet on. She's a good woman. You need to pull your head out of your ass so you don't lose her. After all, she fell in love with you while you were homeless and didn't bathe frequently, so you know she's a keeper.

I've called in some favors, and we're going to do everything in our power to get your name cleared. Let these people do their jobs. This is their forte.

Be kind and grant me a few final wishes, would you?

—Let go of the guilt.

—Share your burdens with the one you love.

—Tell Faith you love her. (You're wondering how I know you haven't, aren't you? It's because I'm intelligent. And you're a man. It's that simple.)

—Marry her and make some beautiful babies.

—Teach those kids that bathing regularly is important. (I have to bust your chops one last time.)

—Whenever you drink iced tea or hot cocoa, I hope you remember this old bat fondly.

Go and live your life, because you deserve it.

I'm grateful for the time I had with you. You were the son I'd always wished for.

Sincerely,

Pauline Cartwright-Donohue

Silence engulfs the room. I raise my hands to press the heel of my palms against my eyes in an attempt to stave off the tears. That she took the time with her arthritis-ridden hands to write this, to go to all this trouble for me…is overwhelming. I wish like hell she were still here for me to thank her.

"Let us do our jobs, Mr. Sullivan."

At the man's quiet words, I drop my hands from my face and nod. "Thank you."

Long after I sign the paperwork signifying I've appointed them as my legal representatives, I lie on my cot and stare up at the ceiling. It takes me a moment before I realize what I'm doing.

I lie here, a man who committed himself to a solitary existence, against forming any bonds whatsoever. Yet right now, I find myself missing those individuals who forced their way into my life and permanently embedded themselves.

Father James.

Pauline.

Faith.

People I'm not related to—people who have no obligation to me whatsoever—managed to creep past my defenses and were able to peer beneath it all to notice an ounce of goodness left, a bit of potential in me.

If I'm to believe what they say is true, then I need to discover that for myself.

Now, it's up to me to do the rest.

THE GOOD SAMARITAN IS GRANTED JUSTICE

By Faith Connors

In an unprecedented fast-tracking action by the city, the Altman family was delivered a swift and brutal response by Veronica Thomasino, the judge appointed to the preliminary hearing brought by the prosecutor against Simon "Jude" Sullivan. After listening to statements from both the prosecutor and the defense attorneys, Thomasino announced the evidence was not sufficient to sustain the charges, and Mr. Sullivan was to be released.

As for the civil suit the family was trying to proceed with, her response was, "If you were to rob a bank and get a paper cut from the banded money, would you sue that bank?" Thomasino addressed Altman's mother and grandmother, who stood beside their attorney, Mr. Collie. "Do you think that's right? Is that just cause?"

Mr. Collie protested that the family "only wants justice for Timmy," which the judge swiftly issued a correction saying, "No. What you want is money that isn't rightly owed to you. What you need is to start raising your children to know right

from wrong. Teach them that there are consequences in this world. Most of all, teach them to respect others. Teach them it is not okay to touch anyone without their permission."

It is also important to note that forensic evidence has cleared Sullivan from any connection with the death of Darrel Bodner. An arrest has been made in the case, and authorities have taken Benjamyn Leatherwood into custody.

LOCAL EVENTS & THINGS TO DO

The shop owners and nearby residents of downtown Cleveland are planning a "sidewalk celebration" on Saturday beginning at noon to rejoice in the hearing's results. Everyone is welcome, and donations are appreciated as all food and refreshments will be provided free of charge in honor of the Good Samaritan. Figure Eight women's clothing store, Erie Sporting Goods, and Fiore Pizzeria are welcoming any donations to help those in need.

Any monies donated to Figure Eight and Erie Sporting Goods will fund gift cards strictly for those in need. Fiore Pizzeria offers a pay-it-forward dollar pizza slice.

Other local shops plan to participate, and details can be found at www.beagoodsamaritan.com.

34

Jude

LATE JULY

I'm free to go.

As grateful as I am not to be facing charges, I find myself faltering at the prospect of re-entering the world where everyone knows my secrets. It was a hell of a lot easier to live in the shadows where no one knew my name. Light might brighten things, but it also illuminates imperfections; it encourages closer inspection.

Everything I don't want.

"The judge would like a word with you first."

I'm escorted into the judge's chambers, and I still struggle to recollect this woman is the fragile, terrified person I pulled from a wrecked vehicle long ago. She looks well, healed, and put together. Judge Veronica Thomasino is undeniably one intimidating judge. The way she commands a courtroom is impressive. Now, standing beneath her steely gaze as she inspects me, I feel much like a bug under a microscope.

"Please sit." She gestures to one of the large leather chairs on the opposite side of her desk before she takes a seat.

I slowly lower myself into the chair and brace myself for what's to come.

"I'm not entirely satisfied with things."

I attempt to school my expression to rid it of the combination of wariness and panic.

She leans her forearms on her desk and links her fingers together. "I want you to gain closure. To talk to someone, Mr. Sullivan, who is a professional so you can finally move on from this. Otherwise, you'll never have a future." She reaches for the newspaper sitting at one end of her desk, slides it across the sleek, shiny mahogany, and taps a perfectly manicured finger on the byline. "And I'll bet hard money there's one woman who would like to share that future with you. But even so"—she leans back in her chair, regarding me carefully—"you need to do this for you. First and foremost. It's well overdue."

As much as her words grate on me, drawing open raw wounds, I know she has a valid point.

She reaches for a file folder and flips it open to withdraw what appears to be two printouts. Sliding them my way, she eyes me with a pointed expression. "I have two recommendations. One is for a therapist near Fort Bliss, and the other is located here in Cleveland."

I stare down at the papers and hesitate even though I know I've already made my choice. The easy route would be to choose the local therapist and stick around here, but I can't.

With the Fort Bliss recommendation in my hand, she dismisses me from her chambers, wishing me the best. I stride to the door, and when my hand rests on the handle, her voice makes me pause, but I don't turn around.

"I owe you a lot from that night." Her tone is different from before. It's gentler, softer, more muted. Heartfelt. "Thank you, Jude."

THE HUMIDITY HITS me like a wet blanket, nearly suffocating in its intensity. *Welcome to Texas.*

By waiting for me when I walked free with my identification in hand, Kane saved my ass. He also ensured Father James would watch over Scout in my absence. My cousin and I boarded a flight from Cleveland to El Paso; the latter would be a short drive to Fort Bliss.

Turns out, I owe him big-time since he's ensured everything back there hasn't gone to shit. I didn't even bother to ask how he got the driver's license I'd left lying inside my wallet on the kitchen counter in the house.

Kane presses the key fob to unlock the rental car but doesn't immediately slide inside. He tips his head back and inhales deeply. "Now, *that's* the smell of home." His mouth twists into a wistful smile. "Good to be back." Even beneath the dark sunglasses covering his eyes, I feel the weight of his gaze on me. "Ready?" His tone is gentler, cautious.

I clench my jaw against the rush of memories and offer a curt nod before opening my door to settle on the passenger seat.

Kane navigates through traffic with ease, and I'm grateful for his silence, for him allowing me time to prepare for this. The shops and gas stations pass by in a blur as my mind recalls that final conversation.

"You're never here! This isn't what I want anymore!" Katie's voice echoed throughout the house we called home, the hardwood floors contributing to the acoustics.

I ran a hand through my short, trimmed hair, my temper fraying thin. Lately, all she did was pick fights with me. I tried—God, how I tried—but it was like she'd suddenly woken up one morning and decided being married to an Army guy wasn't what she wanted.

That I wasn't what she wanted. And that stung like hell.

"This is my job," I replied wearily.

"Well, if you re-enlist, I might not be around for it."

I stared at her in disbelief and horror. It was like someone gut-punched me. Everything I did, I did for us. I didn't fuck around; I didn't blow money on strippers or prostitutes like some guys. I was a family man.

At this moment, I was at a loss.

"Katie." I glanced at the time, hating the fact that I had to leave on another deployment and this was my send-off. Another part of me resented that she'd bring this up now, knowing I needed to have my head right.

"Can we just talk about this more once I get settled?" I pleaded with her. I'd have access to email and could Skype during deployments.

"Fine." She turned away and began to rifle through the mail.

I stepped closer, hoping to get a goodbye kiss, but she shrugged me off. I steeled myself against the hurt and retreated two steps.

"See you soon, babe. I love you."

Greeted only by the sound of painful silence, I stepped through the door and closed it softly behind me.

That was the last time we talked. She'd avoided my calls home and my emails had gone unanswered. I'd resented not having more time with her that day. That I didn't suffer from being late and getting my ass reamed out, just to try harder to make her smile and get one last kiss.

"Fuck." The muttered expletive escapes my lips and lingers within the silent confines of the car.

"Not your fault, man."

Kane's quiet words fail to calm me, especially when he pulls into the driveway and parks the car.

"Want me to come in with you?"

I don't answer immediately. I'm too busy staring at the house I'd once thought of as a home. The place I imagined growing old in. Having kids play in the backyard.

Now, it only serves as a bad memory. Tainted not only by our final words, but with the knowledge that she—*they*—died here.

I offer a faint shrug without tearing my eyes from the house. "Whatever you want." I quickly exit the vehicle before I chicken out and the dread in my gut wins. In my clenched hand is the key Kane handed me earlier. I slide it into the lock and push open the door slowly, cautiously, half expecting to hear her call out to me.

All I'm greeted with is an eerie silence.

My boots are loud against the hardwoods, the inside clean and not from anything I did. Once the forensic team came through, the police department had given Katie's parents the number for a company that specialized in cleaning and repairing scenes like that since I was still deployed and it took some time to track me down and get me shipped home. My mind flicks through a mental Rolodex, sifting through what stuck in my brain from the police report and the photographs I know I shouldn't have seen, but I'd asked—demanded to. Maybe the cops took pity on me in some way, thinking I'd gain closure from it.

The sliding glass door leading to the back of the house sparkles, no longer shattered from gunshots. The flat-screen television that had been dropped in haste is still missing. Pools of blood no longer gather on the wood floors. The walls are now rid of the blood spatter.

I slowly plod down the hallway to our bedroom and

cross the threshold. Our bed is exactly the same, and I lower myself down on the edge of the mattress, leaning forward to rest my elbows on my knees, and gaze over at the framed photo on one bedside table. The two of us on our honeymoon in Key West—we were both tanned and smiling happily, like a couple truly in love.

"We were happy once, weren't we?" I whisper raggedly.

Footsteps sound down the hallway, and moments later, Kane pops his head in. "Hey, man." His voice is gentler, more subdued. "I just got off the phone with a realtor. If you're sure about this, I'll tell her to get the ball rolling, and we can swing over there and you can sign the paperwork."

I nod slowly. "Sounds good."

"Okay. I'll wait for you in the car." He's already starting down the hall.

I rise from the bed and grasp the picture. Lifting it, I trace a finger along the curve of her smile. "This is how I want to remember you."

When I place the photo back on the table, I heave out a long, heavy sigh. Without another look around, I leave the room and exit the house to join Kane.

I need to sell the place and finally sever this tie.

AFTER ENTERING THE CEMETERY GATES, Kane drives along the winding path leading to the left and finally draws to a stop, putting the car in park. With one arm resting on the console between us and his other hand loosely gripping the steering wheel, he turns to me.

I stare out the window toward the lines of gravestones and hesitate before turning to face him. "I might be a while."

“All I got is time.” His smile is muted, tinged with sadness.

Without another word, I exit the vehicle and walk to the third row of graves, making my way along the well-manicured lawn to two graves I haven’t visited in years.

Fresh flowers adorn each, which I’m grateful for. I place a hand upon the top of the stone, welcoming the singeing burn to my palm from the heat it’s absorbed from the hot Texas sun. Dropping to a crouch, I trace my fingers along the engraved name and the words beneath it.

Katherine Sullivan
Beloved daughter, wife, and mother

I lean my forehead against the stone. “I’m so sorry.” My eyes burn beneath the shade of my sunglasses, and I squeeze them closed. “I’m sorry I wasn’t there to save you. You’ll never know how much I wished it had been me instead.” My throat clogs with emotion, and I welcome the cool trickle of tears down my cheeks as I grip the top of the gravestone. Silent sobs wrack my body as I repeat in a ragged whisper, “I’m so sorry.”

Slowly, my tears subside. I slide my sunglasses to rest on top of my head and rise, peering down at Katie’s grave. I swipe my cheeks of the wetness, and my voice is hoarse, gravelly, thick with emotion. “I’m sorry I wasn’t enough. But I’m not planning to make that mistake again. I, uh”—I break off as a surge of nervousness rushes through me —“met someone. I think you’d like her. She’s amazing. Brave. Has a heart of gold. I’m trying to get my shit straightened out, though. Because I can’t come to her like this.”

I shake my head and lower my focus to the grass at my feet. “I want you to know that I loved you. Always. And I hope you know that. Hope you realized that somehow." I take a step back and grip the tense muscles in the back of my neck. A part of me knows I need to move the few feet to my right, and I dread it, but it must be done.

When I finally draw to a stop at the next grave, my knees buckle, and I drop down to the grass.

Baby Sullivan

With palms splayed flat against the gravestone, I'm at a loss for words. I'm unable to stem the tears that begin to flow freely once again, and I pray she knows I would've done everything in my power to protect them both if I'd been there.

I pray she understands I would've loved her, would've tried to be the best father for her.

"I failed." I lay a heavy fist against the grave in angered grief. "I wasn't there to protect you like a father should."

I'm not sure how long I stay kneeling with my hands braced against the stone before I'm drained, my eyes finally dry but tight and swollen. When I pull myself upright, I drag in a deep breath before exhaling slowly.

"I'll do better next time. I promise."

With those words in my wake, I slide my sunglasses back over my eyes and walk back to the car.

***

A day later, I'm nervous as hell, palms sweaty, chest tightening painfully the closer we get to their house.

"You got this." Kane's reassuring words barely penetrate my panicked state. We park in the driveway, and he turns to me.

I nod slowly. "Thanks, man." After exiting the car, I stride up to the door of the small, humble one-story home. When I ring the doorbell and wait for an answer, I can't say exactly what I'm expecting, but it's sure as hell not the greeting I receive.

"Sully!" Katie's mother nearly knocks me over with the force of her hug. "Oh, sweetie," she mumbles against my chest, "we've been so worried about you."

"Marjorie? Who's at the…?"

My eyes flick up cautiously to Katie's father, Alan. He stills, his features displaying shock at first, but when he recovers, his expression morphs into an odd combination of painful remorse and relief.

"Sully." Tears fill the man's eyes as he approaches. "It's so good to see you, son."

A few minutes and some heartfelt tears later, we've all gained composure as we sit in their living room and sip some sweet tea.

"It's not your fault, sweetie." Marjorie shakes her head, features etched with sadness. "We could never hate you. As much as it devastated us, it was made so much worse when you disappeared." She peers down at the tissue in her hands. "We ended up losing all three of you."

Fuck. I'd never even considered that when I left. I figured it would be easier on them if I was out of the picture.

"Regardless of the circumstances between you two and the status of your marriage," Alan interjects somberly, "you were and will always be our son."

Marjorie lets out a slow exhale. "She called here after she'd finally taken a pregnancy test. It seemed like she wanted to complain when all she'd been given was a gift, and I gave it to her straight." Her soft brown eyes lock with mine. "I said, 'You knew what you were getting yourself into when you married him. You knew he'd likely be away for periods of time doing a job he believed in. I understand you miss him, but giving him an ultimatum is just wrong.'" She shakes her head sadly.

"Son, you didn't do anything wrong." Alan's deep voice is oddly soothing. "We both know you would've done everything in your power to protect them if you'd been there."

Marjorie reaches for my hand and holds it tight while looking me in the eyes. "It's not your fault."

Her words chip away a chunk of the enormous weight I've been bearing.

And I know it's a step in the right direction.

35

Faith

FOUR MONTHS LATER–NOVEMBER

I place a shaky hand on my stomach, which is heaving violently, plagued with nervous anxiety. One might assume being surrounded by my own art would be comforting, and under other circumstances, that might be true. Tonight, though, I'm surrounded by men and women dressed to the nines, sipping champagne and commenting on the sketches adorning the walls of the gallery.

Sure, I'd dreamed of this happening one day, but that's all it had ever been: a dream. Now that it's become a reality, the urge to be violently ill is all too overwhelming. Which is why I'm on the upper level, overlooking the main section of the gallery, where everyone is gathered, as I try to gain some semblance of composure.

Add in the fact the majority of patrons are congregating near the one sketch I warred with myself about whether to even display, and my stomach walls take on the actions of a churning sea.

"Your sketches are exquisite."

I don't turn at his voice. I'm far too busy trying to calm my nerves.

"It seems fitting that's the piece garnering the most attention."

I fix my eyes on the sketched portrait of Jude. His eyes appear haunted, features troubled, and I'd included snippets from news headlines bordering him.

"Anonymous sources say he's an angel in disguise"

"This city's savior"

"Rejuvenated humanity"

"Our local superhero"

I allow my eyes to trace over each feature of his face, and like every other time, I return to his eyes. The eyes I'd convinced myself had love in the depths. Love for me.

I was a fool. But it sure didn't stop me from committing my delusions to paper. In the depths of his eyes, I'd inserted in the darkness of his pupils what I wished with all my being was actually there.

The reflection of a silhouette of a particular woman's face. My own.

I heave out a long breath and glance at Father James.

"Even now, you still love him?"

I turn away from his inquisitive gaze and refocus my attention on the sketch, answering honestly. "That was never in question." My voice cracks on the last word. I squeeze my eyes closed and will myself not to lose it here—not now. Not on an important night like this.

"Is that true?"

Every particle in my body freezes at the sound of that voice. My heart instantly recognizes it and promptly begins hammering, practically threatening to beat right out of my chest.

Father pats my back, and I open my eyes at his retreat. Slowly, with trepidation intermixed with the masochistic yearning to see him again, I turn and face him.

Jude stands before me wearing a well-fitted black suit, a

button-down shirt in a blue that brings out his eyes, and black dress shoes. His collar is unbuttoned at the top, and he's not wearing a tie, but that's not what has me nearly gasping in surprise.

There's an overall lighter air about him. His hair is shorter, and his features aren't as severe as they once were. He drags a hand over his now freshly shaven jaw before shoving both hands in his pockets, showcasing a deep vulnerability.

Jude steps toward me until only a foot of space separates us. His eyes don't leave mine.

"I'm sorry." He swallows visibly, his gaze searching. "I'm sorry for hurting you. For not being honest. I was in a bad place, and I wasn't sure how to get out. Wasn't sure I deserved to. And you came along and changed things… unexpectedly. You showed me how it could be to live again. But"—he hesitates—"I wasn't ready."

I remain silent, so fearful of grasping at hope.

"I went to see them." My eyes widen at his sudden admission, but I nod, encouraging him to continue. "I went to their graves." He drags in a deep breath. "Then I went to see my in-laws." Jude runs a hand over the back of his neck and winces. "It was pretty emotional, but we talked for a while and they, uh"—he breaks off and clears his throat—"said they never blamed me."

A tear breaks free and slips down my cheek at his words.

Jude looks alarmed. "Please don't cry. Especially now, on your special night. I'm so damn proud of you." His voice cracks with emotion. He appears at a loss for a moment before continuing with, "I just wanted to let you know I've been seeing a therapist and to say…thank you."

My stomach drops, and my hope plummets to the ground. *He wants to thank me?*

As if hearing my internal question, he steps forward, his eyes flaring with intensity. "I want to thank you for believing in me when I couldn't believe in myself. For showing me what it's like to be loved just for me." His voice deepens, husky with emotion, and his features turn half hopeful, half wary. "I'm hoping you'll find it in your heart to give me a second chance. To let me prove that I'm good enough for you. That I'll stick around and won't let you down. That I'll always be here for you. That I love everything about y—"

His words are cut off by my lips crashing into his. I startle him, but he quickly recovers. An arm snakes around my waist while the other moves to cup my nape as though he's afraid I'll move away.

I kiss him with all I'm worth to show him I never once stopped loving him. Not once.

When our lips finally part, we rest our foreheads against one another. In barely a whisper, a hint of wonder laces my words. "You came back to me."

He moves back to gaze deeply into my eyes. His thumb skims along my cheekbone in a whisper of a caress. "There was no way I'd be able to survive without the one person who not only taught me to live again but also how to love again."

"I love you so much," I whisper.

His voice is thick with emotion. "I love you back."

"Wait." I ease back slightly. "What about…your name?" I wince. "No offense, but Simon sounds odd. You'll always be Jude to me."

His tender smile makes my stomach flip. "Simon might be my birth name, but I came out of this feeling like a different person." He pauses for a beat. "I think of myself as Jude now."

He glances around the gallery. "So, about this

sketch…?" There's a hint of mischief in his voice. "One might say I was an epic muse, wouldn't they?"

I shove at him with a laugh before sobering and leaning back. "Feel up to being my muse for a while longer?"

He shrugs casually. "I could pencil it in for the next few decades."

A smile spreads on my face. "Wanna keep me around for a while, huh?"

He nods. "If I have my way."

I reach up and slide a hand to the back of his head, guiding his lips closer to mine. "You have yourself a deal…" I stroke a fingertip along his strong, smooth jawline. "If you'll do me a favor."

His husky, heartfelt whisper curls around me. "Name it."

"Grow back the beard?" I offer a hopeful smile. "Because I have to admit, I miss it a lot right now."

His grin is lethal and so damn sexy. "Consider it done."

"You'd do that?"

"Faith…" His eyes skim over my features as if memorizing my face. "I'd do anything for you."

HOURS LATER, I'm escorted from the gallery in a daze. Exhausted, a bit overwhelmed, but most of all, happy.

"So, what happens next?"

We draw to a stop at my car parked in the small lot around the corner from the gallery. I tug my scarf a bit tighter to ward off the harsh chill from the night air and sag against the door with a sigh. "Next?"

Jude's expression borders on bashful. "Do you plan to stick around here?"

I wrinkle my brow in confusion. "I hadn't really thought about it..."

He steps closer and braces one gloved hand on either side of me, caging me in against the car. A soft smile plays at his lips. "If I can convince you to marry me and persuade a certain priest to do the honors, maybe I could talk you into running away with me to Saint Augustine and sell your art there?"

A stunned gasp is all I can manage. His eyes are imploring as he continues. "I know of a little house not far from the beach with a porch perfect for a bench swing. And"—he dips his head, his lips grazing along my cheek as he speaks—"two large art galleries nearby."

"Maybe."

He leans away, nervousness etching his features. "Maybe?"

I glide my hands up along the smooth fabric of his jacket. "As long as you promise never to leave me again. Because I want forever with you."

His eyes take on a fierce intensity. "I promise, Faith." He cradles my face in his hands, his thumb skimming along my cheekbones with a reverence that robs me of breath. "And forever with you still won't be long enough." Then his lips descend to mine in a kiss that's brimming with love and promise and so much hope.

The Good Samaritan has finally found his redemption.

Epilogue

JUDE

Saint Augustine, Florida

It's days like these, when the sun slowly rises in the sky, a myriad of colors splashing against the horizon marking the late morning, that I love most. Our simple cottage-style house isn't fancy, but it's home. I'd discovered the listing for it after it had gone into foreclosure and jumped on it for a great price. It has private access to the beach across the street, and it's a quiet, peaceful area with a fenced yard for Scout to enjoy.

Most importantly, though, it has a large front porch where I quickly installed a bench swing. It's where Faith and I spend much of our time with hot cocoa or iced tea in hand, basking in the gorgeous weather and relishing in the ocean breeze that alleviates much of the humidity. Her sketchbook is never far from her these days. The well-known art gallery down here has commissioned her for numerous pieces, and agreements are in place to make large prints of some of her works.

The foundation we started together has flourished with

the attention and support of the media and donors throughout the state. The Good Samaritan Foundation provides all-encompassing assistance to the homeless. Clothing, food, toiletries, shelter, resume and job search assistance, job interview coaching, onsite staff to assist with grants and loans for those who wish to take college courses, and daycare for those who have finally regained employment and are trying to save enough money to leave the shelter.

"Such a beautiful morning." Her murmur draws me from my musings. I glide us back and forth gently, her head against my shoulder, my arm draped along the back of the swing. Scout lies in the corner of the porch, warming himself in the small section of sunlight. He's certainly taken to the warmer climate like a champ.

I take in the sight of her in the ankle-length sundress, the way the fabric gathers tightly around her midsection that's growing each day with our baby.

"It is."

When she raises her head and catches my admiring look, she groans and runs a hand over her belly. "I feel enormous."

I place my hand over hers and plant a light kiss to her temple. "Don't talk about my wife like that."

Her soft laughter gets carried away by the breeze. "I'm glad you have the day off."

"Me, too." Normally, I run down to the shelter on Saturdays to ensure things are running smoothly, but since I hired a director, my schedule has eased considerably.

She snuggles closer, and I gaze across the road at the long pathway leading to the beach. I've come a long way from where I once was, and though Faith played a vital role in helping me change course, I'd be remiss not to recognize the others who impacted me as well.

Father James. Pauline. Kane. Hell, even Judge Thomasino played an important role in helping me finally move past everything.

The sound of an approaching vehicle draws my attention. When the mail truck stops at our mailbox, I'm already halfway down the driveway. Our postal carrier gives a little wave and then continues on her way. I grab the items stuffed inside the mailbox and make my way up to the porch. There are only a few envelopes; mostly junk mail, one bill, and—

The familiar handwriting has me slowing my steps.

"What is it?" Faith calls out.

I speed up my pace and settle beside her again, tucking the other two envelopes beneath the seashell paperweight we use for the napkins before ripping open the envelope.

It's another handwritten letter, much like the last one.

If you're reading this letter, it means you finally got smart and took my advice and married that sweet woman. I had two letters written—this one and another one in which I basically read you the riot act. Be glad you're getting this one.

The instructions were to send this letter to you once you found your way. I have to admit, this one is harder to write because I'm heartbroken I won't be around to witness any of it. I wish I could tell you in person how proud I am of you.

You were called the Good Samaritan by many because, although you couldn't see it at the time, everyone else could easily see the wonderful, giving, and good man you were and are.

I look forward to watching over you and Faith and your little ones. Know that it will be done with such immense pride and love. You may not have been my son by blood, but I will always think of

you as my own, and I know that this time around, on this particular road you're traveling, it will be the gorgeous scenic route with easy navigation, because not only are you a good man, but you also have the love of a good woman who will stay by your side.

Sincerely,

Pauline

P.S. You better still be bathing on the regular.

Faith sniffles as she reads it beside me. "I really wish I could've gotten to know her." Her glistening eyes rise to mine. "I owe her so much." She reaches up to touch the side of her head where her hair covers up the cochlear implant area.

"So do I." I fight back the emotion threatening to break free.

We sit for a while with the seagulls and ocean waves the only sounds in companion to our thoughts.

"I think I've decided on a name."

I glance at her in surprise. We've gone 'round and 'round trying to determine a name that fits, to no avail.

She nods thoughtfully. "I think we should name him Paul, in honor of Pauline."

I pull her closer and press a kiss to the top of her head just as a large gust of wind blows hard enough to flutter the wind chimes hanging from one corner of the porch. It makes me smile because maybe, just maybe, that was a sign of her approval.

"I think it's perfect."

FOUR MONTHS and eight days later, on the sunniest, near-cloudless day, Paul James Sullivan entered the world hollering up a storm, feisty as ever. Faith and I looked at one another and smiled because we knew his name was not only fitting, but that Pauline would be proud as hell.

Later that night, as I watched my wife close her eyes, a happy yet exhausted smile playing at her lips while our son nursed, I understood.

Sometimes we lose our way. Sometimes we have to lose everything in order to find the good in ourselves. To rediscover faith not only in oneself but also in humanity.

And if we're really lucky, there are angels among us who help guide us along our journey.

I was luckier than most, because not only did I find my way, I also gained even more.

I found my Faith.

THE END

Note from the Author

To locate your local food bank for volunteer opportunities, you can use this link:
http://www.feedingamerica.org/take-action

DIVE! is a documentary which served as inspiration for part of this book. It's both eye-opening and heartbreaking to witness the vast amount of food which goes to waste each day—simply discarded into dumpsters by stores throughout the United States—when it could be used to feed those in need.

Never allow the choices you've made or your past mistakes to define you.
You have the ability—and choice—to be remade.
Always have faith.

Dear Reader

If you would be so kind as to leave a review on the site where you purchased the book, it would be appreciated beyond words. Once you've done so, if you send me an email at rcboldtbooks@gmail.com with the link to your review, I'll send you a personal 'thank you'!

Please know I truly appreciate you taking time from your busy schedule to read this book! To stay up to date on my future releases, you can sign up for my mailing list (I'm the most anti-SPAMMY person ever—promise!) via this link: http://eepurl.com/cgftw5.

If you enjoyed Faith and Jude's story, be sure to check out my other books:

Standalones

Out of Love

CLAM JAM

Out of the Ashes

BLUE BALLS

He Loves Me…KNOT

Tap That (with Jennifer Blackwood)

DITCHED

The Teach Me Series

Wildest Dream (Book 1)
Hard To Handle (Book 2)
Remember When (Book 3)
Laws of Attraction (Book 4)

He Loves Me...KNOT Excerpt

PROLOGUE
EMMA JANE

"Bless her heart."

This—the quintessential Southern phrase "bless her heart"—is the ultimate kiss of death.

The irony isn't lost on me since I just avoided my own kiss of death, figuratively speaking. Instead of walking down the aisle, I'm trudging along the Pensacola Beach boardwalk in my wedding dress.

Alone.

With tear-stained cheeks.

Two elderly women peer at me, blatant curiosity etched across their features, and one turns to the other to hiss, "I wonder if the groom left her."

"Would you blame him?" the other woman responds, disdain dripping from her tone. "She's got a"—she utters the next words much like they're absolutely scandalous—"*nose piercing.*"

My sunglasses conceal the dark glare I direct at them,

so with a dismissive huff, I continue plodding along, swiping a hand across my tear-streaked cheeks. Judging by the black smudges on my fingers, my waterproof mascara clearly lied.

Damn jackass mascara.

Damn jackass groom. I'm starting to see a trend here…

The longer I walk, the more stares I get. One little girl in a tutu bathing suit points at the top of my head and squeals with joy, "Look! A princess!"

Damn jackass tiara and veil my mother insisted I wear.

I march over to a large trash bin and—without any finesse whatsoever—begin tugging the pins holding this awful tiara-veil combo in place. As I'm attempting to remove it, agitation takes over due to my sad lack of progress. I bunch the veil in my fists and give it a firm tug from my elaborate updo. Bobby pins shoot and ping in various directions, and I distractedly pray no one gets too close and loses an eye. Shoving the obscene length of fabric in the trash, I feel a bit lighter.

The June sun beats down on me as I stand on the stamped cement of the boardwalk, the heat radiating through the soles of my favorite flip-flops. My eyes flutter closed as I inhale a deep breath of the salty Gulf of Mexico air.

God, I love this beach. It's always been one of my favorites, especially since it takes just under an hour to drive here from Mobile. The water is a gorgeous shade of blue-green, and the sand is perfectly white and free of pesky shells. Any other time, I'd be kicking off my flip-flops and running toward the surf. Now, though, I have different priorities: a stiff drink. Or ten.

Or twenty.

The challenge is finding a place where I might not draw attention—*er*, as much attention. I slowly survey the nearby choices of bars and restaurants lined up along the boardwalk; I scan and dismiss them one by one.

"No…no…no…n—"

Wait a minute.

One particular sign snags my eye. It has an outline of two men standing back to back, their forms filled with a swirl of rainbows and the name Be-Bob's written in script-like font beneath it.

A gay bar.

Perfect.

With my key ring clipped to my small wristlet, I stalk over to the bar, doing my best to ignore the startled looks and gawking from other beachgoers. Tugging open the heavy door, I step over the threshold and into the brisk air-conditioning.

Into a place where I might find slightly more acceptance.

I slide my sunglasses to rest atop my head and take a moment to allow my eyes to adjust to the dimmer light. There are only about eight people scattered about, chatting over drinks. When I don't earn more than a brief glance before they return to their own conversations, I breathe my first sigh of relief. Most of the patrons are likely indulging in the great weather and enjoying a Saturday at the beach, not looking for refuge and hiding out like I am.

I scan the framed photos adorning the walls, which feature local drag queens and scantily clad male models before striding over to the bar. I hoist myself up onto a worn leather barstool, and catch the eye of the only bartender behind the counter. He appears to be taking inventory of the liquor, if his clipboard is anything to go by.

When he turns around and gets the full visual of me,

his expression is priceless as his eyebrows nearly hit his hairline. I'd laugh if I had it in me, but I'm emotionally spent.

As he regards what's visible to him from the top of the bar on up to my hair, his light brown eyes soften and the corners of his mouth tip up slightly. Without batting an eye, he reaches below the counter and produces a wet wipe. I gratefully accept it and he rests his forearms upon the lacquered surface, regarding me with interest as I rid my cheeks of the dark mascara streaks.

The bartender waits until I'm finished and then accepts the wipe from me before tossing it into the trash.

"Well, I can't say I've ever served a runaway bride before." My makeup-fail savior appears to gauge me, as if expecting me to burst into a river of tears.

Funny enough, the drive here has expended me of those and I'm firmly entrenched in the anger stage of my fiancé's betrayal.

I prop an elbow on the bar, rest my chin on my palm, and offer what I know is the weakest excuse for a smile. "There's a first time for everything, right?"

He doesn't immediately answer, eyeing me curiously until his lips stretch into an easy smile. His eyes do that little crinkly thing at the corners, and he has what I call "kind eyes."

Then again, I remind myself, *what the hell do I know?*

I'm clearly not the best judge of people. That much has become all too evident.

The bartender reaches out a hand. "Casey."

I grasp his hand, noting his impressive manicure. This guy's cuticles are better than mine, and I love the shade of metallic gray polish on his nails. "Nice to meet you, Casey. I'm Emma Jane."

He reaches beneath the bar and I hear a clinking as he

scoops ice, before he brings a cup into view. Then he works his magic and pours in a bit of this and that from one bottle to the next. Finally, with flourish—and a maraschino cherry tossed in—he slides the plastic cup across the smooth surface.

"It's my special secret mix. I call it"—he leans in toward me and lowers his voice, his eyes dancing with mischief—"the Panty Dropper."

One of my brows arches as I stare back at him with dismayed skepticism. "I hardly think I'm a prime panty-dropping candidate right now."

Casey lifts a shoulder in a half shrug, his eyes flickering over my shoulder before returning to me. His smile grows wider. "You never can tell."

With a tiny laugh, I shake my head and wrap my lips around the straw to take a sip of this concoction he's made me. Just as I swallow the sweet drink, I both feel and smell a person sidle up next to me at the bar.

Hell. The reason I came here was because I thought for sure my chances of getting hit on would be slim to none. But as I glance at him from the corner of my eye, I observe strong, muscled forearms, tanned and sprinkled with dark hair. The scent of him is appealing and masculine, with a cologne that doesn't overpower. Just the sight of those arms alone, however, makes me incredibly wary to see the rest of him.

Casey doesn't address the newcomer, his focus still on me. "I'm all ears, Emma Jane. Been told I'm a great listener."

Good Lord. *Where do I even start?*

Before I can answer, the man speaks up, his deep voice booming. "Are you cheating on me, Case?" He makes what sounds like a gasp of exaggerated indignation. "I can't believe you'd betray me like this."

I glance up to see Casey's expression full of mirth, and he rolls his eyes. "You know better. I'm still waiting for you to switch over."

A husky laugh greets my ears, and it sounds far too male—far too appealing—which is why I refuse to turn and look at the man beside me.

"I might switch if you'd agree to root for my team."

"Not gonna happen," Casey scoffs before his gaze meets mine. "Isn't that drink exactly what the doctor ordered?"

I muster up a smile because he seems like a sweet guy. "It is." With a start, I realize I haven't given him my card to pay or to at least start a tab. I reach for my wristlet. "What do I owe you?"

He waves me off. "Honey, that one's on me as long as you promise to dish before we get slammed in a few hours."

A loud exhale spills past my lips. "It's a pathetic story, really."

"Let me guess." Mr. Forearms's husky voice is a deep timbre, amusement threaded in his tone. "You caught him with your maid of honor."

I let out a harsh laugh and fiddle with my straw, using it to move around the ice cubes in my drink. "Nope." *If only it were that simple*, I muse internally.

"Caught him with his best man?"

This time, his suggestion drags a lighter sounding laugh from me. "Not even."

"Well, you know I can't leave here without hearing the story. I'm intrigued."

This guy is something else, that's for sure. His voice is the epitome of sexy, yet, even with all that's transpired, I have zero interest.

Finally, I drag my attention from my drink and my eyes

travel up those muscled forearms, over the bulging biceps stretching the short sleeves of a dark-blue polo shirt, and up to the face that—

My breath catches in my throat as recognition floods me, my eyes widening as I take in the man beside me.

Becket Jones, the quarterback for the NFL team in Jacksonville, Florida. He's a two-time Heisman Trophy winner from the University of Florida and was the second overall draft pick by the Jacksonville Jaguars. Adding to that impressive resumé, he's a Lombardi Trophy recipient and was recently voted MVP. His face is in commercials and on billboards everywhere. Living in Mobile, Alabama, and in a state without a pro football team, most of us either gravitate toward the Atlanta Falcons, the New Orleans Saints, or the Jacksonville Jaguars.

I don't follow NFL as closely as college football, but I'd have to live under a rock not to recognize Becket and his pretty-boy face. Even beneath the brim of the ball cap, which curls under at the edges and draws shadows over his eyes, I'd recognize that wide charming smile of his anywhere. He's slouching against the bar but I know he pushes well over six feet.

His features cloud as he observes my response, his large hand reaching up to tug his cap lower. "Please don't tell me you're going to sell some seedy story about seeing me in a gay bar to a stupid gossip rag."

"Of course not. I'm just..." I falter for a moment. "Surprised."

His chin lifts, gesturing to a couple of guys standing nearby a jukebox, laughing and talking. One of them is wearing a shirt with bright pink flamingos printed on it, along with a yellow feather boa draped around his neck.

"I'm with my brother, Brantley—the one who insisted on that crazy getup—and his roommate, Vonn, whose birthday we're celebrating." His eyes flicker to them briefly, obvious affection in his gaze, before returning to me. "I drove in from Jacksonville late last night to join them."

I nod politely, not sure what to say. "Well, I hope you guys have a great night." I turn back to my drink and studiously take another sip of the dangerous concoction, acknowledging Casey and Becket have fixed their attention on me with unfettered curiosity. This drink is deliciously sweet and I know it's masking the copious amount of liquor Casey put in it. And I can't get hammered. I should—and I *really* want to—but I can't. I have bigger fish to fry.

Like figuring out my freaking life.

With a long sigh, I unzip my wristlet and withdraw my cell phone—whose ring had been silenced—to face the "music" I know is about to blare at me.

Let this be noted as mistake number one. Because I'm certain my phone is going to overheat from the number of text messages and missed calls I've received already. Mainly, the ones from my father.

Dad: You'd better get back here now, young lady.

I continue scrolling past all his other messages until I get to the last one, time stamped from about five minutes ago.

Dad: Consider yourself disowned. Don't even think of coming back to this house after the way you've embarrassed everyone.

Huh. Well, thank heavens I'd already thought of that and had made a quick stop at the house before driving here. I'd scooped up the items I'd need most, knowing my father's reaction would be extreme. Maybe I was delusional, but I'd hoped it wouldn't come to this.

Just as I'm about to place my phone back in my wristlet and avoid the remainder of the painful messages sure to come, another one comes in.

Dad: Forget your job at the magazine. It's done. You're done. You did this, Emma Jane.

My chest tightens, and my stomach churns sickly. I knew it was coming but it doesn't make it any less devastating. I'd worked my ass off for *Southern Charm Lifestyle* magazine at their new location in Mobile. I know I have the potential to rise up in the ranks.

But now it's gone. Poof. All because of my father. The one and only Davis Haywood, city councilman, owner of the local newspaper and the city's largest magazine, and commercial developer galore. He has the money and power to make things happen in Mobile.

I just never thought he'd use that money and power against his own daughter one day.

"So." Becket startles me from my own drama-filled thoughts. "You might not know this about me, but I was brought up to be a gentleman."

I regard him warily, unsure where he's going with this. "O-kay," I drag out the word slowly.

"This means I can't leave you sitting at this bar, staring down at your phone, looking like your puppy just died."

I shoot him a hard glare that would normally cause people to rear back...but then I recall that this man faces the risk of being tackled by two-hundred-plus-pound men on any given game day.

So as much as my dangerously narrowed eyes might

flare with the "Don't even go there" vibe, my glare does nothing.

He looks around first before slipping his ball cap around on his head, the brim now at the back. And honestly, on any other grown man, it would look juvenile. On Becket Jones, however, it actually looks cute.

Casey slides a bottle of water to him, which Becket uncaps before downing half of it. Resting his arms on the bar, he playfully nudges me with his shoulder.

"Go ahead. Spill."

Exhaling loudly, I peer up at him skeptically. "You really want—"

"To hear all the sordid details?" He grins at me, nearly blinding me with his pearly white teeth. "Absolutely."

Shaking my head at him, I take another sip of my drink and toy with my straw, making the ice cubes clink together in my cup. "Fine. But don't you dare give me a *bless your heart* that's chock-full of pity."

"Deal."

Letting a long sigh loose, I answer, my voice muted and laced with pain. And I hate the way it sounds.

"I'm running from a man who doesn't really love me."

About the Author

RC Boldt currently lives on the southeastern coast of the U.S., enjoys long walks on the beach, running, reading, people watching, and singing karaoke. If you're in the mood for some killer homemade mojitos, can't recall the lyrics to a particular 80's song, or just need to hang around a nonconformist who will do almost anything for a laugh, she's your girl.

RC loves hearing from her readers at rcboldtbooks@gmail.com.

Stay Connected to RC:

Facebook: https://goo.gl/iy2YzG

Website: http://www.rcboldtbooks.com

Twitter: https://goo.gl/cOs4hK

Instagram: https://goo.gl/TdDrBb

Facebook Readers Group:
https://www.facebook.com/groups/BBBReaders

Acknowledgments

THE GOOD SAMARITAN
Copyright @2018 by RC BOLDT

Editors:

Tamara Mataya
Editing 4 Indies
Diamond in the Rough Editing

Proofreaders:

Judy's Proofreading
Deaton Author Services

Cover:

James Critchley Photography
Charlie Garforth, cover model
Cover Me Darling, cover designer

My husband and daughter who support me every step of the way—I could never do this without you both. Thanks for bringing me wine when I'm exhausted and I've hammered out *allll* the words, and mimosas for when the manuscript wouldn't save my changes and I'm about to burst into tears because technology hates me.

My readers—I'm not even remotely kidding when I say that it's still surreal to know that I actually *have* readers. That's the honest truth. I am so grateful for each and every one of you who spend your hard-earned money on my books. Thank you for allowing my characters to be a part of your escape from this crazy thing we call life! It's an honor and privilege I don't take for granted.

Jen B., Lauren S., Hazel J., and Kata C.—you three ladies graciously volunteered to read the rough draft of this and helped me refine it to be what it is. I'm grateful for not only your friendship but for your support and feedback.

Heather, my publicist—I could never manage to thank you enough for always being there to help me and guide me along the way. Having you by my side on this journey is, by far, one of the best decisions I ever made. <3

Marisa, my cover designer—You knocked this one out of the ballpark! Thank you for always being so helpful and going above and beyond to help my vision come to life.

Tamara, Julia, and Jenny—you ladies are my lifesavers. Thank you for helping me refine this story!

Sarah, my Australian BFF—Thank you for being by my side from the start of this crazy journey. There's no way I would've survived without you and your unfailing encouragement! #LYLT

Judy and Julie—Thank you for being the best proofreaders on this earth and putting up with me!

My team of betas—Thank you for all of your feedback and help with this book!! I can't express how much I appreciate you ladies!

My readers group—You are the greatest, most supportive bunch I've come to know. I adore you all so much!! <3

Patrick W. (A.K.A. Patricio)—For letting me pick your brain on the medical aspects of this story. I take full responsibility for any errors and liberties.

The douchebag who lived across the street—Your muffler drove me insane and I firmly maintain that you're compensating for something. But I have to say, when I was up late trying to finish this book and thought I'd hit the wall, you would start up your car (to go wherever it is you went at midnight), and that loud-ass muffler would give me the jolt I hadn't realized I needed. I'm not thanking you because I still believe you violated some sort of noise ordinance, but maybe you helped me a *tiny* bit. I also think those gaudy flashing lights on your rims and outlining your windshield are a bit much, though, but whatevs.

My mother—You've been a devout Catholic your entire life and, thanks to you, I still feel a tinge of guilt over my boisterous retelling of how Father James could've left the priesthood for *me* instead...if only I'd attended the local university instead of the one farther away. Thanks for lighting candles for your smut-peddling daughter's soul. I love you. Sincerely, Your favorite child.

Joseph James—I once knew you as Father James when I was a senior in high school. Wherever you are, I hope you're happily married with lovely children (and grandchildren). I'm not saying I wouldn't be filled with great pride if you thought about the curly-haired eighteen year-old Italian girl and reminisced about missed chances, though. But, really. I hope your life is everything you imagined it to be and more. Trust me, I ended up with the right man.

Although, now that I think about it, he kinda resembles you… ;)

Made in the USA
Middletown, DE
23 September 2018